GOOD FRIDAY PUBLISHING PRESENTS

JOY R WASHINGTON

A QUIET PLACE

COPYRIGHT© 2011

ISBN-13:978-0692551301
ISBN-10:0692551301

HEART TO HEART

Giving honor to God who blessed me with the creativity, and the gift of storytelling, I give you all the praise. None of this would be possible if it weren't for you. Thank you with all of my heart. To my parents, Molen and Isaiah Washington Sr., for blessing me with that front porch experience, and handing down your gift of telling stories, I love you and thank you so very much for all that you taught me and all of your prayers and faith in me. To my ladies and now gentlemen at the Marcy library who support and believe in me, and fought so very hard for my first collection to become a part of the library, much love and so much thanks. To my two best friends in the world, my two sisters, Marie and Sundae Sue Washington, I love you for believing in me when I couldn't believe in myself. Thank you for pushing me when I wanted to give up. I love you so much. To Fran who has fought for me and believes in me so much, I love you. To Ed who is a mentor and a dad, and an inspiration. And finally, Sue my special angel on high who gave me this title on the top of the staircase when we all were going through it. This book is especially for you. Here is your book. May you enjoy it on a puffy, Joyful cloud in Heaven.

Chapter 1

Come to think of it, there wasn't a lot to do in Oak Grove, California. It was a peaceful, but small coastal community where life was simple; old folks still hung laundry on clothes lines and talked over wooden fences. It was the type of town where everyone knew their neighbors, and family was important. The young however, made the most of what they had; spending their weekends at either Echo Park, or the Dollar Theater. The movies were old, and nostalgic, but they allowed them to dream.

Somehow it was enough for their tiny, quaint town where time didn't seem to be in a hurry, and living was easy. For Oak Grove was their small village; their tiny corner of the world, and their little quiet place. It was a warm weekend as Mr. Wells sat on his side porch scrapping caked on burnt grease from his wife Pauline's cast iron skillets. It was another one of his projects that he would take a day to do.

With a pitcher of lemon aid by his side, his favorite tin cup beside him and nothing but sunshine and time on his side, there he sat working as if his bread depended on it. It was his life now. Since he had retired from the railroad years ago, it was the next chapter in his seasoned lifecycle. He took on many projects like that now. Solomon would often stop his bike in front of his house and watch him. He was a gracious old man, earning every strain of silver hair that flowed through his head. Life was a project for him, and watching him scrap the thick black oil off his wife's cast iron skillets, was like watching time.

"Woo –woo!" Kamari whistled. "Come on Solomon," he stopped his bike at the corner.

Mr. Wells looked up and tilted his cap. Solomon waved, got on his bike and rode as fast as he could to catch up with Kamari and the others. By the time he reached Echo Park, they were breathless from laughing at Tommy Parker from sliding into the same patch of mud that he'd been sliding into since he was six.

It was as if he didn't see it; like the plump green grass around it had secretly hid it, but it hadn't. Tommy was big and brown skinned; around six feet six, and he always wore a matching Dodger baseball shirt and cap turned backward on his head.

He was blind as a bat, but he could hit a baseball into another city. Playing for the Dodger's was his dream.

"Looks like you let some stink get on your jeans Tommy." Boyd teased. Boyd Carson was a skinny black kid who ate almost as much as Tommy, but to look at him you wouldn't know it. He was good looking with hazel eyes, and a comedian at heart. Boyd could stop a skunk from spraying him with one of his jokes.

Tommy laughed and dusted the mud off his butt. "You kiss my…" he stopped cold as Tori Hunter and her pals passed by. The echoes from the boys' laughter didn't even touch his ears. He watched Tori like he eyed a curve ball; intensely focused, not even blinking an eye. She was his home run. But of course, he was shy around her, and he swore to himself that he'd never let on just how much he liked her.

Immediately Boyd started in on Tommy. He sat on the peeling blue bench in need of a paint job with a goofy look on his face. He sat pretending to be so zoned out as if nothing could shake him. Of course Tommy leaped at him, and Boyd made a run for it.

Tommy was big, but he was quick; an oversize Gazelle in motion, he matched Boyd step for step. Solomon and Kamari followed disturbing the girl's conversation and their lunch. The boy's startled them with their horseplay, and Boyd and the others caused their cold drinks to spill.

"Damn you Boyd Carson! I swear you and your sorry friends will pay for this." Ruby stood as she yelled at all of them.

"Men," Tori snapped.

"You mean boys. It's just another pathetic way for Tommy Parker to get another stare at you." Ginger wiped the table with a clean cloth.

"Please!" Tori said. "Tommy's got his eye on one thing, baseball. Have you ever seen him hit a ball? Boy can play some baseball."

Tori was medium height around five feet six; medium build. Her eyes were caring and as brown as rich soil. Her skin matched her eyes, and she was a mix between a young Dorothy Dandridge, and a young Lena Horne; no clue of what she wanted to do with her life.

Ruby was thin, chocolate, and pretty, and dreamt of being a journalist. Her hair was full, thick, and as black as the night sky. She worked with her mother who owned her own salon.

Ruby's hair was always styled nicely even if she wore it in a simple ponytail, or a sophisticated French roll. Ruby was no stranger to styling hair, and her pal Ginger Maples was no stranger to style and fashion.

Ginger was petit and cute with sassy short hair. Her clothes were always color coordinated and stylish. Even her shorts and tee shirts had pizazz. She designed her own clothes, and prior to school letting out for summer, she was bombarded with orders and forced to turn some down. Ginger was an entrepreneur at heart. Sewing and designing garments came natural to her. She had dreams, big dreams. And it would start with getting out of small town Oak Grove, and going to New York University come fall.

Ginger craved big city life; busy streets, crowded subways, and a city that suffered from insomnia. She tried to convince her friends of that, but they didn't seem that much interested in New York.

Tori, who was still searching for her dreams, didn't think that a State as big as New York was a place to go soul searching. Although she too wanted a place away from singing crickets and solitude, New York didn't quite suit her idea of home.

Ruby on the other hand knew what she wanted. She wanted to attend Stanford University, major in communications, and become the next Oprah. It occupied her mind a lot; as much as Solomon. Unlike Tori and Ginger, she didn't mind the singing crickets, and the quiet. It, coupled with the older ladies at the beauty shop, offered her stories, and one day she would have the opportunity to tell them.

Ginger looked over across the way at the boys goofing off. She shook her head at them as she spread out the checkered red table cloth over the peeling blue bench. "I swear," Ginger sighed. "They can be so immature. Fooling around with them, it's a wonder I haven't lost my appetite."

"Tell me about it." Tori poured more punch in their cups. "Don't they usually go to the mall on Saturday's?" Ruby passed out hot steak sandwiches her dad had made for them. He owned a little diner that he had inherited from his grandmother.

Over the years, he expanded and added outside dining with ground fire pits, and lighting. The place was always full, and the food and smiles kept customers coming back.

"With our luck, maybe they'll leave and go down to the Gingerbread?" Ruby said. The Gingerbread was a small strip mall where the teenagers hung out a lot.

"Yeah right," Ginger said. "The chance of that happening is like asking Tommy Parker to stop gazing at Tori."

"Now, you know you need to stop." Tori wiped her mouth that showcased a little sneaky grin.

"Come on now Tori. Everybody in Oak Grove knows that boy has got the hot's for you." Ruby talked with her mouth full.

"And everybody knows that you've got the hot's for Solomon Garrett." Tori smiled and sipped her punch.

"And I'm not denying it neither. I'm gonna marry him one day." She said it confident as if she knew the date, time and place.

Ginger and Tori went wild. This time they caught the boys' attention. Boyd of course treated it as a calling of some sort. He began mimicking the girls in the few words he had learned from taking German in high school, making his partner's howl.

Boyd was loud and noisy enough to get Ruby's attention. She knew that he was only reacting because of her friends who had gotten out of control at a secret confession that mistakenly rolled off her tongue. She wanted to throw something at Boyd, but there was nothing to throw at him except her shoes, and she happened to like her shoes.

"You can calm down now." She frowned at them. "Now, who's acting immature?" Ruby picked up her cup and drunk some of her punch. "I know I shouldn't have said anything."

"Well you did," Tori smiled.

"Mistake," Ruby ate more of her sandwich.

"Hush, Ruby." Ginger placed melted cheese, and grilled mushrooms in her mouth. "We'd of found out sooner or later. We always knew you liked him, just never knew you wanted to marry him. I'll design the wedding gown as long as I'm the matron of honor."

"You would say that." Tori laughed. "She's got loyalty because I've known her longer."

"When the time comes, you both will be matrons." Ruby smiled and shook her head.

"Yeah, well if she wants that designer gown for free," Ginger laughed and took another bite of her sandwich. "In all truthfulness girl, he may be fine and all, but you know he's a player."

"Yeah Rue, you know he got eyes for many. You remember Tiffany?" Tori said.

"And Sasha, Daphne, Brittney, and so on; tiger's don't change their stripes." Ginger said.

"None of them were right for him," Ruby took another bite of her sandwich.

"Girl please!" Ginger sat her sandwich on her plate.

"Rue, don't make excuses for him." Tori chewed on melted cheese and grilled onions. "After all, his name is Solomon."

"Amen to that." Ginger poured more punch.

"Well, I see a different Solomon." Ruby's pleasant demeanor had changed.

Ruby saw past his charm and good looks; past all the desperate females who would give anything to gain his attention and pull out every trick in the book to be his girl. She saw deep beneath his layers to the core of his soul. The playboy that soiled his reputation, and tainted his image was not the man she waited for. Eventually the poison would spew from his veins, and when it had ran its course they would come together, and all the leaches would be gone.

Ruby sat quietly finishing up her sandwich. A warm June breeze wiggled her hair from behind her ears, and tossed her bang over her eyes; forehead, and back over her eyes again. Whatever Tori and Ginger were saying about Solomon, she grew weary of hearing it. She'd heard it all before. Why couldn't they talk about summer, boys, proms, and being seniors come fall?

Why couldn't they laugh about conversations that they would never allow their parents to hear? Why couldn't they be making plans for college, dorm life, and naughty sleepovers? Why did it somehow always have to revolve around Solomon and how much of a player he was? If they only knew how much it hurt her when they talked like that?

She stole her bangs from the feisty winds, and tucked it tight back behind her ears. She balled up her paper that her sandwich had come in, and threw it into the trashcan. Across the way was Tiffany, one of Solomon's many girlfriends. She was one that was sickly devoted to him. No matter how many others he messed around with, heard rumors of fooling around with, or even caught him with, he couldn't seem to get rid of her. This one was the one that Ruby disliked the most.

She stared at Tiffany and Solomon. Tiffany's body was pressed against his as he sat with his legs slightly opened on his bike with his hands around her waist, and much lower than they should be. She became furious every time she saw it. But yet, her feelings hadn't changed for him. Sometimes she wished they would. Sometimes she wished for another to come along and sweep her off her feet; for Solomon to become insanely jealous and do all sorts of crazy things to woe her, only for her to deny him, and ride off into the sunset with her knight on the white horse. "Like what were the chances of that happening?" She said to herself.

She rolled her eyes from a distance and as she turned away from him, she captured his gaze. In awe, she stared back. She was stunned that he actually stopped to look at her. When she recognize what he was doing; how he was staring at her, she became nervous and turned back to her pals. What she didn't recognize was that they had seen it to.

"Look at him." Ginger tossed her cup and sandwich wrapper in the trash.

"Humph!" Tori shook her head, packed up everything and shut the picnic basket. "Ask me," she looked at her watch. "He's doing it to make you jealous. I just hope that you don't bite."

Ruby's expression was priceless. Solomon noticing her? And more importantly, her friends acknowledging his sudden interest. Her memories of Solomon were simple. In the second grade he pulled her hair; which was why she fussed with her mother to put her hair up where he couldn't pull it. However, her mother relented to ponytails, and darling barrettes; and, the boy that he was resorted to pulling her tails.

In the fourth grade, he buried her brand new pink shoes in the sand; seventh grade, he chased her across the field with a baby lizard, and now he dated every girl in Oak Grove except for her and her pals of course. Now, according to Tori and Ginger he was noticing her? She didn't know what to make of it? Could it be that her luck was changing with Solomon?

The thought of watching Solomon and Tiffany was more than she could bear. She slid her purse over her shoulder, and lifted herself up from the bench; suddenly she and everyone else in the park heard the famous bells. Immediately the park emptied, and folks were scrambling to be the first in line. From a distance, she could see the little red truck and the huge snow cone that decorated it. It had become a Hallmark in Oak Grove. For the moment, her mind had left Solomon and Tiffany, and centered in on a juicy rainbow cone, always her favorite. Instead of leaving, she found herself along with her friends, walking toward the pond, where Mr. Mosley always parked.

Mr. Mosley had been selling snow cones for over fifty years. He was a kind old man with the sweetest eyes. His snow cones were a trademark in Oak Grove. After five decades of service, he was still going strong and showed no visible signs of slowing down; retiring didn't appear as though it were in his vocabulary. He had to be approaching eighty; but, he was doing what he loved.

His authentic sounding bell cued folks to know when Mosley was courting their neighborhood. And like some sort of summonsing, or calling, they immediately stopped what they were doing, surrounded the old truck that had faded somewhat, and stood in line eagerly. Today was no different. It was hot and dry. The need to cool off was imminent. Before Ruby's eyes, the park seemed to have emptied, and lines were beginning to form around Mosley's truck.

Mr. Mosley was old and moved a little slower, but he was always prepared: Two huge barrels full of smoothed ice; several bins of tasty syrup he made from scratch and hundreds of paper cone shaped cups. Only one thing changed, Mr. Mosley had hired his great grandson Kameron for the summer.

Kameron was a junior at Cornell University in Ithaca New York. He came to Oak Grove to work on his project and learn his

Gramps business. He felt the only way to embrace that part of his heritage was to make Oak Grove his home for the summer. Kameron was tall, approximately six feet five, and extremely handsome with a scholarly look about him. Kameron was fair skinned with caramel eyes, and he had a killer smile that would make any female melt.

Oak Grove was a far cry from New York. He was still adjusting to the clean air, wild flowers, picturesque views, and the town's quaintness. Things were simple; people and family seem to matter. The sun dried linens, jeans, and tee shirts by outdoor clotheslines in the backyards of the elders who trusted God's sun over man made dryers. Oak Grove was that town of yesteryear that you read about long ago in history except this one never left. It hung around somehow. In New York, he napped over noisy traffic and construction. Here, he tossed and turned to crickets, yellow moons, and quiet.

Kameron was beginning to feel the rush of orders come in. His Gramps began to call out orders and Kameron was quickly filling them. While the crowd was gathering in lines in front of the truck, he was making cones in the back, waiting for specific orders to come up.

"Grandson," Mr. Mosley cleared his throat. "I need 10 rainbow cones; heavy on the syrup.

He quickly put the syrup on the cones, adding extra syrup as his Gramps had asked. "Here you go Gramps," he said holding the cones in a tray that his Gramps had made. Mr. Mosley smiled; took the tray, and handed them to the ones who bought them.

Kameron was a quick study. In two days, he learned the secret to mixing his great grandfather's famous syrup out back, in a tiny refurbished farmhouse where he created his legendary syrups. There was a certain thickness, flavor, and a molasses type of look that his Gramps looked for. After fifty years of mixing the serum, he knew the right mix with his eyes closed. His sense of smell alone let him know when the mix was perfect, and when it was off.

Kameron was quite impressed at how his grandfather took something as simple as flavored syrups; smooth ice, paper cones, and created a business that lasted over fifty years and made more than an adequate living, and created a family heirloom all at the same time. He continued making snow cones in the back of the truck, hardly able to keep up with the orders as a steady flow of them kept coming in.

He was hot, sweaty and tired, and had lost count of how many snow cones his Gramps had sold. It seemed the only way the orders were going to stop, was if they ran out of ice which was very likely at the pace in which the orders were coming. He had worked up a sweat scooping up ice to pre-make the cones, and dug for more cups to fill. He didn't see how his Gramps had done it for so long. From the outside, it looked easy almost too easy, but behind the simplicity of it all was a lot of hard work.

Ginger, Tori, and Ruby stood next to each other underneath the shed tree, blessed by a cool summer breeze but bothered by Boyd and the others. Of course, Tommy gazed at Tori when she wasn't looking his way, and when she turned in his direction, he easily focused his eyes on something else. As they slowly inched their way to the front, Boyd poked Tommy in the back of his leg. He fumbled forward, but caught himself. Baseball had taught him that skill.

To his surprise, he used it without thinking.

He started after Boyd again, but he and Tori's eyes met. He couldn't turn away if he wanted to; though he tried really hard. As if he were under some sort of spell, his whole body appeared paralyzed and he could neither stop his eyes from gawking nor his stiff frame from moving.

He could imagine how goofy he looked just staring. Tori was the last person he wanted to appear silly in front of. Nor, did he want her to discover his secret. However, his eyes had given it away and it was obvious that Tori knew how he felt.

Tommy's secret was out, and had only confirmed what Ginger had known all along. Excited, she poked Ruby in the side, and Ruby winced at Ginger's acrylic nail pressing into her flesh.

"Ouch!" Ruby frowned. "Are you losing your mind?"

"Look," she tilted her head towards Tori and Tommy.

"What!" Ruby grinned. "See, I knew she always liked him."

"You know Tori." Ginger folded her arms across her chest.

"Yep, knows what she wants, but not quite sure how to get it." Ruby snickered and watched Tommy muster up the courage to start a dialogue with Tori, which was more than Solomon had ever done to her.

She glanced over at Solomon and Tiffany kissing as if nobody else existed in the park but the two of them. It made her sick and of course jealous. Was she really that invisible to him? It did make her wonder at times if she were too skinny? Not cute enough? Too boring? Not popular enough? What was it? She sighed, taking a long deep breath, plundering; it stomped her. Ruby stopped herself as her thoughts were beginning to make her crazy.

She watched Tiffany in shear disgust and envy do all the things to Solomon that she wanted to do with him: Like, hold him in her arms and whisper sweet nothings in his ear. Press her body so close to his that she could feel his heartbeat, and kiss him until the sun went down. Ruby stared at the two of them for reasons she couldn't explain. However, because she resented Tiffany, in an odd way, she had a choke hold on her attention.

She had tuned everyone out except the two of them. It was as if she was studying Tiffany and not aware of Tommy, Ginger, or Tori trying several times to gain her attention so that she could take her snow cone. Kameron cleared his throat, wiped the sweat

from his brow, and asked for her name. Ginger nearly choked on her

cone at the sight of him; even Tori paused, staring at this handsome

new stranger. Tommy shook his head, and rolled his eyes at Tori.

"Her name's Ruby."

"Thanks man." Kameron said. "Excuse me, Ruby!"

As if something had snapped, she turned trying to cover up

her embarrassment. She stood looking like a deer in headlights.

Ruby didn't dare look at her friends. She just wanted to hide and

quick.

"Your cone is about to be Kool-Aid in five seconds here."

He smiled.

"Sorry," she looked sheepish.

"Let me make you another one, and I'll take this one."

He went back to the back of the truck and scooped up more

of the dwindling ice. Ginger pricked her in the side with her acrylic

nail again. "Girl, do you see what I see? That man is fine. Did you

look at him?" Ginger ate from the top of her cone.

"I hadn't noticed." Ruby frowned.

"We all could see that." Ginger shook her head.

"Ruby," Kameron handed her a fresh snow cone.

"Thanks, sorry for the trouble."

"Oh, no trouble at all," he said, finding himself gazing at Ruby who was obviously engrossed with someone else.

As he stood eating the cone she had nearly let melt, he couldn't help but stare at her, while Ginger persisted in gazing at him. He didn't even see her. Ruby had his full attention. Poor Tommy had no one's attention, not even Tori's. His Demeanor changed and in his face was a hint of jealousy at how even Tori was caught with a jaw dropping look at Kameron.

"I'm outta here," he said, rejoining Solomon and his posse.

"Tommy, where are you going?" Tori yelled.

"Hit some rounds," he turned, knowing he was lying.

"Tommy…"

"Gotta go," he said, cutting her short.

She watched him join his boy's and watched them leave. She sighed, turned, shaking her head, clueless as to what she had done to make Tommy leave when he had finally broken the ice with her.

She ate more of her snow cone that was beginning to turn to mush. Ruby stood next to her eating her cone with an inquisitive look in her eyes.

"What's up with Tommy? He's acting kind of weird all of a sudden." Ruby said.

"I have no idea. One minute we were talking, the next, he's acting funny style." Tori looked concerned.

"Well, I wouldn't…" Ruby stopped herself as she couldn't believe her eyes. "You seeing what I'm seeing?"

"Oh yeah," Tori grinned, forgetting about Tommy for a moment. "I think she's stomped."

"Yep," Ruby whistled.

Ruby's whistle had suddenly taken her out of her zone. In ways she would find hard to admit to Ruby, suddenly she was beginning to understand how Ruby felt about Solomon. There was something about him that was different from any of the boys she liked.

Maybe that was it? They were boys, but this handsome stranger in Mr. Mosley's truck was a man, and she wanted him.

Though she had rejoined her pals on the bench, underneath the shed tree, her mind and eyes were on Kameron, and she was hearing only half of a conversation.

Her mind posed a million questions. Who was he? Where did he come from? What relationship was he to Mr. Mosley? And what in the world was he doing here? He had her attention and she was determined to learn more about him. She was sure that Ruby must have heard something about him in the shop. The women who made it their business to come to Ruby's mother's salon knew everything; nothing got by them. So, how did he roll into town without as much as a whisper? Ruby had some explaining to do.

Kameron pulled off his glasses and wiped his forehead with the back side of his arm. He was hot and sweaty and welcomed the thick breeze that swept through the window of his grandfather's truck. He put his glasses back on, and noticed his Gramps walking brisker than a man his age should. As he approached the truck, he assumed he was with a group of his friends. They were laughing and talking like old men.

"Hey Gramps, we're out of ice." Kameron stuck his head out of the window.

Ruby and Tori were too engrossed in talking about Tommy Parker's sudden interest in Tori and his stunning bold move, that they didn't even hear Kameron call out to his grandfather. But, Ginger did and, of course she became excited.

"You hear that?" She leaped from the bench. "You hear that?" Ginger couldn't contain her excitement.

Tori and Ruby paused. Their eyebrows slanted and a hint of annoyance stood bold in their young faces. It was obvious that she hadn't been listening and she was skating on a thin block of betrayal.

"What are you talking about? Did you hear one thing that Tori was saying?" Ruby asked.

"Does she look like she was even trying to listen?" Tori rolled her eyes.

"I was listening." She said, lying of course. "But, I was also trying to get the dirt on who that fine man is in Mr. Mosley's truck. Now, I know who he is, he's Mr. Mosley's Grandson." Her eyes sparkled.

"So," Ruby said. "Tommy Parker just made a major move on Tori, and you didn't even hear the spicy details. Who cares about what his face on the truck?"

"Really," Tori agreed. "Just so you know, I'm not repeating the details."

"Fine, but don't act like you didn't notice him. I saw how you looked at him, and Tommy obviously saw it to." Ginger said.

"So, he's cute?" Tori said.

"Fine is more appropriate, and the both of you are gonna help me get him." Ginger looked his way.

Tori and Ruby looked at each other. A surprised look loomed from their faces. They giggled somewhat bewildered, trying to figure out if Ginger was serious or not. Ginger was one who was not easily impressed. She was the one who had a long list of criteria's for her man. And, she vowed to stay single until she found the one who would adhere to every single condition that was inscribed on her scroll. Ruby tested her theory.

"Does he at least fit one of your benchmarks on your list?" Ruby said.

"Oh no you didn't," Tori laughed.

"See," Ginger had to snicker. "Don't get me started on you girl. You were too busy staring at Solomon and Jezebel to even notice him."

"Whatever!" Ruby laughed, and finished her snow cone, knowing that she had gotten her.

Kameron placed the out of ice sign on the truck and the few straggler's that stumbled in appeared disappointed as their eyes met the sign on the truck. Ginger of course was watching it all, thinking of a way to mosey over to the truck, and officially introduce herself without appearing hard up or desperate. But, staring at him only made her draw a blank. Ruby stood placing her bag over her shoulder. Tori gathered her picnic basket, and placed her back pack purse across her shoulders.

"Ready," Ruby said.

"Yep," Tori said. "This heat is starting to get out of control."

"Tell me about it." Ruby said, noticing her pal gazing at Kameron. She hunched Tori and both stood smiling, watching Ginger melt. Ruby couldn't help herself.

"Wouldn't it be easier if you just went over and officially introduced yourself?" Ruby teased.

"I'll get my moment." Ginger said, placing her hand bag on her shoulder still eyeing Kameron.

"I bet you will." Tori said.

Kameron was still hot and his red polo shirt was soaked in perspiration. Beads of sweat rolled down his face as he cleaned and dried the tin buckets that his Gramps used to place extra ice in. Unable to endure the heat any longer, he pulled off his shirt with only a thin, sleeveless, cotton tee shirt beneath. His body felt cooler, and it was as if the removal of the shirt allowed his body to breathe. As he stacked the buckets neatly inside of each other, he noticed the girls leaving. He stopped briefly and watched them for a moment. Somehow his eyes became transfixed on Ruby and the sway of her hips, and her long shapely legs walking with spunk and confidence. He liked that. He liked it a lot.

Temporarily, he had forgotten about the buckets, and finishing the task of taking down the truck, and making it ready for the next day. His attention was elsewhere, which is why when his Gramps placed a hand on his shoulder, he jumped a little. His

Gramps teased and balled up both his fist, and tossed around a few

jabs.

"Got something on your mind son?" He said.

"Just trying to keep up with you is all," Kameron put up his

dukes and threw a couple of playful jabs at his Gramps.

He picked up the buckets, and his Gramps smacked him on

the back. It was a proud smack; a smack that Mosley men had given

their sons for generations. They headed back to the old red truck

with the faded sun at their backs; the blistering day starting to cool.

It was a long day, but a productive one. They sold everything, with

nothing left except for empty tin buckets, and an old garden hose

that Mr. Mosley took with him to wash down his buckets after the

ice was gone. It was an odd way of learning about his heritage. But,

he had been warned by his father and so it was something in which

he had come to expect. What he didn't expect was to be taken by

Ruby. He looked over his shoulder again as if he would see her, but

his eyes met an empty park, and a faded orange sun. They loaded

the truck and drove away

Chapter 2

The day was still, but the sting of summer persisted. From a distance, it seemed as though Oak Grove was deserted. It appeared that the only sign of life that existed were in the salons and the barbershops. Ladies despite the fierce heat were getting their hair styled, and the men were going bald, or at least getting their hair cut close.

Ben Nelson had a 42 inch flat screen television mounted to the back wall of his shop. He was a Dodger fan and he loved the game of baseball. His shop reflected his love of the sport; memorabilia from the Brooklyn Dodgers, a signed baseball by the late Jackie Robinson, along with an autograph photo of the young Jackie and Ben smiling as they stood side by side. His place was more than a barbershop; it was a huge piece of history.

It was the first thing that everyone noticed when they walked in and what they looked at when they walked out. Ben was a historian in his own right. He knew the game of baseball like he knew the right cut for a man's hair. His customers were in admiration of his knowledge of the game. They loved the fact that he was a walking encyclopedia regarding Dodger History.

Solomon on the other hand had grown up in Dodger mania. Before he could even speak, there were pictures of him dressed in Dodger gear at the ball park, sitting happily on his grandpa's lap cheering, clapping, and swaying his Dodger balloon, smiling. He had seen it all; heard it all, but unlike his grandpa, Dodger fever never quite captured his restless spirit.

At an early age, he learned from his grandpa to not only cut hair, but to trim, style, and master the art of pleasing a customer. At the tender age of twelve, Solomon had earned a chair, a brand new set of clippers, and to his dismay, his future. He saw it all, the thinning of his cold black hair; the invasion of snow white hair waiting patiently under the sealed roots of black. He saw the potbelly from beer, and the mouthwatering soul food that tricked a slim waist at seventeen. Their stories would become his stories, and by the time he was thirty, he'd become one of them, and his son would inherit his chair.

He smiled his grandpa's smile and placed a long apron around his customers' neck. He learned over the years to talk and jive respectably with the old men. He enjoyed them, appreciated their wisdom, and he was mesmerized by lots of their stories of rising from nothing to standing tall in their own shoes as men.

As they had struggled, survived, and rose up from the ashes to take ownership of their own lives, he wanted the same opportunity and choices. He didn't want kind old men, or destiny handing him his grandpa's barbershop. It had to be more to him than that, but how was he supposed to seep through this cloud that hovered over him to find it?

"Didn't bring your bag of Lays barbecue potato chips with you today Mr. Fletcher?" Solomon smiled.

"Ah damn," Mr. Fletcher snapped his crippled fingers. "Don't tell me I sat on my butt and left them chips on my eating table in my kitchen?" He frowned.

Mr. Fletcher was 92. His family was one of the first families to live in Oak Grove. He was one of the first planners in the city and still sat on the board today. He was medium height, brown skin, eyes hopeful, and optimistic. He still attended church on Sunday's, and took his 5am stroll with his dog lady.

He still kept the community garden, and when he saw patches of distress in the city, he'd marched down to city Hall and get a waiver to beautify the property. Mr. Fletcher pulled out his cell phone, which always cracked Solomon up, about to dial his wife's cell.

"This ain't gonna work son. I gotta call my Dottie; see if I can't get her to bring them on down here?" He started to dial.

"I think I can fix that Mr. Fletcher. I got you covered on that end." Solomon smiled, and pulled out a bag of Lays barbecue chips.

"Well I'll be got dog," he said, surprised. "That's some good looking out there."

"Thanks," Solomon grinned.

"Say Ben," He said.

"Yeah," He turned off his clippers briefly.

"Better keep this boy here, I tell you, he definitely worth the salt in his bread." He held the bag of chips up proud.

Ben winked at Solomon. "He's a keeper. This will all be his someday."

Solomon sighed and subtlety rolled his eyes. "A little off the sides and the top Mr. Fletcher." Solomon turned on his clippers.

"You got it son. You sure know the old man by now." Mr. Fletcher dug into his bag of barbecue chips.

Solomon trimmed his already thinning hair, and removed the subtle whiskers from around his chin, and slapped some nice smelling after shave on his face. His mind was elsewhere, but he learned how to file his dreams in a safe box inside his head and talk the jargon that made him a favorite at the shop.

"Oh," he laughed. "Mrs. Fletcher gonna have her way with you now." Solomon joked with Mr. Fletcher.

"Been a mac my entire life son," Mr. Fletcher stood, did a funky dance move and turned an old man's turn.

Solomon roared and the men in the shop echoed behind him. Mr. Fletcher always knew how to make him laugh even in the midst of private turmoil. He paid Solomon his twenty-five dollars, and then surprised him with a huge twenty-five dollar tip. Solomon reached in his cabinet and took out his cash box, about to give Mr. Fletcher back his change.

"Nah, nah," he waved his hand. "You a good condition kid, always doing right by the old man, and all the other men who come sit in your chair."

Solomon smiled wide, shook Mr. Fletcher's hand, and thanked him. He glanced over at his grandfather, but his Grandpa just smiled and gave him the thumbs up sign. He smiled back. But he felt something inside, and whatever it was, it gave him permission to explore his own dreams.

"No problem got to take care of my peeps." He fist bumped Mr. Fletcher, glad he allowed him to be seventeen.

"You're a good man." Mr. Fletcher patted his shoulder. "God got something for you son, and you hold onto that, you here."

"Yes sir." Solomon said.

His eyes widen a bit at Mr. Fletcher's words. Mr. Fletcher said it with a conviction as if God had specifically sent him there to say it.

"Look at him," an old man joked. "He's ready to hop right up on outta here and go find him a honey to spend it on."

The shop again became engulfed with laughter. The laughter of old men who had been seventeen, and could laugh at their immaturity, and their know it all view on women.

Solomon laughed with these elder men, but little did they know that he had a way with women to.

He didn't know what it was, but to the young ladies, he was like a magnet. He loved it of course, but to choose the one was always an issue for him. Before he could even begin to form any sort of a relationship with a potential girlfriend, he'd be swooned by another female, and another, and so forth. Like a blood thirsty vampire, he needed something from all of them. He had gotten his face slapped a few times, but they always came back. And if they didn't, there were always droves of new ones wanting him.

He couldn't explain it, but it empowered him, added a few manly hairs on his chest. Despite his mother's constant badgering about this trait that he developed from his no good father, only angered him and troubled him. If she only knew how much it hurt her son and drew him into behaviors that affected his sexual cravings, she would have stopped immediately.

It was busy in the shop and the men despite the heat kept coming. His grandpa and the men had tuned into Dodger baseball. His grandpa had started his dictionary of facts about his team.

And, he swore on a stack of bibles that Manny Ramirez's contract would not be renewed for the next season, and that his boy Tommy Parker would take his place. Scouts were already looking at Tommy Parker and lately they had begun to visit his home and bombarded his grandmother and grandfather with calls.

His grandpa loved Tommy Parker's athleticism, his focus, and passion for the game. In his mind, Tommy had all what it took to be part of a team that was a legend. He knew that if Jackie Robinson, Sandy Koufax, and Don Drysdale where alive, that they'd be pursuing Tommy, and they too would want him on their team. He listened to the men, and talked with his customers, and every time he heard Vin Scully with his famous, "going, going, gone," and his grandpa and the patrons celebrating, he'd turn and look at the television and see the scoreboard at the ball park flash homerun.

He watched his grandfather and he could see that he was content, had lived his life, and settled into his special place. He wondered if that would ever be for him. He finished another customer; thanked him, swept up the hair, and tossed it in the trash.

A soft knock tapped on the wooden door above the screen entry. Ruby walked in with steaming trays of fried chicken, okra and tomatoes, cornbread, and peach cobbler. Solomon saw her hands were full and rushed to assist her. She tried to hide her smile, but it managed to break through. Her eyes were glued to Solomon like she truly belonged to him. And though the men were engrossed in the baseball game, even they could see her fondness of him. And like old men did, they grinned, hunched each other, and tried to help her out.

"Say Solomon, why don't you offer the lady a plate?" Mr. Fletcher winked at Solomon. "There's plenty and there's no need for all this good food to go to waste."

"Oh no," Ruby felt a bold rush inside of her head. "I have to go. Tori had a dentist appointment, and I'm only filling in till she gets back. Besides, I have three ladies at the shop waiting on me."

"Sounds like they got you on the run, don't they honey," Ben said, handing her a crisp fifty and she handed him back a ten.

"Yeah, I'm used to it." She caught a glimpse of Solomon. "Enjoy," she turned, and took another look at Solomon, and rushed to the door.

"Say Ruby," he bit into a piece of peach cobbler. "Bet Mrs. Pauline made this peach cobbler?"

"She did." She said.

"Almost as sweet as you," Solomon stunned her with his flirting, and for a minute she was taken by it.

Suddenly, she remembered yesterday, and all she could see was him and Tiffany lip locking; like it was just happening, it fueled her with anger. She stared at him briefly, and for a moment she forgot how much she loved him. The shop grew silent again, and despite the baseball game, the men sat watching her and Solomon, wondering how she would respond.

"You must be talking about Tiffany. You know the one you just couldn't get enough of in the park yesterday. Gentlemen, enjoy your lunch." She smiled at them and rolled her eyes at him.

Laughter suddenly breathed life into the shop again, and Solomon was completely embarrassed. He reacted the only way he knew how. He swallowed the rest of his cobbler and went after Ruby.

"Hey! Hey!" he caught up with her at her father's Red Chevy Silverado truck. "What was that all about?"

"I'm in a hurry Solomon."

"So, you're jealous huh?"

"Please I..."

Solomon overtook her lips with a voluptuous kiss. Before she knew it, she was locked in his arms kissing him like he was hers. It was better than what she could ever have imagined. Something had snapped inside of Solomon and he found it hard to pull himself away from Ruby.

The men had totally left the Dodger game. They couldn't resist seeing what they thought may be poor Solomon getting his face slapped and a few choice words. So, they peeped out the windows, and some stood on the wide porch only to see Ruby snuggled in Solomon's arms smooching.

Some were stunned and opened mouth, including Solomon's Grandfather Ben. Mr. Fletcher, being the man that he was, spared them no privacy to their moment. He clapped and whistled. Stunned out of her heated trans, Ruby leaped into her father's truck and sped off.

Solomon stood watching; a huge smile covered his lips, and made its way up toward his handsome face. Ruby of course reacted differently. She had been busted by old men in a barbershop who were no different than the old women at her mother's salon, and like them they would talk. However, she didn't want to deal with her father on that matter. What was she thinking? Solomon made her dizzy, and she couldn't help herself.

Her heart pounded crazy in her chest. Her head was spinning as if she was drunk, and she was so overjoyed that she was liable to float away. She took several deep breaths trying to calm herself as she pulled up in front of her mother's salon. She put the truck in park and celebrated; stomping her feet on the carpet and bopping up and down, screaming as though something grandiose had occurred in her life. For her it did?

She pinched herself, and winced a little. She pulled down her dad's mirror, and looked at her lips to see if they looked kissed. She couldn't tell, but they felt different. It felt like it was supposed to happen, and like he had meant it.

She couldn't wait to tell her pals Tori and Ginger. This would be their topic of conversation for weeks. She speed dial for Ginger, as she felt her heart thumping ferociously, like an untamed drum. It rung twice, then Ginger answered.

"Hey," she said, as she paused from hemming a garment she was making. "I've been trying to call and so has Tori. What's going on?"

"Are you standing or sitting?" Ruby got out of her father's truck.

"Sitting, why? Should I be standing?" Ginger laid down her garment and stood.

"Solomon and I were kissing girl." Ruby felt the rush all over again.

Ginger screamed from the top of her lungs, and Ruby joined her as she stood outside of her mother's shop.

Chapter 3

Ruby's screaming and excitement outside of the shop captured her mother's attention and a few of the women in the shop as well. Precious paused from wet setting her customer's hair. For a moment, the shop was quiet; absent of old lady gossip, venting, relationship advice, and news they hadn't gotten around to from the previous time. Precious walked toward the big picture window and looked at her daughter and she knew that a boy was involved.

She took a deep breath and shook her head. She had hoped that this part of her life would show up after college, but Ruby's hormones had taken a detour, and she was so unprepared for this part of her life to take place. She walked to the wooden screen door, and stepped out on the porch.

"Uh-oh," Mrs. Amy said, "It's a man involved I know it."

"Girl, it's summer," Mrs. Fletcher peeped out of the window. "You get a mix of nature, hormones, and summer, and you know it's the season of love honey, and she at the age…"

she paused her speech, listening to Precious at the window.

"Ruby Amber Wells, what in God's name is wrong with you?" Precious placed her hands on her hips. "You got folks in here waiting on you girl."

Ruby met her mother's eyes and her conversation with Ginger stopped abruptly. "I have to go Gin. My mama's out on the front porch."

"Did you forget that you've got three women waiting' on you?" Her mother frowned.

"Mama, you know that I had to do a delivery for daddy since Tori had a dentist appointment." Ruby put her cell back in her purse. "Sorry I'm late."

Precious sighed staring at her daughter, and with one look in her eyes, she could see her own: young and swept away by love. Of course she didn't mean for it to happen, but it did. It's what happened to girls Ruby's age and from experience Precious knew that there was little that she could do about it.

Without prying too deeply into her daughter's soul, she could see the teenager inside upgrading to a woman. As a mother, it was a celebration and a curse. She too had fell victim to summer and its spell of love many years ago, and now it had gotten her daughter. However, love would have a fight on its hands.

"What?" Ruby said. She could see in her mother's eyes that she felt something, and her mother was not the type that would let issues rest.

"Maybe that's what I should be asking you?" She folded her arms.

"It's hot mama, and like you said I've got ladies waiting."

"Oh, so now its suddenly hot, wasn't hot five minutes ago," Precious said opening the door and smacking Ruby on the butt.

All eyes were on Ruby the moment she walked into the shop. Ruby saw the same look in the eyes of the old ladies that she had saw in her mother's eyes. She avoided their deep inquisitive looks, and scurried back to the back in a rush to put her purse up. She heard them giggling and teasing her mother.

She put on her apron, and took a deep breath before she went out to the lobby to call Mrs. Fletcher back to the wash bowl. The shop resumed its voice again with some of the older women teasing

Ruby.

"Girl, he must be something special for Ms. Ruby to be late." Mrs. Fletcher said.

"Um-hum," Mrs. Amy said, flipping through an Oprah magazine. "Who is he?"

"He is no one." She lied. "Come on Mrs. Fletcher, let's get you started."

"Girl, tell the truth and shame the devil," Mrs. Amy said. "You can't keep secrets in small towns."

"Not this one anyway," Ruby's voice trailed off down the hallway.

"So," Mrs. Amy said. "You do have a honey, but just choosing not to tell. You hear that Precious?" She teased.

Um-hum," her mother said. "Secrets got a shelf life."

"That's the truth." Mrs. Amy laughed.

"I am not gonna even answer that." Ruby brought Mrs. Fletcher back to the front and placed her underneath the dryer.

Mrs. Fletcher took her head from underneath the dryer briefly. "Child please," she said. You don't have to. It's that

Mosley boy. From what I hear, all these young girls are at him."
She placed her head back under the dryer.

Ruby didn't say a word. She was thankful that Mrs. Fletcher
had it all wrong. Now, she could breathe a sigh of relief. By the
time they did get to the truth, their theory would have taken a detour.
And, she'd cross that bridge when she got to it.

"Is it time for your rinse today Mrs. Odette?" Ruby adjusted
the water and began washing her hair.

"I suppose it is." She said. "When you get my age, them
grays will fight you. They wait a lifetime to take root, so I guess
they got a right."

Ruby laughed as she rinsed the shampoo out of her hair, and
began washing it again. Mrs. Odette was Tommy Parker's
grandmother, and Ruby could see where Tommy had gotten his
stocky build from along with his gentleness. Mrs. Odette did more
listening than she did talking. But, when she did say something in
the shop she captured everybody's attention, even Mrs. Amy paid
attention.

Mrs. Odette and her husband Clive owned and operated their

own dairy farm. They pretty much serviced the whole town with milk, eggs, butter and fresh produce. Odette had inherited the entire farm from her Grandfather Red who was part Pomo Indian. During summers when tourist came, Mrs. Odette allowed visitors to pick fresh produce from her small produce farm and pay at the small storefront that Tommy ran.

Tommy and his grandfather were always bringing over loads of items to her father's restaurant. Her dad had an account with them and everything her father and his staff prepared had to taste like it had been fresh picked from someone's garden and it was. Ruby emptied the bottle of dye and massaged it gingerly into Odette's roots, covering the gray.

"Child," Mrs. Odette patted Ruby's arm. "You got some blessed fingers. I could go to sleep behind you scratching the dirt out the old girls head."

"Thanks." Ruby smiled. "I do my best."

As Ruby began rinsing out Mrs. Odette's hair, Solomon had come across her mind. She could dwell on his kiss forever, and ever. What would Tiffany and the others think?

She played it in her mind over and over again, but she worried; worried about the men at the barbershop. For the men at the barbershop were just like the women at her mom's shop; nosey.

Though they hid it, they stood shoulder to shoulder with the women wanting to be the first to be barriers of juicy hot news. What troubled her was that the women in the shop were the wives of the men at the barbershop, and that what happened between her and Solomon would get back to her parents, and all hell would break loose. She had heard it all too many times, the women in the shop talking about Solomon's father, how much of looker he was, and how he had a reputation with the ladies. Solomon bore the habits of his father and so, they were talked about as if they were one in the same.

Just when she put the finishing touches on Mrs. Odette's hair, her cell phone vibrated against her thigh. Without looking, she knew who it was, and she knew that somebody had talked. She wiped her hands, and answered.

"You know you've got bad timing." She said.

"Screw you." Tori said. "I had to hear it from someone else and I'm pissed."

Tori could barely talk for the excitement she felt. Ruby snickered, and excused herself from putting conditioner in Mrs. Odette's hair.

"Excuse me Mrs. Odette, be right back." She said, stepping outside the back door, which led to a full backyard and a nice patio with a beautiful view.

"Tommy told me what happened." Tori was still excited. "And, I don't appreciate hearing it from him."

"Brother, just what I need," Ruby took a deep breath. "You mean Gin didn't tell you? She called me just as I pulled up at the shop."

"She did, but Tommy got to me first. So, what happened?" Tori sat on the bench outside of Ruby's father's restaurant.

"Tori, I'm here at the shop. I don't think I want my mama to be hearing what happen between me and Solomon." Ruby peeped in on Mrs. Odette.

"You know she's gonna find out. You know how folks talk around here." Tori smiled.

"Well, she had better not hear it from you." Ruby said. "Look, I gotta go, can't keep Mrs. Odette waiting."

"Call me," Tori said.

"Later, I promise. Bye," Ruby hung up.

Ruby took a deep breath, placed her cell back into her apron pocket, and returned to the wash bowl to finish conditioning Mrs. Odette's hair. The moment she had feared arrived. How long would it take the chain of gossip to travel her mother's way? She paused, thinking how she would try to defuse it when it showed up.

"Okay Mrs. Odette, time to head for the dryer." She placed a clean dry towel around her neck, and placed the wet one in the bin where the laundry service would pick them up.

"Alright baby," Mrs. Odette said.

Ruby gave Mrs. Odette the latest Oprah magazine, and an ice cold Coke from the refrigerator, and set her under the dryer for forty-five minutes. From the wash bowl area, she heard laughter and dirty jokes, and things that old ladies got embarrassed about when she heard it. She loved the looks in their eyes; caught being young again and in love in theory in the back seats of cars, and forbidden beds that mama's and grannies took belts to.

All they could do was laugh loud and hard. And, in the same sentence, resort back to who they had become; delightful old women that warned her and all young girls approaching that place in their lives, was to run like hell; get all what they could out of life, and then fall in love. But of course, most didn't listen. They knew it all at seventeen. Years later, they would pay an ugly price. She rinsed Mrs. Fletcher's hair; grabbed more conditioner and towels, peeped in on Mrs. Odette, and turned down her dryer a bit.

"You weren't supposed to hear that little girl," Mrs. Amy dried her eyes from laughing.

"Not supposed to hear lots of things Mrs. Amy," She said with a sly grin. Ruby gave Mrs. Fletcher an orange soda that was cool not cold, and a bag of coconut stacks. Anything too cold gave her chills. She always talked about how cold her blood was, and how she drove her husband Corey nuts about being so cold natured.

It was amazing how from just one of them sharing something as simple as that, that other stories evolved, and soon the relationship experts immerged. Soon they would forget that Ruby was in the shop and they'd get old lady again. Suddenly Ruby would hear her mother say, "Hey now, my babies in the room." Ruby laughed nothing she hadn't heard before.

That's what she loved most about the shop, listening to the laughter of wise women who had risen from journeys in their life. Be it their thorns, hardships, or just plain old bad luck, they had learned all too well how to recycle life's adversities. She loved that about them and hoped she'd be able to do that someday. Ruby put her last client under the dryer and took solace on the porch swing.

The air outside was warm. The wind had bent the sting of the heat somewhat; to sit outside was bearable. The chimes on the porch danced to the restless winds, and the sign just above it rattled sort of the way Solomon had rattled her earlier. Without a doubt, she knew that things would be different between them. It scared her as much as it excited her. Perhaps her Grandma Pauline was right about love and summer? For, there seem to be a powerful ingredient in the stillness of summer that induced a potent element that spoke to the powers of love. Today it had spoken to her and the way Solomon kissed her had whispered in his ears as well.

She sat with her eyes closed; the wind gently pushing her in the porch swing. She envisioned Solomon and her walking by the lake holding hands; him saying something goofy she laughing, and him chasing her only to catch her, and kiss her. She saw him feeding her pizza and kissing the cheese off of her lip; and surprising her with bouquets of Tulips and Morning Glory's. She'd be the envy of all the girls who had dated him prior and suddenly they'd be banished from his existence.

Ruby was so taken by her dreams that she didn't hear the alarm she had set; nor did she hear her mother call her the first time, but the second time had gotten her attention.

"Ruby," Precious stood outside the screen door.

"Yeah," a blank look appeared on her face.

"Timer went off girl; didn't you hear me calling you?" Her mother said.

"I was thinking about the program at Stanford." She lied. "I could finish in four years instead of five." Ruby lifted her body from the swing.

"Five years will be just fine with me," Precious placed an arm around Ruby and kissed her on the cheek. "They'll be plenty enough time for college and dorm life."

Ruby smiled; happy she had temporarily fooled her mother. Secrets in Oak Grove had a shelf life. So she was constantly thinking of ways to break the news to her mother and father before the townsfolk did. She re-entered the shop and walked into a conversation about God and faith. It was another trip down memory lane and quite the sight to see. Old ladies in large green plastic hair curlers, flipping through magazines, sipping on cold cola's and frosty fruit juices, talking over thick, hot smoke from curling irons, and pressing combs, was a snapshot of life in the beauty shop and Oak Grove.

She tapped Mrs. Fletcher and took the station next to her mother. She noticed that her iron was already plugged in and that tiny smoke began to seep up from the stove and sway than disappear into thin air. She knew that her mother had turned it on; in fact, she had always turned it on. Habit probably. No matter how much Ruby asked her not to she did. Ruby had gotten used to it, and now, she sort of expected it. She rubbed coconut oil over Mrs. Fletcher's hair, and began pressing it and listening to the women.

"Girl," Mrs. Amy said. "I see that Mosley and his wife got that handsome grandson of theirs visiting." She said. "From what I hear, he's from New York; attending college there they say." She looked over towards Ruby. "Have you met him Ruby?"

Ruby was totally caught off guard. For a minute her thoughts had knotted up inside her head and she didn't know how to respond. She pretended to cough as if something had gotten into her throat. She held up one hand as if she were going to answer them. They paused waiting.

"Yeah," she said. "He was working with Mr. Mosley yesterday on the snow cone truck. He made Gin, Tori and I snow cones." Ruby blew on the pressing comb and turned Mrs. Fletcher around in the chair facing the front door pressing her last strand of silver hair.

"Is he handsome?" Mrs. Fletcher asked. "Go at him honey, them Mosley's got plenty of money."

"Mrs. Fletcher." Ruby laughed as she sprayed oil sheen on her hair. "I thought you said we should marry for love…"

"And for money," she paid Ruby. "I'm old baby and let me tell you." She took a seat by the window. "There ain't nothing worse than being in love and broke."

"Your secrets out Mrs. Fletcher," Ruby said, and all the old ladies laughed hard.

But, that's why they liked her. She was young but somehow she understood their culture though she was way too young to live it. She called them Mrs., and answered yes Ma'am, helped them in and out of their chairs, chilled their sodas and juices and listened to their stories as if they were her own. She even laughed at the promiscuous days of their youth. On top of all of that, she made them look and feel beautiful, and they worshipped her for it. Though she was only seventeen, they felt like she was one of them. For not every seventeen year old was privy to this circle.

She listened to more talk in the shop. It was like church on a Sunday except the subjects kept changing from one extreme to the next. It was the life of the shop and she had grown used to it. It was the way older women communicated; the way they got things off of their chest, the way they let things go.

It was a classic moment; a connection with women who shared seasons of struggles as well as periods of glory, and listening to them was like a relaxing warm bath. If she weren't blow drying Ginger's mother's hair, she could have easily fallen to sleep. Ruby twisted Jasmine's hair, and then placed a clip on top of it. Ginger's hair was her mother's hair, full, thick, and auburn. Jasmine Maples was easy. She loved her flip with a little spice at the top, and Ruby made it work for her all the time.

"Mrs. Maples," Ruby said. "You mind if I wet set Mrs. Odette real quick?"

"No baby," she smiled. "You go right ahead and do your thing."

"Mama, can I use your station?" She asked

"Yeah, baby, go head." Precious smiled.

Ruby slid over to her station and pulled out the soft pink plastic curlers. Mrs. Odette was tender headed and she couldn't take the hard plastic curlers. She liked a lot of curls and only liked for Ruby to slightly pull out her curls into ringlets. As she worked on Mrs. Odette's hair, she couldn't help but think of Solomon and how he had stunned her with a kiss. It would be on her mind all day. She only hoped that it would be on his?

Solomon couldn't escape the teasing he had gotten from the elder men. He didn't seem to mind it at all. He had been contemplating his move on Ruby for a while now, but because she was different from all the girls he messed with, he needed something fresh and today was it. Like a chess game, he needed to contemplate his next move.

"So how come you didn't tell us that you were digging on Miss Ruby?" Mr. Fletcher said.

"I wanted to show y'all." Solomon grinned.

"What, show us your mac skills?" Mr. Fletcher laughed."

"You cannot be a mac with that one." His Grandfather said. "She is one of the good ones. If you want her, you had better toss that black book, because she ain't having it." He laughed.

"She's been into me forever Pops." He said to his Grandfather. "I got this."

"Really," his Grandfather said. "Y'all better tell this fool something."

"Son you will get your feelings hurt if you try and treat her like the other ones." Mr. Fletcher said. "Go home boy and listen to Ray Parker Jr. He tells it like it is don't he Ben."

"Breaks it down," His Grandfather said. "He'll see. She's a Wells."

Solomon just smiled not taking his Grandfather or the rest of the older men seriously. He knew how Ruby felt about him. Look how long she had waited for him? He couldn't wait to converse with his boys.

Ruby was just about done. In between thinking of Solomon, she tuned into the gossip at the shop. Mrs. Amy and Mrs. Fletcher knew everything, nothing got past them. Somehow she had caught the tail end of a conversation about Ginger going away to college in New York.

"I don't understand for the life of me why my child wants to go to college all the way back in New York." Jasmine watched Ruby style her hair. "I am so not ready for that."

"I bet she's ready though." Mrs. Fletcher said. "These young folk scare the death out of me. They ain't ever been around the corner, and will jump at a chance to go to the other side of the world. Talk to that girl. She can go right to a school in Los Angeles and do what she needs to do about this fashion."

Ruby couldn't help but laugh. Mrs. Fletcher was very animated when she talked, and she was a natural born comedian too. Ginger would not want to hear that for sure. She was very determined to go to college in New York. For her, it was where her dream of being the ultimate designer would begin. It was all she talked about, and she kept a pocket calendar in her purse where she placed a big red X on SAT clinics, application deadlines, and of course graduation. Ginger and New York seem to have a weird sort of connection. And, one way or the other she would get there, even if she had to walk.

"They'll all end up at the same college." Mrs. Amy said. They're shadows of each other wherever one goes the other will follow. You can bet on that." She looked over towards Ruby.

Ruby blew on the curling irons and laughed as she began curling Jasmine's hair. Without a doubt she knew where she was going. She loved Ginger as if she was her own sister, but she couldn't picture herself in such a large city that never slept. On that note, Oak Grove had spoiled her, and she liked the sound of restless crickets, humming birds, and soft train whistle's in the distance.

Precious blew on her curling iron and looked at Ruby. She knew for sure where Ruby was headed; Stanford. It was all she talked about. In fact, she was pressing both of her parents to let her graduate early so she could attend in the fall. She of course wasn't ready for her daughter to take on adult life at seventeen. However, adulthood whether she liked it or not was slowly coming onto the seen as evident by the boy who had captured her vulnerable heart in love.

Ruby sprayed Jasmine's hair with a light oil sheen and took the smock from around her neck. Jasmine paid her and gave her a warm hug. Ruby swept and cleared her station, placed all the soiled towels in the bin and took off her apron. She grabbed her purse out of the cabinet and sat it on her station briefly.

"Well," she said, placing her purse on her shoulder. "I'm going." She turned, picked up her mother's Coke and took a few sips. "Did you need anything else mama?"

"No baby, I'm good." Precious said. "Where you headed from here?" She asked.

The door opened and the chattering amongst the women stopped briefly. Ruby turned and her whole demeanor changed. She nearly fell into her mother's styling chair at the sight of Solomon standing there with a red bag in his hand that said Jerome's beauty Supply. He spoke friendly to all of the ladies, but his eyes stayed fixed on Ruby.

"Hi Mrs. Wells," he said, walking towards her. "My pops wanted me to bring you these smocks. He said he'd borrowed some and just kept forgetting to bring them over." He looked Ruby up and down. "Hey Ruby," he grinned.

Ruby swallowed hard, and she hated the look that weighed in the eyes of the women, and of course her mother. She wanted to disappear. What in the world was Solomon doing there? She was sure that the smocks had probably just been sitting there at the barbershop. Mr. Nelson and her mother often borrowed items from each other and would send over supplies sometimes months later. Why now would he bring them over?

The women in the shop watched intensely. Ruby knew they were watching her, and she knew that they knew something. She could feel her mother's eyes and she fought hard not to turn to face her. One look at her mother and her secret was stolen from her, and she could not let that happen, at least not this way.

"Ruby," her mother said. "Didn't you hear the boy speak to you?

"Hey Solomon," she said.

"What's up?" He stared. "Okay, if I sit them here." He asked.

"Sure honey." She said, with her eyes solely on Ruby.

"How's that mama of yours baby?" Mrs. Fletcher said.

"She's fine. She's doing another double at the hospital." He said.

"You know baby," Mrs. Amy said. "You are every spit of your daddy; handsome just like him. Bet you got a lot of girls chasing behind you?" She glanced over at Ruby.

Ruby said her good-byes and rushed out of the shop. As much as she adored Solomon, she wanted to smack his face. He should have known better. Little did he know that he had given the ladies at the shop permission to pry, and her mother a license to act on her instinct. One look at Solomon staring at her daughter and bringing over smocks that she had forgotten she had even borrowed, told her all that she didn't want to know.

Chapter 4

Ruby drove up to her Grandpa's place in a hurry. Grandpa Wells was out back replacing the broken legs on his wife's redwood lounging chairs. He knew it was Ruby by the way she drove up; fast, anxious, and needing a listening ear, not a lecture. He could tell by the way she pulled in the driveway that she was hiding something from her mother. He knew she needed her good old Grandpa to listen and help her do the hard thing; tell her mother the truth.

He was her sound board and most of the big deal things at her age came through him first; lots of times before her best friends. He put the last nail in the chair, and turned it upward facing him. It looked new, and he knew his wife would appreciate it. It was her favorite chair to sit in during lazy summer days, and she knew eventually that her husband would get around to fixing it.

While he waited on his granddaughter to come through the back gate, he began fixing the matching lounge chair. Ruby sat in her father's truck talking to Ginger and Tori. Tiny hairs still stood perfectly straight on her arms, and her heart thumped lively in her chest.

"I can't believe he did that." Ruby shook her head. "I'm sure my mama and the others have figured it out by now."

"So," Ginger said.

"What do you mean so?" Ruby said.

"Well for one," Tori intervened. "You don't have to hide it, and after a while once your mama's cool with him, she not gonna trip."

"Yeah, Rue, she trusts you. She knows you're not gonna be like them other hoochies that Solomon's been messing with." Ginger pent a zipper in a skirt she was making.

"Tell me about it." Tori said.

"And that's another thing Rue; you had better set this fool straight, and quick about whose number one." Ginger began putting her sewing materials away.

"Come on now Ginger, stop acting like I just fell off a turnip truck." Ruby smiled and waved at her Grandpa. "Just because I really care about Solomon doesn't mean I'm stupid."

"Hey Rue," Tori interrupted. "If Solomon made some dumb excuse to bring some smocks that's probably been sitting at his Grandpa's shop for an eternity, then he must be really into you." Tori grinned.

"Well," she exited the truck. "He picked the wrong time to show it."

"You watch," Ginger put her things away. "If Kameron starts doing stuff like that, Girl I…"

"Spare us the details." Tori smiled.

"Potty brain," Ruby said. "Listen, I'll see y'all in about an hour. I'm feeling kind of sticky and I need to take a shower."

"I'm sure it will be cold." Ginger teased.

"Shut up." Ruby laughed. "See you guys," she said and hung up.

She lifted the latch to the back gate, and walked to the back patio where her Grandpa was working. She kissed his cheek, and poured them both a glass of sweet tea her Grandpa had made earlier.

"What are you doing Papa?" She sipped sweet tea.

"Oh, what I've been trying to do for some time now, fix these chairs for your Big Mama to sit in again. The old man just getting around to it." He said as he finished working on the new leg he put on the chair. He turned it around, shook it hard, and shook it some more. "Sit in it for your Grandpa Peanut."

She sat and felt the sturdiness of his work and his soothing spirit by how peaceful it felt to sit in the chair. "Big Mama will be real happy about this. You know how much she loves these chairs."

"Don't I know it," he laughed, and drank some more of his tea. "So, what brings you here? You know I'm always happy to see you Peanut." He smiled.

"You know I have to check up on you. You know, make sure you not over doing it." Ruby said.

"God knows I appreciate that." He patted her hand. "So, what is it that you don't want to tell your mama?"

Ruby shook her head, and drank more of her tea. "How do you always know?"

"Cause I'm your Grandpa, and I'm old. Age teaches you things."

"Really," she said.

"Yeah, if you smart enough at your age to be mindful, and pay attention, then you'll learn that life is always teaching us something." He said.

Ruby paused, thinking for a minute. Today she had two weird moments occur in her life. She was thrown off guard in both instances, what was life per se trying to teach her? She sighed, her mind a blank. "I don't know where to start?" She said.

"Everything always has a beginning baby." He drank some of his tea.

Ruby paused and wiggled in her seat a little bit, thinking how she would begin to tell her grandpa. How would her Grandpa react if she openly admitted that she kissed Solomon? Maybe she should phrase it that Solomon kissed her? What difference would it make? In her Grandpa's mind, she had to be on the other end of that kissing business. She sighed and poured another round of tea.

"It's hard Papa." She said.

"It's never as hard as it seems Peanut. Ain't nobody gonna hear about it but me." He helped himself to some more tea.

"You remember Solomon Garret?" She said.

"Yolanda's boy," he smiled and drank more tea. "He's the one that zips by on his bike heading up to the park. Most of the time he stops right in front of that gate out there and just watches me like he's looking for something."

"Solomon!" Ruby said, sounding as though she were shocked. "Solomon stops in front of that gate and watches you?"

Grandpa Wells grinned and drank some more of his tea. "Well, I was a Denzel in my day," he said, smiling at his granddaughter. Ruby laughed at his sense of humor.

"The boy is definitely looking for something, and his soul got him searching for it." He finished his tea.

"That's strange." She shook her head.

"Young folks do strange things." He gave her the eye. "So, why you like this boy?"

"He's handsome for one and I see something in him." She wiggled the ice in her glass.

"What do you see in him?" He asked.

"What nobody else sees I suppose." She drank more of her

tea.

"And, what's that?" He turned his chair to face her.

"It's hard to explain." She sat her glass back on the table.

"Try me." He said.

"Well," she paused, thinking. "Most people see him as a player and I don't. I just think that he hasn't found the right one yet."

"Meaning you," he said.

"Well, yeah," she finished her tea.

"I'm assuming that your parents, especially your mother don't know how you feel about this Solomon?" He scratched an itch in his scalp.

"Daddy no, mama, well sort of. He came over to the shop as I was about to leave to drop off some smocks that Mr. Nelson probably had sitting for weeks. I guess I sort of panicked. I'm sure I gave myself away." She placed her hand over her forehead.

Grandpa Wells tossed his head back in a hearty laugh. At the ripe age of seventy-two, he could laugh at the growing pains of puberty.

Ruby looked innocent and in need of advice from someone who had walked that road with the same fears, and had the same worried look, and stressed over a relationship that meant so much at seventeen. He took a deep breath and patted his granddaughter on the hand.

"Peanut," he said. "I suppose that this Solomon is pretty important to you, and what your parents think is pretty important to."

"Yeah," she said, as confusion stood tall in her eyes. "Papa," she cleared her throat. "Can I ask you something?"

"Shoot, I'm all ears."

"Am I wrong for falling for Solomon?"

Grandpa Wells took a deep breath, and turned his stiff body in the chair. "Only you and the good lord can answer that." He said. "But if you want to know the answer to that question, get still, and the truth will reveal itself."

Ruby said nothing, but her eyes said all that she couldn't say. Adulthood was complicated and at seventeen she couldn't understand why adults made life so difficult when it didn't have to be. Or, maybe she was making this too complicated? One way or the other, she was a year away from being a grown woman, and would have to take full responsibility for any decisions that she would make. The thought of it made her dizzy, but it was life. At least she had her papa to guide her. However, she was clueless about what being still meant.

In all of her Grandpa's wise old language, she did manage to figure out at least some of his message. Tell her parents the truth about Solomon; a hard proposition from where she sat. Sad thing about it, she knew that he was right, and she knew that she would have to find the courage to tell both of them and to be brave enough to hear their answer.

She kissed her Grandpa's cheek and stepped inside of the back door that led to the kitchen, and made her way to the shower. Grandpa Wells finished putting the last coat of paint on his wife's chairs. He knew that in a few moments that he'd be hearing the sound of keys coming through the front door, and he wanted to surprise her on the weekend with a big jar of sun tea. God knows she had waited some time for him to get around to fix them. He had a secret place in his tool shed where he could hide them and where she would never notice them.

Kameron had finally awakened from an early afternoon nap. He yawned big with sleep still in his throat. In New York, he would never nap in the afternoon. Life was busy there and with all the noise pollution, it made it nearly impossible to sleep.

He stretched his long legs and yawned once more. This was a quiet that stomped him; a stillness that he had not yet experienced until he came to Oak Grove. It was odd for him being from a city as populated and as chaotic at times as New York. It was taking him some getting used to especially at night listening to the crickets playing violin with their wings and soft train whistles whistling him to sleep.

He looked at the wall clock in his room and it was barley after one. He arose from his bed, showered, shaved and slapped on a pair of shorts and a matching polo shirt. Before he could open his bedroom door, he could smell his Grannies home cooking of Cat fish, deep fried potatoes and sweet white corn on the cob. He slipped on his slippers and rushed to the kitchen.

"Got that cat nap out handsome," she smiled and kissed his

cheek.

"Yeah," he picked up a piece of fish, blew on it and ate it. "Granny, this is so good."

"Thanks baby." She sat a huge platter of Cat fish on the table and called for her husband.

From the back door of the kitchen, Mr. Mosely appeared, dressed in jeans and a polo shirt almost identical to his grandson's, and a matching handkerchief hanging out of his pocket. Mosely was tall and big and Kameron featured the same body build. He smacked his grandson on the shoulder and took a seat next to him and took a piece of fillet cat fish from the tray.

"How you liking our town grandson," he talked with fish in his mouth.

"I like it." He said. "I'm still getting use to the crickets, humming birds, and soft train whistles, but overall I think it's cool." He began making himself a plate.

"Huge difference from New York huh," His Gramps said.

"Yeah," he said, smiling his Gramps smile.

Mr. Mosely blessed the food. Kameron made both his grandparents plates, and poured them tall glasses of sweet tea made by his Granny, then he poured himself a glass. He couldn't remember the last time he had a home cooked meal period. His idea of home cooked was Swanson TV dinners, Marie Calendars lasagna, and mandarin chicken with fried rice from Panda Express. This was all new to him and he loved it. He wondered if Ruby could cook.

Actually, he wondered a lot about her. And lately, he hadn't been able to keep his mind off of her. She was the most beautiful thing he had seen in Oak Grove, and he could tell by the sway in her hips that she was sure of herself. Her eyes were sweet, and gentle, and there was a kindness to her that made him blush. He hadn't gone there to be immersed by Ruby, he went to learn more about his family tree, work on his project, and relax.

"It's been a long time since you've had home cooking like this." His Gramps said.

"Too long," he spoke with his mouth full.

"Well," his Granny said. "You'll get plenty of it around here, and just maybe you'll find yourself a honey that can cook."

She smiled wiping her mouth.

"My lord." Moseley said. "The boy ain't been here a second and here you go trying to already match him up. Women!" He smiled wiping his mouth.

Kameron smiled, sipped some of his tea, and pretended like he wasn't interested in finding any young girls, that he was strictly focused on his project and just hanging out with his folks. Of course, that could not have been further from the truth. At this point, he didn't care if Ruby could cook or not. If they got that far in a relationship, they could both learn. Right now, he just wanted her.

His Gramps helped himself to another piece of fish. "Let the boy just relax and enjoy himself Cassidy."

"He can do all of that and find a nice girl." She ate a piece of her fish. "You found me." She kissed his cheek. "And you're not the least bit sorry."

"No, I'm not." He kissed his wife. "But can't the boy finish college first." He laughed.

"Now Jacob," she said. "You know better than that," she nicked his thigh.

Kameron sat not saying a word. His plate sat empty, his belly full, and no room now for dessert. He was waiting for Ruby's name to be mentioned, and then he would inquire and contemplate his next move.

"So," his Gramps finished his plate. "What have you got to say about all of this?"

"I'm not getting into this." He took his plate and his Gramps and sat it into the sink.

"You think you're smart." His Gramps shook a finger at him.

"Baby," his Granny said. "If you're gonna think on anything, let it be that Ruby Wells." She finished her plate. "She's a cute little something and the girl is going places."

At the mentioning of Ruby's name, his entire demeanor had changed. His Gramps could see it. His eyes danced and his face had a lover's glow. Though he tried, he couldn't hide the smile. He was hooked no matter how much he tried to conceal it.

He cleared his throat. "She's the one that I made a rainbow cone yesterday." He couldn't help but smile.

This time his Granny picked it up. Her smile was nearly as large as his. She liked Ruby. She always had from when she was just a tiny little girl. In fact, she was the doctor that helped Precious bring her into the world. Ruby came out with the most prolific cries. They were pronounced and being minutes old she was announcing to the world that she was here, and that she was going to be something special.

"Really," his Granny paused at the kitchen sink.

"Oh, here we go," Mr. Mosely said.

"Hush, Jake." She said.

"Yeah," he said, not wanting to remember how much she was taken by Solomon. "So," he managed to get it out. "You guys know her?"

"Know her," his Granny said. "Child, I brought her into the world."

"Her daddy owns his own restaurant, the Bread Basket. We have to go there some time. The man can cook." He said. "So, I wouldn't doubt that his daughter can cook." He scratched his scalp. "Her mama owns her own beauty shop, and Ruby works right along side her."

"Interested," his Granny smiled, putting away the dishes.

"Yeah," his Gramps said. "Boy can't hide nothing."

But neither could Ginger disguise her feelings for Kameron. Then again, she wasn't trying to. She had only hoped that time and opportunity would be good to her and that before long she would belong to him. She had already started making herself revealing outfits that enhanced and added to her figure.

She would get Ruby to find the right cut, style and color for her hair. Their first date would be a romantic picnic by the lake with just the two of them. She'd have Tori make all of the food including the dessert and lie and say that she made it. And before, he discovered that she couldn't cook, Tori would have given her cooking lessons, though she hated cooking, and he would never have known the difference.

As she sat waiting in her room for Ruby to blow for her, she began thinking just how she would get to know Kameron, and how she would find a way over to his grandparents' house. Kameron on the other hand was thinking the same thing about Ruby.

He couldn't just show up at the shop, or at her house. It couldn't look rushed, nor could he look desperate and out of control. He sighed. Ginger sighed. He paced. Ginger paced. Ruby pulled up and blew, and for Kameron, the light had suddenly come on.

Chapter 5

Precious sat at her kitchen table with a steaming cup of coffee in front of her. It was Monday, a day off from the shop. Her husband Jacob had taken Monday's off too. It was their time to spend with each other, and get caught up on all the news. Jacob appeared in the kitchen tall, brown skinned and handsome; hair as curly, wet, and black as a raven. Ruby had his hair color and his texture, and her father's smile. Jacob kissed his wife, and poured himself a cup of coffee and began seasoning it.

"Where's that daughter of ours?" He asked with a smile.

"Initially, she said she was headed to the Gingerbread, but with the three of them, who knows." She sipped her coffee.

"Well, it's summer and she's earned it." He said. "You know young people don't ever stay in one place." He laughed.

"That's the truth," Precious said, drinking more of her coffee. "You know she's starting to get into boys, and I think she's kind of sweet on that Garrett boy."

"Oh really," he laughed. "And what would make you think that?"

"He showed up at the shop bringing me smocks from Ben that I even forgot he had borrowed." She shook her head. "Then, the way he was looking at my baby." She sighed. "I got nothing against the boy, but I've heard things about him, and I don't want her dating him."

Jacob laughed. "Well, did you ask her about it? Maybe he's into her, but she's not into him?"

"No, she's into him." She said. "You should have seen how she bolted out of that shop when he came in." She drank more of her coffee.

Jacob laughed hearty. He reached over and took hold of her hand and kissed it, and laughed some more. "See," he said. "That's why you need to get on board with me and let her go to Stanford this fall, baby you know she's ready."

Precious sighed. "I know. I know. She's only seventeen, and Stanford is…"

"Two hours away; an hour if I'm speeding." He took her

to his lap and kissed her. "I think we need to invite that recruiter and that counselor here for dinner." He said. "She'll be fine, and I can have my truck back."

"I'm not getting into that." She said. "I told you not to let her start driving it but…"

"She saving and she's working hard, and she needs something to drive baby come on." He said.

"See," she said. "I'm done." She placed her mug in the kitchen sink. "I'll call the recruiter and Ruby's counselor." She turned to face him.

"What," he saw a concerned look on her face.

"Solomon, just the way he looked at Ruby." She took a deep breath. "I hope I'm not judging that boy Jake. But, I think he's trouble, and Ruby's future is too bright."

"And her father is six foot five with a strong left hook, and with a shot gun," he finished his coffee.

Precious smiled and shook her finger at him. Deep down inside her soul she couldn't shake that feeling about Solomon. Ruby on the other hand couldn't get enough of Solomon. There they sat underneath the oak tree at Echo Park kissing liked they loved each other; Ruby a step closer to the place that she didn't want to be.

She paused from kissing him. He looked as if he were shocked that she did. None of his prior's had done that. By now, they would have been half dressed, getting busy underneath the oak that wouldn't talk. He wanted Ruby badly, but Ruby resisted him and he wondered why?

"I have to say something." She said.

"Say what," he tried to kiss her but she refused; now he was really surprised.

"I'm not going to be some girl that you're just messing around with, and I'm not going to be some chick in your black book that you can call anytime you want." She said.

Solomon sat straight up. He wanted to say something but his mouth wouldn't move and his tongue seemed to be stuck somehow. Tiffney or Daphne would have never have spoken to him like that, nor would any of the rest of them. What was it about her that she could?

"Who said you had to be?" He tried to kiss her again,

but again she refused him.

"I'm serious Solomon. I'm not going to be second to any of them. And, if you want me, you're gonna have to let them go completely. I mean it."

Solomon just looked at Ruby. Who was this pretty young girl giving him demands when she had waited for him through all the honey's he had been through? Every time he looked at her, he could tell she wanted to be with him, and that she loved him. What had she heard? And, what had gotten into her? Or, was it that she was mad that she had allowed herself to wait in a long line of wannabe's? Nonetheless, he was stunned, and to her credit, she had caught him off guard.

"So, I see you're listening to the rumors too," he sat and turned his body towards hers.

"I don't pay attention to rumors. I'm going off what I saw in the park about a week ago." She said.

"I was trying to make you jealous, and I see that it worked." He got smooth on her.

"I'm not jealous Solomon." She lied. "I'm just…"

"Just telling me what you want," he scooted close to her. "I like that about you." He kissed her. "And, let me tell you something, you don't have to worry about them. I want you." He kissed her again. "I want you."

Unfortunately, Kameron wanted the same thing. He didn't have a plan yet. He didn't even know how to approach a girl who he knew had eyes and a heart for someone else. He sighed put on his tee shirt and joined his Gramps at the shed. He knocked and then entered, hearing his Gramps telling him to come on back.

It wasn't hard to see his grandfather's dreams within this place. Next to his work station was a huge blue book with thick bold writing that said: "Dream big and expect great things" Kameron took a peek inside finding old pictures of the farmhouse, and what he wished his business to become. There were also pictures of his granny and their children, his grandchildren, and great grandchildren. It was like he had made them all a solemn promise of success and a most proud heritage. He closed the book as something else had gotten his attention.

Kameron noticed a modest loft upstairs that was barely used. As he climbed the few steps that led to the loft, he felt an instant connection. It was roomy with more than enough room to work or relax. He had wanted to start making early drafts on an intern project that awaited him for the fall quarter, and he already knew the perfect place to begin.

His Gramps wiped his face and took a drink of cold water and sat in his chair. He watched his grandson trot down the stairs and from the look in his eyes, he already knew what Kameron would ask. He smiled and drank more water and turned his body completely to face his grandson.

"Like that place up there don't you?" He said. "Recipe for my syrup I use for my snow cones came to me right up there in that very place."

"Serious," Kameron said, drinking his water, and pouring another glass full.

"Oh yeah," Gramps said. He folded his hanky and put it back into his pocket. "It's yours if you want. I suppose a young fellow like yourself can create some good stuff up there; place is a magnet for ideas let me tell you."

"Thanks Gramps, I'd be honored to use it." Kameron drank more of his water. "I figure that after I help you, that I'll come back here, hang out and see what I come up with."

"Sounds like a plan to me." Gramps said. "But do enjoy yourself Grandson; all work and no play makes Jack a dull boy.

"I'd like that." He said. "But, I don't know anyone."

"What about that Wells girl?" His Gramps said. "She's really pretty, and I can tell you've taken a fancy to her." He smiled.

"I don't know her." He said.

"Well get to know her," he said. "She's an awful sweet girl, and looks like to me that you could use a haircut." He winked".

"Get to know who?" His Granny appeared.

"Nobody nosey," His Gramps said. "Women."

"Men," she playfully smacked him on the arm. "Where would you all be without us?" She said. "Kameron, I'm going to get my hair done tomorrow. Perhaps you'd like to join me." She fiddled in his hair.

"Wow! I must really need a haircut." He said.

Kameron sighed, and Ginger took a deep breath, tired from all the sewing she had done. She placed plastic bags around the garments that she would deliver to the people that had ordered them. Mrs. Amy had three suits for church: Mrs. Fletcher two suits, and two matching hats. Jacob ordered aprons for his restaurant. Tiffney and Daphne miniskirts and mini dresses which she charged double.

A soft knock hit her door. "Come in." She said, knowing that it was her mother.

"Hey you," her mother said.

"Hey," Ginger said, putting her things away.

"You have got your grandmother's genes." Her mother said. "Here you are making clothes, and me, I can't sew on a button." She laughed.

"Well," Ginger looked at her mother. "I can't cook, and you're an excellent one."

"Even trade, I guess," her mother said, looking at the garments that Ginger had made.

It amazed her every time she looked at anything that Ginger had made. No one had taught her to sew. All she ever did was watch her mother-in-law Tess make everything. But, maybe that was all it took. Ginger was her father determined; a go getter, eyes on the prize, and no doubt she would get it. However, Jasmine's fear was that Ginger bypassed her trait, and not let a man get in the way of her dream.

"Mom," Ginger said. "You've got that look in your eyes again, like you and Daddy had a long distance fight." She put her scissors in her bin.

"No we didn't fight," she hugged Ginger. "But, we talked about you a lot."

"Did you talk about getting me a car?" She asked.

"We talked about you going to college further up the coast or in LA." She put her arm around her daughter and they walked out of Ginger's room.

"Not gonna happen mom, New York is the fashion capital of the world. I just feel like my dreams are there waiting on me." She opened up a bottle of Evian water. "And…"

"And what," her mother inquired.

"There might be reasons I want to go to college in

New York." Ginger grinned.

Without even asking she knew what it was a boy. They always had crazy timing and as a woman, she resented them for it. "So," she asked. "Who is he?"

"Am I that obvious?" Ginger snickered.

"Yeah," her mother said.

"It's Kameron Mosely, Mr. Mosely's grandson." Her smile grew wider.

"Oh," her attitude suddenly changed. The Mosely's had money. They were well established and they would most certainly require any suitor to have a college degree. Ginger was definitely talented enough, entrepreneurial enough, and pretty enough, and her dream would not go unhatched.

"Mama," Ginger said. "You zoned out on me again. Did you even hear what I said?"

"Why not invite the Mosely's over for dinner." She said.

"Great, as long as you cook." Ginger said. "So, when's daddy coming home?"

"Next month for a while," she said with uncertainty in

her eyes.

Ruby and Solomon had landed at Rossi's, a small Italian bistro within the Gingerbread mall. They found a small table in the corner by a circular window with a nice view. They had decided long before they got there that they would order a pizza supreme with everything on it except onions and mushrooms. Kamari and his boys were blowing up his phone, impatient with details from their first real date. Tori and Ginger were tempted, but more patient and Ruby appreciated that.

It was better than even she imagined. Beyond his phenomenal kissing was his commitment to be with her and only her. Now Tiffney and the other's would have to stand idled in a sad line of rejection and spoon up envy as they watched her be held in his arms, and kissed. Their time with him had ended as she had predicted; now the Solomon that she had waited for had finally shown up.

They ordered their pizza in between flirting with each other and kissing. At a distance, they looked in love, feeding each other pizza, and kissing the cheese off of each other's lips. It was sight especially when Ruby's parents had entered and caught Solomon

and Ruby in the act.

Chapter 6

The look on Ruby's face was priceless. Out of all the people in Oak Grove, why would her parents decide to dine out at Rossi's tonight? Precious was numb, and Jacob's mouth landed on the floor, then found its way back up to his chin. Out of surprise, he laughed, and Ruby's expression in seeing the both of them made him laugh even more.

He had been warned earlier this morning about her feelings for him. But as a dad with a timeline for dating in his head for his daughter, and in the image he had painted of Ruby had caused him not to worry. However, that all had changed. They both approached their table. Ruby swallowed her root beer hard and her look was sheepish and in trouble; now she was mad at herself for being careless.

Solomon wasn't uncomfortable with the whole thing. So what her parents had caught them kissing. By their reactions, he knew that they were going to make a big deal of it, especially Ruby's mother. The eyes of Ruby's father spoke to him. Ruby was his little princess and he eyed him as if he were researching his soul. The frog, being Solomon had crossed the line and the king had summoned him to an empty table. Jake bent over and kissed his princess on her cheek, and whispered something in her ear.

He caught the eyes of her mother as he left with Ruby's father, and she wasn't that kind lady that called him honey, and reminded Ruby that Solomon was speaking to her. Precious sighed, and looked at Ruby.

"I know what you're thinking." She said, looking over at her father across the way talking with Solomon.

"What am I thinking?" He mother said.

"That I shouldn't be with Solomon, that he's not good enough for me," Ruby said, still looking across the way.

"You know I can't argue with that." Precious said. "What has gotten into you? That boy that you were lip locking with has a reputation girl."

"It's just gossip mama. You know just as much as I do that everybody in this town compares Solomon to his father." She said.

"With good cause," Precious said. "The Fletcher's had to send their great granddaughter down to Atlanta and you know for what."

"Solomon's mama said it wasn't true, that Hillary wasn't pregnant, and that she lied to try and trap Solomon. She never produced no baby."

"Don't play crazy with me girl," she said. "You know they sent her down there to get rid of it." She took a deep breath. "You've got a future and I'm not about to send you nowhere to get rid of nothing."

"So, is that what you think of me?" He eyes watered. "Yes, I like him mama, but I'm not stupid. Give me more credit than that," she stormed out of the restaurant.

"Ruby!" Precious called out to her, but she ignored her. "Ruby!"

Solomon looked shocked and so did Ruby's father. Before he could go after Ruby, he took one look at her mother and he knew not to. Jacob looked at his wife; his eyes asking what had

happen. Before she could try to give an answer, he ran out after

Ruby.

Solomon did everything thing he could not to look in Ruby's

mother's eyes, but she stood in front to him and made certain that he

did. She didn't like his womanizing, and she didn't like him being

with her daughter he could tell.

"I like your grandfather a lot. In fact, he seems like a second

father to me." She said. "I couldn't have gotten my shop off the

ground if it weren't for him, and I'm grateful to him." She cleared

her throat.

"You don't like me Mrs. Wells, and you don't think that I'm

good enough for your daughter just say it." He said.

"Solomon," she said. "I don't have anything against you.

But, you're not for my daughter. She's got a bright future and..."

He interrupted her. "So do I," he said. "I'm not my dad Mrs.

Wells, but you or my mom never seemed to have gotten over the

hurt that he caused the both of you." He walked out of the

restaurant.

Precious felt light headed after his words. She sat in the seat before she fell in it. That was such a long time ago, and how could Solomon have known. It was an old ghost that she had sworn she had buried, but had she?

Ruby was troubled and had found solace in her grandpa's arms, soaking his tee shirt with her tears. Solomon had camped out at Kamari's house in need of a listening ear he could vent into. Kamari heated up some left over Cabbage, cornbread, and roasted chicken and set a plate before Solomon with a pitcher of grape cool aid.

"Thanks man." Solomon said. He blessed his food, blew on it and set the fork of cabbage down on his plate to cool.

"No problem," Kamari said, adding some hot peppers over his cabbage. "Nothing like venting over food," he smiled.

"Yeah," Solomon said, tested his cabbage and ate. "Pops can burn man."

"Yeah, he's a beast in the kitchen." Kamari grinned. "So, what don't you want to tell me?"

"How do you always know?" Solomon said.

"You're my brother man." They fist bumped. "We have a unique connection, and there are some things that you just know. So, what's up?"

"Ruby," Solomon said.

"Ruby," Kamari paused from eating. "She's fine in all man, but you know damn well that she's not your type. She's not Tiffney or Daphne you know that. So, why her and why now?" He asked.

"I like her." He said, biting into a piece of roasted chicken.

"You like her?" Kamari drank some of his cool aid.

"Yeah, I do." He said. "You act like you're surprised man."

"Shocked is more like it." Kamari ate more of his food. "Man come on," he said. "This is me you talking to, your boy. You have never liked any girl you went out with man," he shook his head. "You go after the girls who give you what you want man. And we both know that Tiff and Daphne was bringing it, which is why they're still in that little black book bro." He laughed.

Solomon laughed. What Kamari had said was true. However, Ruby was different. But when it came to both Tiffany and Daphne, he liked them both. Each came equipped with their own set of unique talents. When nothing else was available, all he had to do was speed dial. "What can I say," he grinned. "They got skills man, and why should a brother have to choose?"

"See," Kamari laughed. "That's why you and Ruby cannot work, she's different man and she is not about to go for none of that stuff and you know that." He ate more of his food.

"She check me on that to." He laughed.

"See," Kamari said. "Get out while you can man, or change." He said. "That's the only way you will get and keep a girl like that."

Solomon stopped eating for a minute. His mind had went back to the very first time that he had shocked himself and had stunned Ruby by kissing her by her father's truck. It was spontaneous; done to get a rise out of her and to see if she would be one that would blow up his phone, be in that line of female's waiting for his attention, but she was just the opposite. Something inside of him snapped, and without warning he wanted her like he had not wanted any of the rest of them.

That whole entire day he had thought about nothing but her; which was why he found something to bring over to the shop. He just had to see her. He just had to look in her eyes again, and there was a hope that she would swing him around back and serenade his lips again. Later that day, he had gotten his wish. They laughed and talked underneath the grand oak tree in the park. They kissed and kissed, and kissed some more. And later as the sun began to set, and their stomach's start to speak, and they had headed down to Rossi's, for pizza. Everything was perfect until Ruby's parents showed up.

"Solomon," Kamari nicked his elbow.

"Yeah," he said, the sad look had returned.

"What happened man. You look like you just backed out of life." He said.

"Ruby and I went out tonight. In fact, we spent the entire day together. It was really nice man." He swallowed some of his cool aid.

"So, what happened?" He asked.

"Her parents showed up when we were enjoying some tongue action." He smiled just thinking about it.

"What the hell?" Kamari nearly chocked on his cool aid.

"Her pop called me to an empty table and start talking about how much he adored his little girl; how she had a future, and how he had a loaded shotgun at his pad for any dude trying to interfere with his daughter's plans. The dude is crazy man." He finished his cabbage.

"What?" Kamari said. "See man, take a fools advice and leave that one alone." Kamari finished his last piece of chicken. "Thank God her Gramps wasn't there. He's ten times worst. Ruby's his girl."

"I think her pops was just trying to scare me." He finished his piece of chicken. "But it was her mom that got to me. He said.

"What'd she do?" Kamari asked.

"It's not what she did, but what she said after Ruby stormed out of the restaurant." He shook his head.

"Ruby stormed out of the restaurant." Kamari seemed surprised.

"Yeah dog. I guess she and mom's got into it about me and she split." He said.

"So, what happened?" He said.

"She said that she had nothing against me, which we both know is a lie, but that Ruby had a future as if I don't, and that pretty much she didn't want me to be with her daughter." He said with a deep sorrow looming from his voice. "Man," he sighed. "I'm so sick of people judging me."

"Some of its unfair man, but to be honest, some of it's on you dog." Kamari said.

"I don't need my boy to be judging me right now." Solomon stared at Kamari.

"I'm not you judging man, but let's just put it out there." He said. "Would they have reacted the same if you were Mosely's grandson Kameron?"

"Who?" Solomon said.

"Kameron," he said. "He's here visiting his folks, the Mosely's for summer.

"So," he said. "What's that got to do with me?"

"You got a rep with the ladies' man, and Kameron's got the hot's for your girl." Kamari said. "And that's straight up from your boy Tommy who was an eyewitness dog."

The doorbell rang. Solomon paused his thought as Kamari answered the door. He could tell who it was by Boyd's loud mouth, and Tommy's distinctive laugh, and how he would always tell Boyd to shut up. Tommy's laugh made him smile even when he was in a foul mood. He couldn't explain it. Just like he couldn't explain why he was suddenly so mesmerized by Ruby.

They entered the kitchen and greeted Solomon with fist bumps and manly hugs that women either laughed at, or were in awe over. Boyd didn't wait for Kamari to offer up food, he haply helped himself and fixed Tommy a plate to. Tommy put extra peppers on his cabbage as did Boyd.

"What," Solomon said. "You live here now."

"Oh, he didn't tell you," he talked with food in his mouth. "Got a room at your pad to, Tommy's everybody," he made a crazy face. "I thought you knew." Instantly the kitchen was in uproar.

"So, what's up with you and Ruby?" Tommy asked.

"Drama," he said, looking at Solomon.

"So she caught you cheating already," Boyd said. "You don't play do you man?"

"It's not her man, it's her parents." He said. "They don't want me with her."

"I wouldn't want you with my daughter either." Boyd said. "You poke them and then you dump them." Boyd stood up, did a crazy dance and then made a weird sound, and all of them laughed even Solomon.

"I like this girl." Solomon was serious.

"Then you had better watch this Kameron dude, he's into Ruby." Tommy said.

"See I told you dog," Kamari said.

"Do I look worried," Solomon said.

"Let's see," Boyd finished his plate. "Mom's don't like you. Pops got a shot gun and loaded at that, and now old boy is going after your girl. Bro," he swallowed some cool aid.
"You need to be terrified." He said. "From where I'm sitting it don't look good."

"Shut up man." Tommy finished his meal. But he couldn't

help but laugh.

"My sentiments exactly," Solomon said.

Yo man," Tommy resumed his seat. "I'm serious bro. Watch this Kameron dude man. Trust me, he was not playing at how he was checking out Ruby." He cleared his throat.

"I'm not worried." He said, and the look in his eyes said that he wasn't. Ruby's parents were more of a problem to him than this Kameron could ever be. Besides, Ruby had waited on him not Kameron, and that said a lot.

"Okay man," Tommy said. "But don't say I didn't warn you."

Solomon sat in silence. Ruby sat in agony, more upset with herself than her parents. Her secret was out now, but would she still be able to court Solomon? She sat at the Kitchen table with her Grandfather peeling potatoes. Her Grandmother was making smothered potatoes and steak, and some speckled butter beans she had purchased from Odette's farm.

The scent of the beans went all through the house, and it made Ruby hungry. But, her Grandmother's cooking always had that effect on her. She continued peeling potatoes with her Grandfather, and he seeing Ruby soaked in misery too long made a silly face, and she laughed.

"Papa," she said.

"What," he giggled. "Getting caught smooching ain't the end of the world." He laughed.

"I know." She said. "But mama sure made a big deal out of it." She wrapped the peelings in newspaper and threw them in the trash. "And Daddy, talking to Solomon across the way," she sighed. "God knows what he said to him."

Big Jake laughed. "Well, whatever it was, he won't be pulling nothing, especially since Junior got that shot gun loaded and waiting."

Ruby eyes widen. "Jesus," she said. "I hope he didn't tell Solomon that? Knowing daddy, he probably did." She sighed.

"What you like about that boy?" Big Jake said.

"I don't know?" She said. "I just like him."

"I'm not buying it." He rinsed off the potatoes. "It's gotta be something."

"He's cute." She smiled.

"Cute," he looked at her.

"And different," she said, she called out to her Grandmother letting her know that the potatoes were ready for cooking.

"Who's different?" She inquired. "Kameron," she said.

Ruby frowned. She didn't know where his name had come from. All she remembered about him was that he busted her gazing at Solomon and Tiffney, and he was kind enough to make her another snow cone. She was embarrassed of course even this stranger could see how much she was mesmerized by Solomon. Of course, if he had seen it, it was evident that her parents would see, especially since the way she and Solomon were going at it. She finally answered her Grandmother.

"No Big Mama," she said. "I don't even know Kameron. I was talking about Solomon. But, I'm sure you've already heard."

"You talking about that Garrett boy," she said, preparing the potatoes.

"Yes," Ruby said.

She turned from frying diced onions and looked at Ruby.

It was summer and love had hit her. But thank God Solomon had inherited his father's genes and could never be satisfied with one girl. The trick was getting Ruby to take a closer look at Kameron. She had her ways.

"So," Ruby said. "You don't like Solomon either."

"I suppose that he's a good boy baby." She said, stirring in flour and potatoes. "I know he took them looks from his daddy." She added watered and placed a top over the potatoes to simmer.

At least her Big Mama didn't go nuts like her mother did and neither did her Papa which was why she always shared her secrets with him. Why couldn't her mother have behaved the same way? Maybe her Big Mama didn't have a favorable opinion of Solomon, but at least she didn't judge him like everyone else was doing.

She wondered what her pals would think when they found out that she got busted? Ginger for certain would crack up. Tori would say that she told her so. She was the one prodding Ruby on to level with her folks. However, Ruby refused and fate had dealt her a bitter hand.

She resorted to her room at her Grandparent's house. She

lounged in her retreat and took out her journal and wrote. In writing, she had forgotten about getting busted, and the anger that she felt toward herself had vanished. In a weird sense, she could actually laugh about it, and now she wouldn't have to hide it or sneak around her parents back. They knew. They didn't like it, but somehow, someway things would work out. It had to.

She put her journal a way and embraced the quiet. It was different; a sound that she hadn't heard before. It was a peace; a stillness that had caught her off guard. But, nonetheless it feed her spirit in a way that normal rest could not. She wanted to talk to it, but it wouldn't allow her to. Her requirement was just to listen to it.

When it had finish speaking to her, she returned to her bedroom and sat in the middle of her queen sized poster bed feeling a sense of ease. She paused for a minute, called Tori and Ginger and told them the news. Ginger howled in laughter as she had predicted, and so did Tori which surprised her.

"Did you not see this coming?" Ginger laughed.

"No," Ruby laughed.

"Rue, your parents go to Rossi's a lot." Tori laughed. "I could have told you that."

"I wasn't thinking." Ruby smiled.

"Of course you weren't," Ginger said. "You were too busy kissing Solomon. I hope it was worth it?"

"So," Tori inquired. "Was it?"

"Oh yes," Ruby said. "Solomon knows how to kiss." Ruby couldn't help from grinning.

"I heard that he's pretty good with the other stuff to." Ginger said.

Tori and Ruby paused. An inquisitive silence suddenly hoovered over their conversation. Ginger cleared her throat and tried to refurbish her statement.

"I'm just saying what I've heard." She said. "I wonder how good Kameron is."

"I bet you're just dying to find out." Ruby said.

"I am and I will." She smiled.

"Potty brain," Tori said.

Ruby could smell dinner and she could taste the cornbread

and speckled butter beans. The aroma of the complete meal made her mouth water and her stomach started talking. She invited her two pals over for dinner. Tori accepted, but Ginger refused only because she had previously committed to having dinner and a movie with her mother.

Ruby said her goodbyes, took a shower and sat in front of her vanity set combing her hair. She folded it over and placed it in a lazy French roll with a dainty hair pin in the back to add a hint of elegance to it. She heard the doorbell and assumed it was Tori. As she put on her sandals, she heard her Big Mama say come in, and then she heard her Papa's hearty laugh. As she slipped on her other sandal, she heard a voice that was foreign to her and she couldn't make out who is was. However, Tori would show up any minute, and she did.

As always, she gave Ruby a jingle on her cell to let her know that she was there. This time she heard the soft knock at the door, and before Tori could come to her room, she heard Tori talking to this strange voice. She wondered who it was, but she couldn't make it out. A soft tap knocked on her door and before she opened it, she knew who it was.

"Hey," Tori said, and entered her room, closing Ruby's door.

"Hey," Ruby said, with her hand on her door knob.

"Did you know that Kameron and his Grandparents were out there?" Tori Said.

Chapter 7

Ruby's eyes said all what her mouth couldn't. Her big mama never mentioned to her that guest were coming over. This was odd, even when Ruby was at her parent's house, and her grandparents were having guest, she would always mention it. It had to have been a spur of the moment thing.

Maybe Mrs. Cassidy and her grandmother were conversing and one thing lead to another. Mrs. Cassidy probably mentioned that she had made either a carrot cake or a red velvet one. Pauline most likely stated that she had made smothered potatoes, steak, and all the fixings to go with it, and that was it, the invite was on. However, in Ruby's mind, something was out of place. Even Tori had a weird look in her eyes.

Ruby sighed. Tori raised an eyebrow, and both exited out of Ruby's room. The moment Ruby appeared in the family room, suddenly everything went dark, and only he and Ruby were in the room. She was beautiful in her Hawaiian print mini dress that

Ginger had made for her. It showcased Ruby's figure in ways that only Kameron could appreciate.

His eyes were like mini digital camera's with a save button. He snapped, saved, and snapped and saved again, until he had her body locked in his mind. Ruby hugged Mrs. Cassidy and Mr. Mosely. Kameron looked on wishing and wanting it to be him.

"Ruby," Mrs. Cassidy said. "Have you met my grandson Kameron yet?" She asked.

"We met at the truck a few days ago." He intervened. "I made her a rainbow snow cone." He smiled, starring at her. He stood extending his hand.

His hand was like a glove and her small hand fit perfectly into it. As they shook hands, he held her hand as if he didn't want to let it go. The two grandmothers' had seen all that they needed. Tori had seen enough to know that Ginger was in trouble. She watched Kameron look at Ruby, and it was obvious that he was in love with her. He never took his eyes off of her, and he was still holding onto her hand when Ruby introduced him to Tori.

"Kameron," she said. "You remember my friend Tori." She said.

"Yeah," he said, though he didn't. "Hi," he said, shaking her hand, but he didn't hold it like he held Ruby's.

The only one of them that he remembered that day was Ruby. The other two might as well have been invisible. It was Ruby he saw that day at the park, and he had been seeing her in his mind ever since. Tori watched Kameron stare. She wondered if Ruby had noticed at all. She had too, it was just too obvious, besides Ruby seemed somewhat uncomfortable; that had to be what it was. She couldn't wait to ask her.

"Peanut," Big Jake said. "You and Tori take this young man and show him around the place."

"Okay," she said, glad her Papa had broken the silence. "I guess we can start down the hall." She said.

Kameron arose from his seat and followed the both of them. Ruby gave him a tour throughout her grandparents' house. She showed him the house as if she were a realtor. She showed him each room, and gave a little history about each of them. Tori followed not saying a word just watching and observing Kameron more so than Ruby. Until today, she had not seen real love. However, Kameron had showed her what it looked like, and it had nearly taken her breath away.

The quiet room in the corner seemed to have gotten his attention. He stopped by it and looked at it intensely. It was as if something was drawing him into it. Inside, was a wall mural that decorated the entire walls with perfect blue skies and puffy white clouds? There was a blue sectional to match the perfect blue sky; a huge white family bible with bold red lettering on it, sitting on the polished cherry wood table. In the corner, was a provisional alter patient and waiting.

"Can I go in," he asked.

"Sure," she said, looking at Tori. "It's my grandparents' quiet room." She said. "They pray in here, meditate in here, and be quiet in here," she joked. Kameron laughed.

"I like it." He said. "You can feel the serenity in here." He came out of the room and stood next to Ruby.

Pauline ringed her dinner bell and both Ruby and Tori knew what that meant. Tori had eaten over Ruby's Grandmother's house too often, and every time Pauline rung the bell, she rushed to the table. Ruby turned to face Kameron and his eyes were already there awaiting hers. Tori took serious notice.

"It means dinner's ready." She said.

"Great," he smiled. "I hear your grandmother is a great cook." He said

"You got that right." Tori had finally opened her mouth to speak.

Big Jake blessed the food, and like a big Sunday meal, everyone helped themselves to steak, smothered potatoes, speckled butter beans, cornbread and a huge pitcher of sun brewed sweet tea. Kameron made sure he set next to Ruby, and Tori made sure that she had just the right angle in her chair, giving her the perfect view to continue to watch Kameron.

"You sure don't get food like this in New York." He said. "Mrs. Wells, this is delicious."

"Thank you baby," she said. "You are welcomed here anytime." She looked over at Ruby. "So consider yourself having two places to eat at," she winked at him.

Tori nicked Ruby's foot under the table. Ruby nicked hers back as if she knew why Tori was nicking her foot underneath the table. Now, she was starting to put two and two together. It wasn't just an odd coincident. It was more than two old chums talking over the phone and telling each other about their dinner plans and what they were cooking up for dessert.

She wondered what her mother and father would think about this. Would her father pull Kameron to the side, probably not, and would her mother lecture her like she did with Solomon? Probably not, the Mosely's and the Wells went back and were already an extended family long before both she and Kameron were born. To his credit, Kameron was just being nice, and Ginger already had her invisible claws in him, and she was not about to give up Solomon.

Jasmine was known for her spontaneity, and today just happened to be one of these days. Ginger had just assumed that they would dine out in Oak Grove probably at Rossi's, but her mother had pulled a fast one on her. Jasmine drove nearly three hours to San Francisco, and Ginger was inclined to think that it was more than for dinner. She loved San Francisco. It was like a mini New York on the bay, and it also hosted some of the biggest fashion shows in the world, and was home to some of the most incredible fashion designers. She had honestly thought about going to school there, but there was something about New York that had a hold on her.

The smell of the bay had her longing for fresh caught fish and chips. But, it wouldn't be right to be in San Francisco and not go to "All of It." All of It was a soul food buffet that truly did have everything. From collard greens, to tea cakes, it was the place for southern food, and the history of southern cuisine and culture. For every meal one ate, there was a history lesson, and the entire experience was just as fulfilling as the food.

Ginger yawned and stretched her legs. "Just dinner huh," she said.

"I felt a little impulsive and I thought that my daughter needed to get away and breathe a little." She said, finding a parking spot at All of It.

"Are you trying to coast me into going to school up here?" Ginger said.

"No," She said. "Why would I do that?"

"Mama, let's face it you don't want me to go to New York, and since we've had our mother daughter dinner dates, we've never come this far to eat dinner." She said.

"Well, every day is different baby. I'm starving, so let's go eat." She placed her arm around her daughter and entered the restaurant.

They sat in a corner overlooking the bay. The smell of deep fried catfish had captured Ginger's nostrils and she rushed to the area where the fish was. Her mother had taken to the other side filling her plate with barbeque ribs, collards, black-eyed peas, and cornbread. Ginger on the other hand settled for Catfish, chips and a heaping bowl of macaroni and cheese. They blessed their food and began eating.

"So, what's the real reason we came all the way here?" Ginger asked her mother.

"Why does there have to be a reason?" She said eating.

"Mama, come on," she said. "You don't drive three hours for dinner."

"Baby, it's our favorite restaurant, you know that." She drank lemon aid.

"Are you and daddy okay?" She asked.

"We're perfectly fine baby come on, I wouldn't lie to you." She wiped her mouth. "I mean how can we not be fine, we hardly ever see each other with his crazy, grueling schedule." She said.

"Doesn't it bother you," she asked. "I know it bothers me." She paused eating for a minute. "I know it's his job and all, but I feel like I don't even know my own dad."

"Baby no," she stopped eating. "He loves you so much, and the first person he always asks about is you." She stroked Ginger's face. "Besides, he texts you all the time, and because of his work, your college is paid for even if it is in New York, which I hope the hell it isn't." She said and resumed eating.

"I know, but Ruby has her dad with her all the time. She drives his truck, and..."

"And Ruby's parents cannot afford to pay for her to go to Stanford; do you know how much debt their going to be in? And, I can imagine, that new truck is killing them."

"Ruby hasn't said anything." Ginger drank root beer.

"The Wells are proud people baby. I give Precious and Jacob credit for going after what they want, owning their own businesses, but it really hasn't paid off for them financially. Because of your father, you don't have to worry about that."

"Then, why don't I have a car yet?" She asked.

"You know your father said that you couldn't get a car until you graduate high school." She ate.

"What do you say?" Ginger said.

"High school, now finish eating your food."

Ginger ate more of her meal and headed back to add another piece of fish to her plate, and another helping of macaroni. Her mother reached over and tasted a piece of her fish. Her eyes danced and she pinched off another piece. "Oh Jesus," she said. "If I could steal this woman away from here I would."

"Tell me about it." Ginger took a rib from her mother's

plate. "Mama, did you know that the Mosely's grandson was here visiting his grandparents."

"I think you told me about that." She said. "Have you met him?"

"No, but I want to." She said. "He is so fine, and he goes to school in New York; Cornell I think."

"Ginger," She smiled seeing herself in her daughter.

"Well, he is. Can we invite him over for dinner next week?" She asked.

"We'll have to check with your father first." She said.

"Are you kidding me?" She said. "He's not even here yet."

"I am now." He hugged Ginger tight, then kissed his wife.

Ginger screamed loud. Everyone in the restaurant looked over at their table. She grabbed her father again and hugged him. Now she knew why her mother had driven three hours for dinner. She hadn't seen her father in three months. When he texted her days ago, he was in China. Before that Africa, prior to that London; now, he was here sitting right next to her. Point being, how long was he staying?

Did she have him for a week, or two, or a month? If only she could have him forever like Ruby had her dad. However with her dad and his line of work was just too much to ask. Ginger looked at her father again in disbelief. He wrapped his arm around her, and kissed her cheek.

"I just can't believe you're here." She said.

"I flew nonstop just to see my little girl." He kissed her cheek again, and then stole a piece of her fish.

"Want me to make you a plate?" She said.

"Yeah baby, and don't forget to load me up on some of that catfish." He dove into her plate. "You look beautiful as ever." He kissed his wife's hand.

"Thank you darling." She said, watching Ginger go from station to station so happy in making her father a plate.

"So, you're really going through with this." She said.

"Yes," he said. "Baby, we talked about this. My baby girl is practically grown, and my wife without a real husband." He sighed. "I don't want to spend another moment away from my daughter, or my wife." He said, eating another piece of Ginger's fish. "It'll be fine. Trust me, I got this." He reached over and kissed her.

Ginger sat a mixed plate of catfish, and ribs in front of him. Then,

she went back and brought him a plate of cornbread, and collard

greens, along with a tall glass of sweet tea. Though she loved

everything on his plate, to eat it in the same meal would send her

stomach in turmoil. Her farther however was a native of Louisiana

and had an iron stomach.

"So," she sat next to him. "How long is it this time?"

"How long do you want it to be?" He talked, while eating.

"Don't ask me that daddy." She said.

"I'm asking." He wiped his mouth.

"Forever," she finished what was left of her catfish.

"Forever it is," he drank some of his sweet tea.

She wanted to disbelieve him but his eyes were too sincere,

and her mother's as candid as his were. She paused from eating her

macaroni. "Really," she said.

"Really," he said. "I'm not missing another moment of my

little girl growing up, or being with that fine woman across the

table." He winked at his wife. Jasmine smiled, but underneath her smile was uncertainty.

"You're serious." She glowed.

"Very," he said. "If you can handle your dad taking the train into San Francisco four days a week for the rest of your born days, then I guess you got me forever." He said.

"Yes!" She hugged him. "Yes, yes I can." She was nearly moved to tears. "Mama, isn't this great news?"

"Yes," she managed to smile, but her eyes said something totally different.

Jasmin's eyes weren't the only eyes reading something different. Though she tried to make herself believe that Kameron was being friendly, she came to a hard truth that it was more. It was the way he held her hand after he had shaken it. The way his eyes followed her and took detail pictures of her body. No matter how she moved, looked over towards him, or had to make eye contact with him, his eyes seem to never leave her. More than that, it was how they looked at her, like he loved her, and like he had already claimed her as his

She was Solomon's. She had waited on him way too long to

not be into a relationship that she didn't want. And besides, Ginger
was crazy about Kameron and she had to find a way to get them in
the same room so that he could look at Ginger how he looked at her.

"Big Mama," She said. "Tori and I will clean up here."

"Okay Baby," she said.

"I'll help." Kameron said.

"Kameron, you're guest. We got this." She began clearing
the table.

"Ask my Granny how I kick her out of the kitchen at home."
He winked at his Granny.

"I'm not too fond of it, but he does." Mrs. Cassidy smacked
him playfully on the behind.

"I'll start with the trash." He said. "Come on Ruby." He
starred at her. "You have to give me a chance." He winked.

His wink made Ruby nervous and she nearly dropped the
plates, but Kameron had quick hands and he captured them, smiled
back at her and took them into the kitchen. The look in the
grandparents' eyes was the look that she didn't want to see. They
looked like they were getting a glimpse of true love forming; even

her Papa's eyes showed it. Pathetic was Tori, she had the same look in her eyes that the grandparents' had, and Tori knew better.

She knew that Ginger was crazy about Kameron and that she was as crazy about Solomon. But then again, neither Tori nor Ginger ever liked Solomon for her. She constantly heard from both of them how much of a player Solomon was, and how Ruby could do so much better. Ginger even tried to set her up with Kamari, but Kamari just wasn't her type. Tori had her waiting until she went to Stanford.

She would definitely pull Tori aside and let her know what time it was, and remind her that Ginger was both their friend and that both of them were going to help her get Kameron no bones about it. Tori smiled at her as they arrived in the kitchen. Kameron had taken out the trash and before he got back in the door, Ruby had a word with Tori.

"Remember," she said. "It's Ginger who likes Kameron." She peeped out the kitchen window. "And, we have to get the two of them in the same room. We..."

"We don't have to do anything." Tori wet the dish cloth and

put soap detergent on it. "Rue," she looked out of the kitchen window as well. "I know you've seen how he looks at you. He's got the hot's for you." She looked out the window again, and saw him coming. "It's not going to matter if their standing shoulder to shoulder. He wants you."

"Well…" Ruby was interrupted

"Well what," he came in on the tail end of the conversation.

"Well what college do you go to?" Ruby asked.

"Cornell University," he said, standing next to her.

"That's a great school," Tori finally got out of the observation stage and said something.

"Just what I was thinking," she looked over at Tori wiping down the counters.

"So," he eyed Ruby. "You thinking of coming there?"

"No," she said, placing the dishes in the soapy water. "I'm going to Stanford come fall hopefully?"

"Whoa," he said. "Stanford, talk about great schools," he said. "Why Stanford, if you don't mind me asking."

"I know this is going to sound crazy, but when I was in the third grade my class when on a field trip there. I was hooked and I've dreamt about it ever since. Everything that I've done in school has been for Stanford." She said. "I've been accepted there already, but it's just a matter of convincing my mother to let me skip my senior year at King and go this fall. She sighed, "Tall order."

Kameron paused from washing the dishes. He knew that she was more than just a pretty face. It was something about the way she carried herself and at the tender age of seventeen she was paving the way for her future. He was impressed, and his eyes showed it. Tori liked what she was seeing. So, she snuck out of the back door without Ruby or Kameron noticing.

She grabbed a spare basket from the Wells unused closet. To her, it was a perfect time to pick fresh apples and peaches to make deep fried peach and apple fritters for Tommy. She liked the way Ruby and Kameron fit together. If only Ginger could see that she was to Kamari what Kameron was to Ruby.

Whether Ruby liked it or not, it was going to be her job to make sure Ginger recognized that Kameron had a fetish for Ruby.

Plain and simple, Ginger was just going to have to understand that Kameron had eyes for Ruby.

Kameron had already made up in his mind who he wanted and it didn't matter what Ruby or Ginger tried to do. Ruby hadn't noticed yet that Tori had slipped out of the kitchen and had landed in the orchards. She was too busy engrossed in talking about Stanford to have noticed.

"So," Kameron asked. "What do you plan on majoring in?"

"Journalism," she said without hesitation.

"Oh, so you're a writer," he smiled, as his hands touched hers in the soapy water.

"How'd you know?" She paused from putting the dishes into the dishwasher. "You're the first person who's ever asked me that." She was impressed.

"I don't know?' He said. "I just knew."

"Really," she said, taking the silverware from him. By accident she touched his hand again, but she hadn't noticed.

"Yeah," he said. "Have you written anything?"

"Yeah, but it's raw, just my first draft." She looked at him.

"I'd like to hear it some time." He handed her a dish and gazed into her eyes.

"I never had anyone ask me that before." She dried her hands on a dish cloth.

The way he stared at her scared her. For an empty second, there was an awkward silence more so for Ruby than Kameron. This was all wrong. Kameron belonged to Ginger. She had claimed him the day that she had seen him on his Grandfather's truck. And, he had claimed Ruby at the same time he had gotten her attention; his heart had erupted in a love that he had not felt before, and had thrown him off of his feet.

In that moment, she noticed his hand in hers, and she gently took it away from him. It was an inept moment for her, but for him it seemed to have come natural. She cleared her throat and tried to avoid his eyes. But she couldn't as the two of them were alone. Suddenly she noticed Tori had vanished and had left her by herself with Kameron. She was sure it was done on purpose and it was.

Like magic, she unexpectedly showed up in the kitchen with a basket full of apples and peaches, along with a devious smile.

"Peaches and apples for the fritters you requested." She said.

"And how long ago was that request," Ruby said, rolling her eyes at Tori.

"Delays don't mean denials," she licked out her tongue. "So, Kameron," she smiled at Ruby. "How do you like our little town?"

"I like it a lot." He said, looking at Ruby as if she were the reason for his love of the place, and partially she was. "But," he said. "I'm still getting use to these noisy crickets at night." He said with a smile.

"We happen to love our crickets." Ruby said. "And, they don't make noise, they make music."

"Now, that's a different take on it." He laughed. "But," he said. "I do enjoy watching the beautiful fire flies at night light up the sky. Never, would you see anything like that in New York."

"Ginger loves New York." Ruby said.

"Who's Ginger?" He said.

Tori couldn't help it. She burst out laughing. Ruby however had egg on her face. Kameron looked clueless, but he did wonder why Tori found what he said so funny. Nevertheless, Ruby wasn't done, and in her mind, she wondered, why Solomon hadn't called her yet?

Chapter 8

The beauty of Oak Grove had showed its face. The sky a perfect blue, the grass a solid emerald green, and the leaves on the trees a ripe hunter green. The scent of wild Sweet Pea flowers perfumed the much cooler summer air. The flowers had grown there since the town had existed and finally they had shown up.

Before Marcus could settle into his home, the news had gotten out that he was home. Marcus was the darling of Oak Grove. He was an all American in basketball; very intelligent, and had earned a full scholarship to Morehouse University in Atlanta Georgia. In four years, he had graduated top of his class, married his high school sweetheart, and went to work right out of college working for a fortune 500 company making six digit figures in international business. And, on top of all of that, he and Jasmin had a beautiful baby daughter. He was the epitome of success.

It appeared that life had shined bright on Marcus. He was living his dream until Jasmin started over indulging in their finances. Their elaborate life was quickly sinking fast and he had no choice but to put in for a transfer, take less money and try to dig his family out of a hole that his wife had gotten them into.

Maybe he was partially to blame. He lived out of a suitcase, and saw her and his baby girl days, weeks, or a month or two at a time. She had Ginger to raise, an unfulfilled life, and she allowed frustration, and resentment to get the best of her. Before she could grasp it all, they were in trouble and on the verge of being broke.

Of course there were rumors, some had the Maples on the verge of losing everything Marcus had worked so hard for; others gossiped about Jasmin spending Ginger's entire college fund, and others whispered that Jasmin was stepping out on Marcus. From where he stood, the rumors simply weren't true. He may have lived out of a suitcase throughout his career, but when he did come home, he would have seen the signs of a wife having an affair.

Despite the gossip, it was a stunning day for a celebration. It was Ginger's job to get her father out of the house for a while. She had strict instructions from her mother and Mrs. Fletcher, and she followed them verbatim. Besides, it gave her and her father time to get caught up on years, and reacquaint themselves with one another.

They easily drove up the coast towards Saratoga for lunch first and then the mall. It was one of her favorite spots. Sometimes she, Tori, and Ruby would make the half hour drive and nearly spend all day up there. Now, she could make the trip more often with just her and her dad the way Ruby and her dad just spent time alone together.

Solomon had taken a lunch break in between his next client. It was Mr. Fletcher and he was cool with Solomon feeding his growling stomach.

"Say Mr. Fletcher is it cool if I take a quick lunch and cut you up in about twenty minutes." He said.

"Go ahead son," he waved his hand. "You ain't got to be in no rush." He said. "The old man ain't in no hurry."

"Thanks man. I appreciate that." He fist bumped Mr. Fletcher.

Solomon left out of his pop's shop and took a seat under the tree. He had a tuber ware full of his mother's okra and tomatoes, and cornbread. Another tuber ware had two healthy pork chops, and in the side compartment, a serving of peach cobbler. As he began to eat, he couldn't help but think of Ruby. He wondered how she was doing. If she were thinking of him, and if she would want to see him again?

Before he could take his second bite, he picked up his cell and called Ruby. Ruby licked the cream cheese frosting from her fingers and answered her cell.

"Hello," she said.

"Hey," he said.

"Solomon," her voice suddenly changed.

"I didn't think you'd call me, or want to see me again." Excitement loomed in her voice.

"Nah," he said. "It's not like that. I've been wanting to call."

"My dad, right," Ruby said. "And my mom, I'm sure." She continued to frost the cake. "Sorry about that."

"Nah, it's cool." He said.

"No, it's not." She said.

"Who are you talking to?" Tori asked, taking the enchiladas out of the oven.

"Solomon," she said.

Tori's demeanor changed. Subtlety, she rolled her eyes at Ruby and shook her head. She paused starring at Ruby for a minute. What she saw in Solomon was beyond her. She was happy about their dating only because Ruby was excited about it. But he didn't suit Ruby like Kameron did. Kameron fitted Ruby like a hand to a glove. With Solomon, Ruby was just another chick in his loaded black book.

"So, can I see you?" Solomon asked.

"Yeah, where," she looked over at Tori as she finished frosting the cake for Ginger's father's surprise party.

"A place where your parents won't show up," he laughed.

"I know just the place." She smiled.

"See you in an hour." He said.

"Okay," she said and hung up.

"Ginger's dad's surprise party is in a few hours, and she will never forgive you if you don't show up." Tori said.

"She won't, or you won't." Ruby said.

"You know this means a lot to her." Tori turned to face Ruby.

"Solomon means a lot to me." Ruby said.

"And to Tiffney, Daphne, and God knows who else," Tori said.

"That was not fair, and that hurt." Ruby's eyes became misty. "I'm your friend Tori. Can't you try and be happy for me, or maybe that's asking for way too much?" She stormed out of the kitchen.

Tori took a deep breath and tossed her mittens down. Precious flung the mail on the table by her station and sat and relaxed while her clients were under dryers. Mrs. Amy had entered the shop. She was always finely dressed even when she was casually clothed. The moment she entered the shop it came alive, and all the unconfirmed news was about to be spread. Mrs. Amy was the town crier and when she entered any building all was gossip.

"Hey ladies," Mrs. Amy said, pulling off her silk handkerchief from her head. "Oh," she sat in a comfortable leather chair.

"Hey Precious, she said. I come to bear news."

"Girl, you are always bearing news." Odette laughed.

"What did you come to bear girl?' Precious laughed.

"Y'all all know that Marcus is back by now I'm sure," she said.

"Yeah," Precious said.

"Word is that he's transferred to San Francisco, taking less money, and get this," she said. "They broke."

"What?" Precious said.

"Say that again," Odette said.

"Who's broke?" Pauline stuck her head from underneath the dryer.

"The Maples girl," Mrs. Amy said. "Didn't I tell you that Jasmin was spending too wild?"

"What!" The women said, Pauline taking her dryer clean off of her head.

"Mama Wells," Precious said. "If you don't put that dryer back on your head," she laughed.

"Girl," she waved her hand. "Just give me a quick minute," she said. "I've got to hear this."

"I'm telling you." Odette said. "So, that's why he's home?"

"Girl that man was making some good money." Pauline said. "According to old lady Fletcher, Ginger's college was paid for in full, do you hear me, with some to spare."

"Well, it's gone now." Mrs. Amy said.

"Gone!" They said.

"All that money," Precious looked stunned. "That's hard for me to believe." She shook her head.

"Well," Mrs. Odette said. "It's not for me when you think about it." She said. "Look at all those expensive cars that she's been buying every two years."

"Yeah, and look at how she'd make them three hours drives down to San Francisco and buy all them expensive clothes from Saks Fifth Avenue." Pauline said. "And ain't spent a dime on that girl," she shook her head.

"That's a shame," Precious checked on her other client. "That's a shame."

"So, you telling us that, that girl of hers ain't got no college fund," Odette said.

"Or, no trust fund," Mrs. Amy opened up a bottle of Coke.

"What!" Pauline said.

"I can't believe this." Precious said. "That girl is her heart. We talk a lot and I know that she's been having a rough time."

"Really," Odette said.

"Yeah, I think when Marcus just whisked off into the sunset and made the money and lived his dream and left her to raise Ginger that did something to her." Precious said.

"I never could understand why she and that Girl couldn't jet set with him at least sometimes." Pauline said.

"Maybe he was stepping out on her? I hope not, but you can never put nothing past a man living out of a suitcase like that." Odette said.

"True," Mrs. Amy said. "But from what I heard Marcus wasn't the one stepping out, it was her. That's another reason why he's home, and will be working up the road in Frisco girl."

The shop went nuts. And as much as Precious was telling her mother-in-law to get back under the dryer, it all went on deaf ears. Pauline got excited and smacked the table a couple of times. Odette tossed her magazine on the floor, and had to catch her sweet tea before it fell. Precious plugged up her dryer and began drying Pauline's hair. The shopped roared as Odette and Mrs. Amy wiped happy tears from their cheeks.

"Where you get all this juicy news from?" Pauline said.

"I heard the Fletcher's having a not so friendly husband and wife discussion." She said. "I walked up on them and you could have bought old lady Fletcher for a nickel child."

"I bet she denied it didn't she?" Pauline said.

"Girl, how'd you know?" Mrs. Amy said.

"Cause, I know her, old and full of it most of the time." She said. "Lord forgive me." She giggled.

"Mama Wells," Precious said.

"I don't see anybody denying it." She said.

"That's the truth," Odette said. "Always talking about somebody and half the time she's getting her facts wrong."

"Maybe this will quiet her down some since her prize Godson is in trouble." Pauline said.

"Maybe?" Odette said. "By the way, where is that Ruby," she asked.

"Over at Tori's helping with the food." Precious said. "And still upset with me." She laughed.

"Oh, cause you busted her kissing that Garrett boy," Mrs. Amy said. "Child let her be mad, honey she don't need that one." Mrs. Amy sat back in her chair. "He's just like his daddy. Good for you."

"Let's just hope that she don't try and sneak behind your back." Odette said. "I'm not saying that she will, but you know these young folks."

"Odette, don't be wishing nothing on me." Precious said. "We had our little talk and she knows I meant what I said. And besides, her daddy had a talk with Solomon."

"You won't have any more problems out of him." Mrs. Amy said laughing. "Jake got a shotgun, and I'm sure it's loaded." She laughed again.

Ruby parked her father's truck behind the old gristmill. As she stepped out of the truck, there was Solomon, smiling like a treasure cat. He walked toward Ruby and took hold of her waist, smiled and kissed her passionately. He took her by the hand and guided her to a blanket that was already spread out for them.

She sat and he sat and before long they were immersed into kissing again. Ruby loved every ounce of it. Solomon wanted more. Ruby felt herself slipping and doing something that she may regret. She pulled herself back from Solomon and took a deep breath.

"What?" He inquired.

"I'm not ready for that." She said. "I came here because I wanted to see you, not to make out."

Solomon sighed, and disappointment stood boldly on his face. He tried to hide it but he couldn't. He wanted Ruby more so than he had wanted any of the other ones. What was it about him that Ruby was pushing away? If this had of been either Daphne, or Tiffney, the old gristmill would have been a blistering inferno. With Ruby, it was lukewarm at best. He didn't get it.

"So, what do you think is going to happen if we do it?" He asked.

"I don't think anything because I'm not going to do it." She Said. "Like I said, I'm not ready."

Solomon sighed, and underneath his breath, he grunted. This was not the answer that he wanted to hear. He liked Ruby, but he had needs. How was he supposed to be faithful to her if she didn't want to assist him with his pleasures? She was making it nearly impossible for him to not seek pleasures elsewhere if she weren't willing to supply his needs.

"You're upset with me aren't you?" She could read the expression on his face.

"No, no," he lied. "I guess I'll just have to wait to show you how much I care about you." He kissed her.

"I can tell by the way you kiss me." Ruby said, gazing into his eyes.

Solomon wrapped his arm around her and sighed again. This wasn't exactly what he was expecting or looking for. Behind the old gristmill just he and Ruby, no mom with glaring eyes, and no dad with a loaded shot gun at home waiting. This seemed like the perfect place to have his way with Ruby, but Ruby wasn't willing to let herself go, but he would keep trying, or dig out his black book.

"So, are you going to Ginger's dad's surprise party tonight?" She asked.

"No," he said.

"No," She turned looking at him. "I'm going to be there."

"You have to be there, that's your girl." He said.

"I can't believe that you're not coming." She said. "Me being there should be enough."

"Me and Ginger are not the best of friends." He said. "Girl knows how to get up under my skin. It's her dad's night, and I'm not trying to let her make me ruin it."

"Are your folks coming?" She asked.

"They told me they were." He said.

"So, you're just going to be all by yourself when you could be with me." She kissed him.

"Well, why don't you skip out early and come over." He kissed her back.

"I don't see Ginger letting me do that." She said.

"You're killing me Ruby." He said.

"You sure you won't come." She said.

"Nah," he said. "She needs to enjoy her pop." He said with a sad look in his eyes.

After all these years Ginger's father was returning home, his was three hours away and never chose to visit. He sent Money on Solomon's birthday, Christmas, and during the school year when Solomon played football. He had the best shoes and football equipment, but what he really needed was his dad, but as usual, he was a no show. In a way, he was jealous. Ginger's father had suddenly returned home, and his didn't care enough about him to even visit on a regular basis.

His pops was getting dressed and his mom had just gotten out of the shower. He would either heat up left overs, or order a pizza. What would his night have been like if Ruby would of aloud herself to be just a little naughty? He could tell that his mother was in the family room by the sweet smell of her perfume before she even said a word to him.

"You sure you don't want to join me and your grandfather tonight?" She said, putting on her high heel sandals. "They'll be plenty of food, and you won't have to sit up here and settle for left overs or some pizza." His mother said.

"I'm not trying to do that mama." He said. "I'm not trying to celebrate somebody's dad coming home when mines doesn't seem to give a damn that I even exist."

"I wish it could be different for you." She said. "But…"

"But what, act like it's alright and wait for another twenty years for him to show up, or come down with some terminal disease and then reach out to his son?" He walked into the kitchen.

"I wish I knew what to tell you." She followed him into the kitchen.

"Well for one, you could stop reminding me how much I'm like him." He said.

"Well, maybe if you stop exhibiting his behavior I won't have to." She said. "And by the way, I don't want none of them girls in my damn house Solomon." She Said. "You here me.?"

"Now that ain't no way to talk to the boy Yolanda." Her father said.

"I just want him to be somebody daddy, and not be like that jackass that I married." She sighed.

"Well, then stop treating him like his daddy, and start respecting him as your son." He said.

Ben knocked softly on Solomon's door. Solomon knew his grandfather's knock and told him to come in. Ben sat next to him on his bed and talked to him, then he wrapped his arms around his grandson and hugged him.

"I love you son." He said.

"I love you to pops." He suddenly felt better.

"I'll bring you back a plate." He said.

"Thanks," he said.

Solomon kicked back in his bed. From his bedroom window, he could hear his mother's BMW start up, and the lights flashing in his window as she drove off. He wasn't about to be alone and angry. He needed a way to release his anger, and he knew just how he would do it. He sped dialed Tiffney, and after two rings, she answered.

"I was waiting on you to call." She said.

"Well," he grinned. "The wait is over, and the house is empty baby." He said.

"So what about Ruby," she said.

"What about her?" He said. "She's at the party tonight. She's more loyal to her girl than me." He said. "Who you loyal to?" He asked.

"Do you even have to ask?" She said. "I'm on my way." She hung up.

Ginger and her father walked into the door, and all Marcus heard was "Surprise."

It was like a reunion but better. He embraced old friends, and if felt like he hadn't left at all. His wife Jasmin however had mixed emotions about his return and his decision to remain in the states. Ginger was just glad to have her daddy all the time like how any normal girl with a working father would have.

She stole him from her mother and from his old friends, and reintroduced him to her pals, Ruby and Tori. He couldn't believe how much they had grown. When he had last seen them they were little girls, now they were on the verge of becoming mature women. Tommy and Boyd had entered from the back door, but between food and talking, they had found their way to the front where the girls were.

Ginger introduced them to her father. Marcus shook their hands, conversed with them for a few, and then he was swept away by his wife, pretending that everything was honky dory and that they were the perfect couple. Tommy stole a kiss from Tori. Ruby smiled of course, but she wished that Solomon was there so that he could do the same to her, even if it meant she having it out with her parents.

Solomon was stubborn. But all she could think about was him being alone at an empty house. She sighed wishing she could be there with him. He grunted and moaned as Tiffney sat atop of him driving him insane. Ruby slipped away to call him, but he didn't answer. She waited a few minutes and then called again, but he didn't answer.

It was still early, too early for Solomon to be asleep. Maybe the boredom had gotten to him? Maybe his restless spirit of not having his father in his life was getting the best of him and all he could do was sleep? She put her cell back into her purse and looked up and nearly jumped out of her skin. There was Kameron standing right in front of her with the biggest smile on his face.

"Hey you," he said, and kissed her softly on her cheek. Ginger turned and saw it and she and Ruby's eyes met.

Chapter 9

The hairs on the back of Ginger's neck stood at attention. What in the world was Ruby doing knowing how she felt about Kameron? Ruby could tell by the look in Ginger's eyes what she was thinking and she knew before the night was over, that she'd have to set the record straight. She watched Ginger steal her dad from guest and head over their way as she made small talk with Kameron.

"So," she said, watching Ginger. "How's it going?"

"Good," he said, staring at her. "I was thinking." He said, as his speech was suddenly interrupted.

"Rue," she kissed her check and whispered in her hear. "What are you doing?"

"Nothing," she whispered back. "Mr. Maples," she hugged him. "Welcome home." She said.

"Daddy," she held onto his arm. "I'd like for you to meet Kameron Mosely, Mr. Mosely's great grandson. He's a very good friend of mines." She stepped away from her father to hug him.

Marcus had that look that only a father could have in his eyes. He could tell immediately that his daughter was fond of Kameron by the way she hugged him, and that she was planning more than to have just a friendship with him. He smiled at Kameron, but as a father, he seized him up. Good thing was that he was a Mosely and Mosely's were good men, and he liked that. He shook his hand, and talked small talk with him. It was Ruby's cue to leave and she did.

Mrs. Fletcher had made her rounds to everyone it seemed. On her way to get herself another glass of punch, she happened to notice Marcus, and Ginger comfy on Kameron's arm. A smile rose from her face, how good Ginger and Kameron looked together. She could see it all them casually dating, then it getting serious, and then the engagement announcement. She paused from pouring herself another glass of punch when her God daughter-in-law came over to see if she could assist her.

"Mother Fletcher," she said. "Is it punch that you want sweetie?" She said. "Here, let me do that for you."

"Thanks baby." She said. "See what I see?" Mrs. Fletcher

drank some of her punch.

Jasmin pulled her hair away from her face and looked directly in front of her, a few feet away. Her eyes sparkled like diamonds in a night sky. Getting the two of them together had been on her mind since their finances had begun to tank.

"Yes," she said with a smile in her voice.

"Don't they look good together?" Mrs. Fletcher said.

"Oh honey yes they do," she said.

"Go on over and introduce yourself, and don't let him leave tonight until you have him coming back this way for dinner." She said.

"Yes ma'am." Jasmin said.

Ruby was board out of her mind. Ginger was entertaining her father and Kameron which she was glad. She knew how much Ginger missed having her father around. Now he was back, and she was spending every awakening moment with him. As far as Kameron was concerned, she was glad that Ginger had come to her rescue.

The way he looked at her nearly gave her chills. It was as if he could read her deepest thoughts and could commune within the most sacred parts of her soul. He looked at her like he should be looking at Ginger, and it made her very uncomfortable. Maybe now that Ginger had him all to herself his affection could begin to turn toward the young lady who wanted him.

Despite Ruby's happiness for Ginger, she was board out of her mind. Solomon had declined to come, and had declined to answer his phone and she couldn't figure out why. Maybe he was as board as she was and the only appealing thing for him was to have watched a movie and gone to sleep in the middle of it. If her parents weren't lurking around she may have slipped away and checked on him. She was tempted, but something told her that she would get caught.

She sighed pulled out her cell again and tried Solomon, but again, she got his voice mail. Solomon was so engrossed in getting busy with Tiffney that he didn't even hear his cell, and if he would have, it wouldn't have made a difference considering how he was making rather marry with one of his black book girls.

"Trying to call that boy?" Her father asked, scaring her.

"Daddy," she smacked his arm. "You scared me."

Jacob laughed, and handed his daughter some punch. "So, were you trying to call that boy," He asked again. "No," she lied. "Can't find Tori, and Tommy, and my batteries dead," she lied.

"I just saw Tori around somewhere with Tommy." He smiled. "Boy's sweet on her," he said. "Now I know why he be slipping in my restaurant eating their nearly every day."

"Daddy," She laughed. "Tommy's sweet, and he really likes Tori. So but out," she nicked his hand.

"I like Tommy." He said. "He's a good kid, and a hell of a ball player and he come from good folks." He said. "Tori's like my daughter, and since her daddy's with the lord, I have to watch out for her and you to." He kissed her on her nose.

"I love you." Ruby hugged her father.

"I love you to." He said.

"So, you don't like Solomon," she asked.

"Got nothing against the boy personally, but I damn straight didn't like the way he was kissing my daughter." He said.

"We like each other a lot." She said.

"You like each other too much. I don't want you dating until you're thirty."

"Thirty," she said. "You're crazy daddy." She laughed. "I'll be in my career, will have bought a house, and a nice car, and…"

"That's my point," he said.

"But, what if it wasn't Solomon," she said.

"Excluding Jesus Christ, it's thirty." He said.

"Well, I'm telling Papa then," she said.

"You tell my daddy and I will deny everything you said." He laughed. He's my daddy, and he'll believe me over you any day." He teased her.

"I don't think that you want to test that out." She laughed. "Thank you for still allowing me to drive our truck." She smiled.

"You're welcome baby." He kissed her cheek. "Now, how did it get to become our truck?" He laughed.

"Cause you and me are the only ones you drive it," she said. "You know, I've saved seven thousand dollars towards my truck." She said.

"Really," he said. "So, can I get a loan?" He teased.

"I've give you all of it if you really needed it, and start saving all over for my truck again." She looked into her father's eyes with sincerity.

Jacob's heart melted. Ruby's heart was bigger than the size of Texas and he loved her for it. He lifted up her chin and placed his face next to hers and hugged her ever so lovingly. Suddenly Ruby's boredom had left, but her father and her Papa had that type of effect on her.

"Can you keep a secret?" He said.

"Yeah," she said.

"Your mama's called your counselor and that recruiter at Stanford and their coming over for dinner on Sunday after church." He said.

"Yes!" She screamed. "Sorry," she said.

"Girl," her father laughed.

Ruby's scream had done one of many things. It allowed Kameron to signal for his Grandmother out of duress. It had gotten

Cassidy's attention and allowed her eyes to land right on her grandson, take his side and whisk him away. And, it allowed her mother to find her.

Ruby's mother waved from a distance and came from the inside around the back by the pool and sat in between her husband and her daughter. She kissed Jacob and he being naughty stole sweet sinuous kisses from his wife. Ruby looked on embarrassed, thinking of how her parents felt when they busted her and Solomon.

"Jesus," she said. "Get a room." She said. "People are looking."

"So," her father said. "This is my baby here. "I earned that."

"And, you get mad at me and Solomon," she said.

"Solomon don't have my permission to kiss my baby girl like that." He said.

"You don't have to say anything because I know that you agree with him." Ruby said to her mother.

"Believe it or not baby, I just don't want to see you get hurt that's all." She stroked Ruby's face.

"Baby, I'm going to get me a plate. You want anything?"

He said to Precious, then Ruby.

"Some of Tori's enchiladas, and big mama's peach cobbler "Ruby said.

"Me too," Precious agreed.

"Coming right up," he said.

"Do you really believe that I would have sex with Solomon?" She asked her mother.

"I didn't think that you would." She said. "But sometimes, when you get caught in the heat of the moment, things happen baby. And, I don't want that to happen to you."

"Mama, I want to go to Stanford bad." She looked at her mother. "And whether you believe me or not, I think about it as much as I do him." She said. "I would never do anything to hurt you or daddy, or initially embarrass you." She looked at her mother. "I like Solomon a lot. I'm not going to lie to you. But, if it bothers you that much for me to see him, then I won't." She said.

Precious eyes displayed shock. Out of the shock, her mouth opened wide and she stared a Ruby for a minute. Maybe she had underestimated her own daughter. Ruby seemed to be mature in ways that she hadn't given her credit for. In that moment she knew

she had to sign whatever documents that she needed to sign for Ruby

to be able to start Stanford come fall. And though she didn't like it,

she had to allow Ruby to see Solomon even though she didn't want

to.

She gathered Ruby in her arms and just held her ever so tight

and wiped tears away from her eyes. She whispered softly in her

ear, "I love you." And then she kissed her forehead. "I don't like

you dating this Solomon." She said. "But just promise me with

him, that you'll be extra careful, and baby please keep your eyes

open, promise." She looked into her daughter's eyes.

"I promise." Ruby said. "I love you too."

"I love you so much." Precious said.

Ginger was livid at Mrs. Cassidy for taking Kameron away

from her. The house was crowded inside as well as outside. To find

Kameron and Mrs. Cassidy was like trying to find a needle in a

haystack. She squeezed, and scooted in between guess, saying

excuse me more than a dozen times. No matter where she looked,

she hadn't found them. In fact, she hadn't seen Mr. Mosely either.

Her hope was, was that Mrs. Cassidy hadn't strong armed Kameron, and talked him into leaving just when she was about to make her move.

If she had, that wouldn't stop her. She would see Kameron around, and by chance she didn't, she would show up at their house with goodies, and see what Mrs. Cassidy would do about that. She sighed and turned nearly bumping into Kamari who felt for Ginger what Kameron felt for Ruby.

"Oh hey." She said. "I'm sorry I nearly knocked you over." She said.

"Nah," he smiled, gazing at her. "It's cool." He said. "That's all iron right there," he patted his chest and flexed his muscles. "I think it's cool that your pop's is back."

"Yeah," she said. "I'm happy about it, an answer to my prayers." She said.

So, you seen Boyd, or Ruby around?" He asked.

"No," she said," actually I haven't seen any of them. "Where's Tommy and Tori?"

"Ah," he grinned. "They took off, sort of into their own thing." He smiled. "You want to get something to eat?" He asked.

"Ah, sure," he had caught her off guard. How come this could not be Kameron.

Kamari had made both of them a plate. It was a mix tray of barbecue, potato salad, and Tori's enchiladas. She was quite surprised that without asking her he knew what she liked. It was probably a lucky guess. She tried to avoid Kamari's eyes, like Ruby avoided Kameron's but Kamari's look was strong and dominant, and even when Ginger managed to look away, his eyes were always on her.

"This is nice." He said, eating. "Thanks for the invite. I know my pops is enjoying. I hear him and your dad went to high school together." He said.

"Really," she said. "I didn't know that." She looked over her shoulder hoping to see Kameron.

"Yeah," he said. "Pretty cool huh."

"Yeah, small world," she said.

Ruby yawned as she pulled back her covers. She rubbed her

eyes and sat for a minute not thinking about anything at the moment. She yawned again and looked at her cell. There were four messages on her cell. She browsed through them, none from Solomon. What was going on with him?

She looked at her clock, and it was 8:30am, by now both her parents were gone. She sat back on her bed for a minute, then she slowly dragged her body to the wash bowl, and then the shower. As she showered she couldn't help but think of Solomon. However, though she tried not to think about it, it did cross her mind if he had resorted back to his old ways and dug up one of his old flames. After all, she had called him three times, and at no time did he bother to answer.

She stepped out of the shower and wrapped a towel around her and her cell rang. She hurried to answer it thinking it might be Solomon, but it wasn't. It was Ginger. She was disappointed, but she had hoped that her voice didn't show it.

"Hey Gin." She said.

"Hey Rue, what's up?' She said.

"Oh nothing much," Ruby Sprayed a silk perfumed lotion on her body. "I have to go into the shop today. I got a couple of ladies that need their hair done." She sprayed her arms and legs. "So what's on your agenda?" Ruby asked.

"I was thinking about hanging out with my dad this morning and maybe this evening me, you and Tori could catch a movie or something." She said

"Sounds good to me," Ruby put on a pair of shorts.

"So, what happened to Solomon last night?" She said. "He's not one of my favorite people, but I wouldn't have mind if he were there with you." She said.

"Ah," Ruby was caught off guard. "He, ah, well, his dad's not really in his life, so…"

"What does that have to do with you?" She said.

"It's not about me Gin, it's about his dad. I guess he couldn't handle it." She put on a cute tee that said *life is a beauty shop*.

"So what was he doing all by his lonesome self?" Ginger inquired.

"How would I know Gin?" Ruby snapped at her.

"Touchy, aren't we?" Ginger said.

"Can we just change the subject?" Ruby said.

"Yeah," Ginger said. "What was that about with Kameron kissing you on the cheek last night?"

"I don't know Gin. I guess he was just trying to be friendly." She placed her hair in a sophisticated ponytail, and sprayed perfume around her neck and on her shirt.

"Well, could you just remind him that it's my cheek he needs to be kissing?" She said.

"Why don't you do that Gin? I assure you that I am not the least bit interested." She put on her big silver hoop earrings. "Trust me," she said. "I am willing to help you out with that in any way that I can."

"Really," Ginger said.

"Why wouldn't I Gin?" She put on her sandals. "What do you have in mind?"

"Mrs. Cassidy likes you." Ginger said.

"Mrs. Cassidy likes everybody Gin." Ruby put on an earth tone type of lipstick.

"Maybe? But, she likes you better than everyone else." She said. "Show up with me to his house unannounced with a tray of Tori's man killing brownies, stay for a minute and make an excuse to disappear."

Ruby Paused from putting on her lipstick. She had seen how Kameron had looked at her like they were the only two in the room, and it frightened her; not even Solomon looked at her like that. In all honesty, she was to chicken to do it. But, what was she supposed to tell Ginger?

"Why don't you and your mom take a platter of goodies over to the Mosely's like a welcome wagon or something and throw an invite for dinner." She put her lipstick away.

"Rue, you're a genius." She said.

"I don't know about that. But my Big Mama tells me that the way to a man's heart is to his stomach." She placed her purse on her shoulder. "Let me know how it goes." She said.

"I will." She smiled.

"I have to go to the shop so I'll talk to you later." Ruby said.

"Later," Ginger said and hung up and fell back on her bed with the biggest smile on her face.

Why couldn't she have thought of that? She could say that she really enjoyed his company and just wanted to thank him for coming to her father's surprise party, and as a token of her appreciation, she brought a tray of brownies for him. After her and her mother were in, her mother could visit with Mrs. Cassidy, and she could have Kameron all to herself. After he ate so many brownies, then she could pop the invite on him, and of course he wouldn't refuse.

She flung open her door, and headed to her parents room, but they weren't there. She called out to them, but they didn't answer back. She went into her father's study, nothing. Now, she was getting scared. As she was about to go into the kitchen, she heard voices escalating, and she followed the voices out back by the pool.

"I did this for you." Marcus said. "I thought you'd be happy."

"How could I be happy Marcus when you took a drastic pay cut?" She said.

"It's not a drastic pay cut." He said. "I'm giving up some bonus' yes, but we'll be fine. The plus side of this is that I get to see my wife and my little girl every day."

"Plus side," she said. "We're practically broke." She said.

"We are not broke." He said. "We just have to juggle some things around." He rubbed his hand over his forehead. "You were supposed to keep watch over the finances, not spend extravagantly was that too hard to ask?"

"I had a daughter to raise; a house to run with no husband to help me." She said. "I was young…"

"And so was I, and I busted my ass every day, every minute, every place that I went. It was always, always about you and my daughter in there." He raised his voice. "So don't talk to me about my decision, about a pay cut," he said. "Something had to give before we hit rock bottom." He turned, placing a hand on his hip. "I expect your support because we are done talking about this."

Ginger stood numb listening at the back door. Her mouth nearly dropped to the floor. She hurried out of the kitchen, grabbed her purse from her room and the spare car keys from the key rack.

She heard her father call her and she rushed out of the door. He stepped out of the front door and called out to her again, but she pulled out of the drive way. From the look on his face, he knew that Ginger had heard everything.

Chapter 10

Solomon hadn't returned any of Ruby's previous phone calls. In fact, it had been three days since she had heard from Solomon, and her instincts were telling her that Solomon had slipped back into his playboy ways. However, her mind disguised as her heart was telling her something else. She was quiet at the shop, not her jovial self. Precious and the older ladies could sense something was wrong.

"Looks like somebody's got man troubles," Mrs. Amy teased Ruby, trying to draw her out of her funk.

"You couldn't possibly be talking about me." Ruby said wet setting Odette's hair.

"Didn't say no name, so I wouldn't have to bare no blame?" Mrs. Amy said.

The older ladies laughed. But, Ruby didn't even crack a smile. She sprayed some sort of oil sheen on Odette's hair to keep the curls in tack. She stuck her under the dryer for fifteen minutes and took an arm full of soiled towels back to the back. Precious followed.

"Ruby, baby," Precious said. "Is everything okay?"

"Yeah, yeah," she lied. "I guess I'm just a little tired."

"What's wrong?" Precious looked worried. "Are you not getting enough rest? Baby, is something bothering you, because if it is, you know you can talk to me."

"Mama," Ruby hugged her mother. "I'm fine really." She said.

"Well, you don't look fine." Precious held her face in the palm of her hands.

"How could I not be mama, my counselor and my recruiter our coming for dinner on Sunday," a fake smile emerged from her lips. "Thank you for doing that, I know it wasn't easy."

"Nope," Precious smiled. "It wasn't, but anything difficult never is." She kissed her daughter on the forehead and hugged her.

"Mama," Ruby said. "How do you know the difference between your heart telling you something, or your head?"

"Your heart tells you the truth. Your head tells you what you want to hear." She said. "Why?"

"No particular reason," she placed the towels in the bin. "I'm gonna take a quick break." She said, grabbing a snack out of the cupboard and went out back to sit.

Solomon had been in a funk since Ginger's dad had returned. He and his mother had been at each other's throats constantly, and he couldn't wait until she left for her long shift at the hospital. Tonight was one of those nights when she would have to stay overnight because she was assisting a doctor with surgery. The house was his. The night was his, and the only music that would ring throughout his ears were the girls screaming out his name. He loved it. Afterward he always bragged to his boys how he had beaten it, and how they couldn't get enough of him.

It was Daphne this time who shared his bed. She was the one he called up when Tiffany was becoming overbearing, and making too many demands on him. Daphne wanted him as bad as Tiffany and the others, but she wasn't demanding. At least she pretended not to be. She played the game of just hanging around and allowing

Solomon to sow his wild oats, believing that when he was finished he'd come back to her, and Tiffany and the others would have egg on their face. As she lay beside him, she couldn't phantom why he wanted Ruby. Ruby was a good girl who would never bed down with Solomon.

Daphne sat up in his bed, and pulled the sheets over her naked body. She stared at Solomon for a moment with lots of questions in her eyes. Usually, she paid no attention to his affairs. She knew his reputation and somehow had come to accept it. She'd just be there when the others had gotten fed up enough to give up on him. She'd be the only one standing and ready to welcome him into her arms, sharing him with no one; at least, that was the plan. She turned her body towards him, and he slid his muscular body up towards his back board; a hint of moisture on his chest.

"I heard a rumor." She said. "Heard that you are messing around with Ruby Wells," she snickered. "That can't be true," she said.

"What if it's true?" he said.

Daphne looked surprise with a mixture of shock gleaming in her eyes. "Are we talking about the same Ruby Wells? The straight A student. Miss Good girl, Miss. Independent" Daphne laughed. "She ain't giving up nothing so you might as well focus on someone who will give you what you want, and what you need." She tried to kiss him, but he turned his face and got out of his bed.

Daphne's eyes were heartbroken. She hated when Solomon treated her like that, and she detested herself for going back to him every time he made a pathetic apology. However, she couldn't help it. No one made her feel like he did; no one she ever dated came close.

She had enough against Ruby without her having to fight with her over Solomon. Body wise, Ruby could not compete with her. Like Daphne, Ruby was not well endowed in places that drove the men wild as Daphne was. Unlike Tiffany, Ruby scared her but she would not let Solomon know it.

"What do you want from her?" She asked.

"Why you getting into my business?" He said, zipping up his

pants.

"I think I have a right." She rolled her eyes, "considering that I'm always in your bed."

He threw his tee shirt over his head and looked at her in a peculiar fashion. She had hit a nerve and made him reach deep down inside, and she could tell because it was all over his face. She smiled knowing that she had struck something in him that he never wanted to touch surface.

"Get your clothes on." He said. "My mama's on her way."

"I thought she was pulling an overnighter at the hospital." She said.

"Things have changed, you have to go," he said.

"If you think that you'll ever get Ruby in bed, you're sadly mistaken." She zipped up her shorts, and threw her tee shirt on.

"Just get out." He said.

"You remember that when you need it and have no one else to call but me." She said, and slammed the back door.

As Daphne slammed the back door, Yolanda came through the front door. Like always, she tossed her purse on the kitchen counter and paused at the answering machine to check her messages. Solomon hurried to remake his bed, and jumped in the shower. He did not want the scent of sex on him, nor did he want another lecturer from his mother about the girls he slept with. He could tell by the sound of his mother's voice that she was tired and had drama at work.

"Solomon," she called out to him.

"Yeah," he was half dressed.

"Solomon," she called out to him again.

"Yeah," he appeared in the kitchen smelling like Dial Soap, and his hair in place. "I heard you the first time mama."

"Well, if you did, how come you didn't answer?" She said, taking a bottle of water out of the refrigerator.

"Well, what is it," he pulled out cold cuts, bread, and mustard.

"How come there are still dishes in this sink?" She drank swallows of cold water. "I told you this morning more than once." She sat her water on the counter. "I'm tired boy when I come home from the hospital; I not trying to come home and do this.

You hear me?"

"I always hear you." He said.

"Don't you be getting smart with me?" She said. "I'm not one of them little girls that you mess with. I'm your mama boy." She stared at him.

"I'm not a boy mama. I'm a man." He rolled his eyes at her.

"Where's my daddy?" She asked him.

"The shop," he said. "Where else would he be?"

"There is such a thing called Dodger stadium." She said. "Come to think of it, why aren't you at the shop?"

"I went in earlier today." He said, taking lettuce, tomatoes, and cheese out of the refrigerator. "Want a sandwich?"

"Yeah," she said.

"Want lettuce, and tomato on it?" He asked.

"Light on the lettuce, a couple slices of tomatoes," she finished her water. "You know daddy really loves that shop. When we were kids it was all he ever talked about." She said. "When mama passed on, he just went for it, and now he's living his dream."

"Yep," Solomon sat a plate down with a sandwich in front of his mother. "Ever stop to ask me what my dreams are?" He said sitting his plate down across from his mother.

Yolanda paused from eating her sandwich. She looked at Solomon as if he had said something foreign to her. As far as she was concerned, his dream was the shop. It didn't take much to see that he liked it, and that he had found a home with the old men who seem to love him and understand him. It was the one thing he was good at beyond the bedroom, and it fit him like a hand inside a glove. What else would he possibly want to do?

"I thought the shop was your dream." She said. "At least that's what your grandfather thinks."

Solomon didn't say a word. He bit into his sandwich and took a couple of swallows of his milk. It was his grandfather that had taken him away from a huge cloud of confusion that he wrestled with as his parents tore each other a part and went their separate ways. At twelve, his grandfather had saved him by inviting him into his barbershop, and introduced him to men who understood his pain and helped him work through it. The barbershop was his solace away from his father's sorry image of being a real dad. And his mother's pitiful excuse of finding ways to remind him of being too much like the man he really never knew.

He had much to thank his grandfather for. He stepped in and took the place of his father when he needed a strong male in his life that cared. The barbershop was his quiet place; a place that offered him more than study pay and tips. It was where the pain of being Bobby Garret's son was erased; where he was respected by real men who loved him in spite of his flaws, and appreciated him as an individual. But, Solomon had dreams of his own, and he wanted nothing more than to be in the NFL like his dad.

"So, what are you gonna do without the shop?" She looked disappointed.

"I'm gonna go to the USC like my dad; play football, and go pro like he did." He opened up a bag of barbecue potato chips.

"Do what." She seemed surprised. "Don't be stupid like your father." She resumed eating her sandwich.

"Damn mama. Are you ever gonna look at me and not see Bobby Garret, but see me your son Solomon?" He left the table and slammed the door to his room.

Yolanda was shocked. Her mouth nearly sunk to the floor. She sat staring at her son in a way that she never had. For the first time, despite his past immaturity, she was seeing a boy evolve into a man.

She knew that she was hard on him, but at times he had demonstrated unacceptable behavior. She searched arduously in her son to find his strengths, but often times she was sorely disappointed. She refused to have him turn out like his father; a womanizing Casanova, who shattered women's hearts, and left an innocent boy to fend on his own. Maybe she pushed him too hard at times? But, it was all out a love that Solomon never saw.

She finished her sandwich and placed her plate in her sink. Her father had just chewed her out a few days ago about comparing Bobby to Solomon. And now, Solomon had echoed in her father's response. She did something that she wouldn't do before. She actually knocked on his door seeking to apologize and hope that he would accept it.

"Solomon," she said. "I just want to say I'm sorry." She

waited for him to respond, but he didn't. He sat on his bed quietly just listening to her. "Can we talk?" she said.

She walked away thinking that he wouldn't open the door. But, when he rose from his bed and opened his door, he surprised her.

"Mama," he said.

"I'm sorry." She said again.

"I'm just tired of always being compared to him." He said. "I may be his son, but I'm not him. It's seems that only Papa and Ruby recognize that."

"Ruby," she said, with a surprise look in her eyes. "Ruby Wells." She said again. "So, you do know something about picking nice girls."

"Yeah, I suppose." He said.

"So, you like her?" She asked.

"Yeah, I just don't know how to show her." He said.

"What do you mean you don't know how to show her?" She sat next to him on his bed.

"I don't. She's different." He looked at his mother like an innocent little boy.

"You ask her out to dinner. You find out what her favorite flowers are and buy her a bouquet." She said. "Nice girls like to be courted baby. They like for you to look at them like you look at no one else, like your looking into the core of their souls." She took hold of his hand. "They just want to know that you care and mean it." She said.

Solomon hadn't felt the softness of his mother's hands since he was a little boy. Somehow it made him feel safe, wanted, and loved. His father however was quite a different story; now he knew why he didn't want children.

He knew now that he had to call Ruby, but what would he tell her? If he told her the truth their short relationship was done. If he lied and she found out, they were done? He had to do something, but what? He decided to check in with his boys for help.

Ruby had finished Mrs. Odette's hair, and Mrs. Fletcher's, and she was working on another client. She headed back to the back to grab some conditioner out of the cabinet as a soft knock tapped at the screen door. Of course, Ruby didn't hear it from the back, but when she came to the front, she nearly dropped the conditioner at the sight of Kameron. Kameron had quick hands and caught it.

"I need a haircut." He fiddled in his hair.

The look in Ruby's eyes was priceless. She wanted to say something but the words just wouldn't come out. Every conversation in the shop was put on hold. Mrs. Amy had taken her head out from underneath the dryer. Odette stop looking at the O magazine, and Mrs. Fletcher nearly choked on her apple juice.

"Haircut," She coughed again, and drank some water. "Ben Nelson got a shop for the men not far up the road." She said. "Solomon cuts hair there to." She said, looking at Ruby.

"I know." He said, looking at Mrs. Fletcher with that Mosely smile. "But, I want Ruby to cut it." He turned back towards Ruby. "Oh, I almost forgot," he said. "I brought you something." He handed her a pink gift bag.

"You didn't have to do that." She said, nearly tongue tied.

"Well he did," her Grandmother said. "Now hush your mouth and open it." She laughed.

The entire shop was on hold. For a moment, time stopped. Mrs. Fletcher sat in the corner by the window with a million frowns in her face. She couldn't understand what all the fuss was over a pink gift bag with no evidence of what type of gift it was. She turned her frail body towards Kameron and Ruby, wanting to see what the gift was so she could spread the word to Jasmin.

Ruby reached down into the bag and pulled out a Red Journal with Stanford University written in bold white writing, and a golden pen sat with Cardinal Pride engraved on each pen. Her eyes danced as she stared at the gift. But, how did he remember? She had only told him once at her Grandmother's house at dinner, making simple conversation. She looked at him to thank him and there was that look again. The same look that gave her chills and placed goose bumps the size of penny's on her arms. It was the gazed that looked deep into her soul as if hers were connected to his.

"Thank you very much." She said.

"You're welcome." He said.

"Girl," her grandmother said. "Don't you know how to thank the man?"

"Big Mama," Ruby said.

"Stop instigating Pauline." She said. "The child did thank the boy." Mrs. Fletcher said.

"Hush," she rolled her eyes at Mrs. Fletcher. "Hug the man girl." Her grandmother said.

Kameron didn't wait on Ruby. He took the cue from her grandmother and wrapped his arms around Ruby's waist, drew her into him and held her, and then kissed her sweetly on the cheek. Ruby was embarrassed and she didn't dare look at the ladies in the shop especially her grandmother. She sat her gift bag on her station, and found her mother's eyes. It was definitely not the look that she had gotten from her when she got busted kissing Solomon.

The way her mother smiled at Kameron's affection towards her scared her almost as much as how Kameron responded to her. The way she read it was that of instant approval. She wondered if it had anything to do with him being a Mosely, or did she honestly believe that he was more suited for her? Maybe it was all her Big Mama's influence. For, she made it no secret how she felt.

"You wanna come back to the wash bowl." She said. "I

need to wash your hair before I cut it." She said.

Kameron haply followed Ruby to the wash bowl. Ruby could feel him watching the sway of her hips, and eyeing her shapely legs. What was she doing so wrong that he wasn't falling for Ginger? His affection was misdirected and she had to find a way to redirect it to Ginger where it belonged, but how?

Mrs. Amy changed seats and took the dryer in the corner facing the wash bowl down the hall. Pauline took the opposite seat and periodically peeped down the foyer. Mrs. Fletcher couldn't stand it and kept her nose in her magazine until her ride showed up. Kameron had showed her what she didn't want to see. He made it clear and obvious that Ruby was the one, and he didn't seem to mind folks knowing it either.

In her mind, Ginger was more suited for him, she was talented, had an entrepreneurial spirit, she was beautiful, and making plans to go back to school in New York. Whether he saw it or not, their paths were already crossing. Ruby was to remain in California and after summer he was headed back to New York. From where she sat, a relationship between the two of them wouldn't last long;

long distance relationships never did. Once Kameron figured that out, he would drop Ruby like a hot cake and Ginger would reign as queen. However, somehow they had to make him aware of that.

"You know," Odette said. "I'm not one to say much, but that boy in there is into your baby girl like jelly goes with bread honey let me tell you." She smiled.

"I was about to say the same thing." Pauline grinned.

"And bold with it to," Mrs. Amy said, watching Ruby adjust the chair.

"Yeah, I see." Precious said. "A far cry from that Solomon," she said.

"Oh y'all are making just too much of that," Mr. Fletcher said. "It's just a journal, and after summer the boy will be gone."

"Well," Pauline said. "We know one thing; he's not interested in that Ginger."

The shop was quiet and the look on Mrs. Fletcher's face was that of defeat and embarrassment. Precious nicked her mother-in-law on the arm, as she tried to stop herself from laughing. There was

quiet snickering going on. Mrs. Amy covering her face with an

Essences Magazine, and Odette with the O Magazine. Thankfully

her ride had shown up, and though she was old and feeble, she

hurried out the door like a woman half her age.

The moment she left out the door, laughter erupted and

gossip and backbiting ensued. Ruby paused briefly before washing

Kameron's hair. And, when she heard the shop explode in laughter,

she knew that whatever had it quiet, it had resumed its voice. She

could only imagine what they were talking about and all of it was

back in the wash bowl. Why did Kameron have to show up for a

haircut, and why did he have to bring her that beautiful gift?

"Just curious," Ruby said. "Where did you get the journal

and pen set?"

"Stanford," he looked up toward her with a huge smile.

"You went all the way there?" She said.

"Yeah," he said. "I'm looking to hopefully get an internship

with this firm when school starts back. Since I'm visiting my

Grandparent's and the firm has a company out here, I interviewed with them out here very close to your campus." He said. "There was a gift shop and I saw it from the window and I couldn't resist."

"Thank you." She scrubbed his scalp. "That was really thoughtful of you," she continued to scrubbed his scalp.

"You're welcome." He said. "I knew you'd like it."

"How did you know that I like to write?" She began washing his hair again.

"You have a rough draft your supposed to read to me remember?" He said.

Their conversation was brief the night that her grandmother had slipped and invited them over for dinner. She barely could remember some of the things that she said to him. But, somehow he remembered everything that she had said to him. Here he was baring gifts over a bland conversation, and Solomon whom she had waited on, hadn't even had the decency to call her. Her heart was beginning to speak to her about Solomon and though she didn't like it, it was introducing her to the plain truth. He still hadn't called.

"So, what's your major?" She asked.

"Engineering, with a minor in architecture," he said.

Ruby placed conditioner on his hair and placed a plastic cap over his head. She lifted his seat only to see his eyes gazing in hers and she nearly dropped the conditioner on the floor again. But like before, he had quick hands and caught it. He placed it in her hands and felt the softness of her fingers and he knew that he would love holding her hand.

"So," she took her hand back. "You're a math person. I hate math." She said about to put the conditioner up. He stood ever so close behind her, placed his hand on her waist and put the conditioner on the top shelf.

"You have beautiful eyes." He stared into her eyes.

"Ah," he had made her nervous again. "I'm going to put you under dryer number four."

She walked him to the front, pointed and put it on fifteen minutes. Now, she was furious at Solomon. When he did call she would certainly give him a piece of her mind.

Boyd, Tommy, Solomon and Kamari sat at an outside table at Berry's eating pork and shredded beef burritos. As Always, Kamari sat by his boy Solomon, and Boyd and Tommy sat next to each other. They never really paid attention to their sitting order. It had been going on since they were kids. The day was nice and Berry's seemed to be the place for Solomon to bare his soul to the guys about Ruby and what he had gotten himself into.

"I need some advice." He said, a slight pause before he blurted it out. "I cheated on Ruby and I don't know if I should tell her?" He ate and then drank some of his root beer.

"Wait, wait," Boyd said, talking with food in his mouth. "Roll that by me again, because I'm not thinking that I heard you right." He smacked his ear in fun.

"Ah man," Kamari said. "Are you kidding me?" He said. "Ruby is such a nice girl man." He shook his head. "You're paving the way for that fool Kameron to step in."

"He's my last worry." He wiped his mouth. "Ruby has eyes only for me." He said. "Fool is just wasting his time." He said. "So, help your boy out, what should I do?"

"I'm still on I've fallen and I can't get up." Boyd teased, demonstrating. The guys roared in laughter. Even Solomon had to laugh.

"Truthfully," Tommy said, sipping on his strawberry shake. "I think you need to end it before it gets ugly man." Tommy shook his head.

"I agree." Kamari said. "Man face it, you're not cut out for one on one relationships," Kamari took another bite of his burrito. "You know it hurts me to say that." He said.

"I made a mistake." Solomon said. "And all I get from my boys is criticism." He said. "You guys know that if the situation were different I'd have your back." He shook his head.

"Go on Maury man and pour your soul out." Boyd unfolded the gold paper on his pork burrito and bit into it. "I don't get you man." He shook his head. "Do you not like women?"

"Wow!" Solomon said.

"Why are you even messing with this girl man?" Kamari said.

"Hold up a minute. Y'all are supposed to be my boys," Solomon said.

"Man, you cheated on your girl." Tommy said. "What do

you expect us to say?"

"Not this bull…" he said. "I forgot that I'm surrounded by saints." He said.

"I'm no saint." Tommy said. "But, I would never cheat on Tori like that man."

Solomon rolled his eyes at Tommy and took another bite of his burrito. It was all a waste of time. He would have been better off at the shop telling the old men his saga. They would have treated him better and had some sound advice for him. He could see he was on his own and that he'd have to make the decision as to what he should do. Some help they were.

"Now, if it were Ginger," Boyd said, "that would be another story."

"Speak to Kamari about that." Solomon said and walked away.

Tommy nearly rolled off his seat. Kamari laughed to. He couldn't get mad a Boyd. Boyd made everything that came out of his mouth hilarious. It was how he walked through life. How he dealt with his valleys, and his thorns. His pop expected much from him and though Boyd never let it touch him, at times it became overwhelming for him.

Boyd's father owned the Gingerbread, the mid-size strip mall that housed anything from ice cream parlors to small mom and pop restaurants and shops. He was a high school drop out with an absentee father, and he wanted better for Boyd. But, to his discredit, he didn't know how to show him. Boyd saw his betterment as pressure. He joked and laughed his way through life and it caused him and his father to be at bitter ends at times. Like Tori, Boyd had no idea what life would render to him after high school. But, unlike Tori, he didn't allow it to bother him. Boyd was a free spirit and he believed that somehow life was rigged in his favor.

Solomon left Berry's upset with his friends. He had called upon them for help and they had thrown him to the wolves, even Kamari. He passed a floral shop on the way out of the Gingerbread and stopped and went in. He didn't know what Ruby's favorite flowers were, but he knew that most every woman loved red roses. He looked at his watch and sent over the flowers knowing that Ruby would still be there. Hopefully that would smooth things over so when he did call she wouldn't be mad at him.

Why hadn't he thought of that all along? Flower's like music calmed the salvaged beast. He didn't need his turn coat friends. He had flowers. He stood a little taller, poked out his chest and walked to his Papa's truck like he owned the world. Ruby could no more resist the flowers then she could resist him. It was time to take his mother's advice and court Ruby and he would start with the flowers.

Ruby had beckoned for Kameron to come to her station. Her mother was kind enough to turn his dryer off and lift the shell from his head. Ruby wrapped a smock around him; the one's Solomon had suddenly brought over to her mother's for no reason but to see her. At the time, it was romantic. Now, it made her sick. She rubbed a light oil over his hair and massaged it into his scalp.

"You have the softest hands." He looked up at her.

"Really," she said. "With all the water and chemicals that touch them," she said, not about to allow him to make her nervous in front of the older women. "So, tell me what type of cut do you want?"

"I trust you." He said.

"Kameron," she said. "Come on, I don't know what you like. Tell me something."

"What would you like on me?" He said.

"I don't know?" She was stunned.

It was one of those moments again where he had completely caught her off guard and it showed. He had placed her in a heck of a position. Whatever cut she gave him, they and he would assume that it was what she liked on him. She wanted to scream but what good would that do. They all waited looking at her to see what she would do including her mother. She took a deep breath and before she could think about it, Ginger had mysteriously entered the shop, and she breathed a sigh of relief. The women breathed a sigh of damn. Seeing Ginger was like seeing misfortune.

"Gin," she said.

"Rue," she looked at Kameron in her chair. "Hey Kameron," she said.

"Hey," he looked, and then looked up a Ruby.

"Have you figured it out yet?" He said.

"Ah," she said. "Gin, how would you like Kameron's hair to be cut?"

"Are you serious?" She said. "What is he doing in your chair?" She whispered in Ruby's ear.

"I'll tell you later." Ruby whispered back. "Now, what's the cut?"

"I like this." She pointed to a picture in a magazine.

"I think it's perfect." She said and began cutting his hair.

Ruby's grandmother looked at her like she was a six year old in trouble. She smiled for the moment knowing that she had outfoxed all of them. Now, it was getting past Ginger and all the questions and assumptions. She could tell by the look in Ginger's eyes that she was not pleased with Kameron sitting in her chair. Her hope was that she didn't see the pink gift bag and so far she didn't. She had finished the cut and happened to like how it had come out, especially since Ginger had picked it.

"There," she said. "All done," she removed the smock from around his neck.

He reached into his wallet, but Ruby put the palm of her hand up and shook her head. "It's on me." She folded the smock. "Mrs. Cassidy's been good to me, and my family." She put the smock aside.

"That's awfully sweet, but..."

"But, no," she said, sweeping up the hair from around her station.

"Ruby, come on." he held a twenty and a five in his hand.

"No," she put her hand up once more.

Kameron walked over to her and placed the money in her hand and held it. "Let me buy you lunch then."

Their eyes met; Ruby dropped the broom as a fierce look stood bold in Ginger's eyes. Ruby had never seen that look plastered in her eyes before and it bothered her. Ginger stormed out of the shop and slammed the door.

Chapter 11

Ginger slammed the front door behind her and raced upstairs to her room. The dress that she was making for Ruby she cut into pieces. She ripped up all the garments that she had made for her and fell to her knees and cried. Kameron had humiliated her and Ruby had shamed her and made her look like a fool.

.   The sad thing was, was that under all the layers of anger, Ginger still cared very much for Kameron. But because he had disgraced her and had openly chosen her best friend over her, made her have it in for him to. Ruby knew how much she liked Kameron, yet she seemed to have her own agenda. Obviously she and Solomon weren't working out so well, or she had recognized that all she was to him was a number in a black book waiting on her turn to be called.

She lay amongst slash pieces of garments crying uncontrollably; wondering what went wrong? Her soul yearned for a quiet place. But what had given her solace, she had destroyed in anger after something that was never meant to be hers. She needed noise. She wanted some sort of sound so that she could rid herself of the gloom messing over her soul. She didn't want to think about Kameron, nor Ruby, and out of frustration and desperation, she called Tori.

Tori's cell made a distinct ring. She knew it was Ginger. She could feel that something wasn't right. She said goodbye to Tommy and switched over to Ginger.

"Gin, what's up?"

"I need someone to talk to before I just snap." She said."

"What's wrong?" Tori asked.

"Everything," Ginger, took a tissue and wiped her eyes. "For one, I heard my parents arguing and long story short we're broke." She said. "And we can thank my dear mother for that," she said. "That's why my dad put in for a transfer." She sniffled.

"Ah Gin, maybe it's not as bad as you think?" She said. "Your dad's here now, and he's going to be working in San Francisco. He's going to be around a lot more." Tori said. "Isn't that what you wanted?"

"Yeah," she said. "But, not if they're going to be fighting all the time." She blew her nose. "Especially about money, and how am I supposed to go to college now?" She said. "And on top of all of that, Ruby is stepping out with Kameron." Her eyes held so much anger in them. I mean, can you believe that? I thought she was so in love with Solomon?" She said. "Apparently not."

Tori's worst fear had come to life. She had warned Ruby and she didn't listen. She was so sure that she could turn Kameron's attention to Ginger. Maybe Ginger would have been a tad upset? Ok, maybe she would have been furious and not have spoken to them for a day or so. But, at least she would have appreciated the truth coming from either one of them, rather than walking up on a train wreck.

Kameron's feelings for Ruby ran deep. When he was around her only the two of them were in a room; no one else existed accept them. Kameron was so taken by Ruby that he didn't even know who Ginger was, and he hadn't registered that Ginger had feelings for him.

Tori knew from the onset at dinner that night that the moment he laid eyes on Ruby that he wanted her in ways that Solomon could not. No matter how much Ginger wanted him, and no matter how much Ruby wanted him to want Ginger, he had eyes only for her.

So, it didn't matter what Ginger wanted or what Ruby wanted, or what she was attempting to do. That hot day at Echo Park while Ruby was immersed in Tiffney and Solomon, Kameron was engrossed in Ruby, and he had claimed her as his own. Tori took a deep breath. She didn't know how to tell the truth without it further hurting Ginger. Maybe now was not the time, but when was there ever a right time to make a tough decision? She sighed and then took a deep breath.

"Have you ever really paid attention at how Kamari looks at you?" Tori said.

"Who cares about Kamari? I thought we were talking about Kameron here."

"Gin, I'm trying to make a point." Tori said.

"What's your point?" She blew her nose again.

"Ruby has nothing to do with the way Kameron feels about her." She said. "I have been wanting to tell you this, but she wouldn't let me. She seems to think that she can turn his attention to you. But, she can't." She sighed. "Gin, I don't want you to get hurt."

The rage in Ginger's eyes returned. There was an awkward silence between the both of them that cut like a knife. Something had turned in Ginger that had suddenly made her feel hateful and unforgiving. Ginger placed her small hands over her nose and life at seventeen had taken its toll on her and she couldn't handle it. Revenge had deceived her young mind and she had accepted it.

"Kamari feels about you the way Kameron feels about Ruby Gin. I don't know how else to say it."

Ginger was lost for words for a minute. She heard what Tori said, but she didn't want to believe what she was hearing. In Ginger's immature mind, it sounded like some sort of plot between Tori and Ruby that had been planned without her knowing it. How did Tori know how Kameron felt? It was obvious that Kameron liked Ruby by the way he looked at her, flirted with her, and took hold of her hand and held it as he asked her to join him for lunch.

What was going on here about her so called two best friends that she was missing? Obviously, Ruby had discovered the real Solomon and had given up the myth of him being the knight on the white horse, and now she wanted Kameron. The night of her father's surprise party Ruby acted strange when Ginger questioned her regarding Solomon's whereabouts. She was snappy and a bit edgy, and she pretended like she didn't have an answer.

When she gave one, it was a shallow. She knew then that Solomon had fallen back into his old habits. Obviously that's when Ruby decided to make a run for Kameron so that her fantasy could be fulfilled.

This was war. She had thought that she would be having this duel with Daphne, and Tiffney perhaps, but not with Ruby who had been her best friend before they could walk. The nerve of Tori and Ruby trying to shove her with the left overs, tossing Kamari at her. Kamari was a boy, but Kameron was a man, and she had seen him first. She dried her tears that day in her room. She shredded the little girl panties and put on the big girl panties. Ruby would be sorry and Tori if she were smart had better decide where her true loyalties' lie.

Tori could tell by Ginger's tonality that Kameron's liking Ruby rather than her was a game changer for Ginger. She knew that she would try and make her choose, that she would never do, Ginger would have to. And from where she sat it seemed like she already had.

"Gin, we've known each other forever." Tori said. "Guys come and go."

"Oh," Ginger sighed. "Go ahead and make excuses for Rue."

"I'm not making excuses for her Gin and you know it." Tori got upset. "It's not her fault that he likes her. But, it's stupid to allow a perfect stranger to come between you and Rue."

"So, you expect me to roll over and go after Kamari now." She said. "It's so like you to choose sides."

"I'm not choosing sides and you know it." Tori said. "You know Ruby better than that. You know she would never do anything to hurt you. Kamari chose you over me, and you didn't see me hating on you about it." She said.

"I don't even like Kamari like that and you know it." She said.

"Rue doesn't like Kameron like that either and you know that, and if you don't you should." She said.

"I know what I saw at the salon. You weren't there." She hung up.

Kameron was clueless by Ginger's behavior at the shop. However, the women knew exactly what was going on. You could see it in their eyes, and you could tell that they had seen it many times before. Ginger had assumed too much and Ruby was trapped between loyalty, and a false reputation of being untrustworthy to a friend whom she beheld as a sister.

Precious gave the signal and the ones who remained at the shop scurried back to the back where the kitchen and snacks were to allow Kameron and Ruby their space. Kameron could see in Ruby's eyes that she wasn't happy and for the life of him he didn't know why.

"Did I do something? Is she going to be okay?" He said.

"No," Ruby placed the broom in the corner. "No she is not," she looked into his eyes without being afraid, and without getting goose bumps or getting nervous by his gaze. "I can't believe you can't see it." She sighed.

"See what?" He said.

"She likes you Kameron. She likes you a lot." Ruby said.

"What?" He said. "Ginger?" He was surprised.

"How could you not know? How could you not see it?" She said.

"Maybe it's because I only see you?" He gazed into her eyes.

"Well, you're not supposed to see me; you're supposed to see her." Ruby said. "And now, you've screwed things up for me. She's my best friend." She said.

"I'm sorry Ruby. I didn't mean to hurt her, but I can't help how I feel." He stood in front of her with his hands inside his pockets.

"And I can't help how I feel about Solomon," she said

knowing that she was mad as hell at him. "And even if it weren't

Solomon, it could never work between us because…"

"Let me guess, Ginger." His eyes were disappointed.

"I didn't mean to hurt you." She said.

"Yeah I know, like I hurt Ginger." He sat the twenty-five

dollars on her station and left.

Ginger's room was sad and messy. There were bolts of

fabric everywhere. It was disorderly and chaotic quite the way her

life was. Her father knocked softly on the door and then opened it.

His eyes widen. It nearly took his breath away, and his mouth nearly

dropped to the floor.

"Baby girl," he said. "Are you okay up in here?"

"Why wouldn't I be?" She said, as she started to pick up.

"You're mother tells me of how you have such a great talent

for making clothes, and I just…"

"Just what daddy," she looked at him like she didn't want

him to be in her room. "Be more organized like my life, or try and

put a good face on when I know we're broke."

"You overheard us discussing," he said.

"Arguing is a better word for it." She said.

"And, none of that is true," he said.

"So what is?" She asked. "Is my college fund safe? Am I going to be getting that car I've been promised since I was sixteen? Did you transfer because you wanted to be with me, with mom, or was it because we are really broke?" Tears formed in her eyes. "Don't lie to me daddy. Tell me the truth." She began to cry.

"Baby come here." He said. "Come here," he held her tight.

The warmth of her father's arms was like a warm bath. She hadn't felt that loved, that safe since she was a little girl. It never mattered if her father was there for a minute; an hour, days, or a whole month, when he was in her presence everything was always perfect. Her mother, God rest her soul tried, but there was always something lacking. Somehow her mother always seemed unsure and it showed up in their life.

She tried to dress it up with her fine and fancy clothes; the way she would have Ruby style her hair like a reigning queen in control of her court, but it was all a myth. Truth was her mother had lost her identity in her father and in his dream that could never be hers. Ginger should have been enough but she wasn't. So, through the talents of her father's mother, she had somehow carved out her own and an identity that no one could take from her, no one.

"Your college fund is safe. I promise." He rubbed her back. "I missed you so much and the truth is, is that I couldn't stand one more day without being here for my little girl every day."
He kissed her forehead. "I am not going to lie to you angel. The bonuses won't be as big, and we will have to juggle some things, but we are in no way shape or form broke." He said.

"We're not," she looked up at him.

"We are not." He said, smiling.

"So, do I get my car when I'm eighteen?" She said.

"Yes." He said. "Yes you do, if not before then." He said.

"Really," she looked surprised, but she believed him. "I'll do anything."

"You don't have to do anything, but just be my daughter." He said. "Now, do I get a free suit?"

"Anything for my dad," she hugged him, instantly feeling better despite the jolt she felt from Kameron.

Ruby could smell her father's biscuits in her sleep. He knocked on her door, and then entered with a tray and six golden yellow tulips in a tall blue vase. She smiled, and scooted up to her head board and yawned a sleepy yawn.

"Daddy," she smiled, removing the silver top off of the tray. "Am I in trouble or something?" She put honey on her biscuit and bit into it.

"You think I would be bringing my favorite daughter breakfast in bed on a Sunday if she were in trouble?" He kissed her on the cheek.

"Probably not," she put honey on both halves of her biscuits and ate. "Oh, these are so good." She talked with her mouth full.

"Why thank you," he said, and stole a piece of her bacon. "Where's mama?"

"In the shower," he winked. "Get ready for church." He said, and stole another piece of her bacon.

"I will." She put more honey on her biscuits.

Her cell rang and it gave the ring of Tori. She finished her biscuit and placed a piece of bacon in her mouth, but it continued to ring like it was determined. "Tori, I know." She said
and picked it up. "Tori, you have the worst timing ever." She said

"It's not Tori. It's Solomon." He said.

"Solomon." She moved her tray from her bed before she knocked it over.

"So, say something," he said.

"The only thing I want to say is good-bye." She said.

"Wait, wait, don't hang up." He said. "Did you get your flowers I sent you?"

"Flowers," she sounded, surprised. "No, and don't be trying to butter me up with gifts because you messed up." She said.

"I'm not trying to butter you up." He lied. I really did send you flowers." He sat straight up in his bed. "Roses, as a matter of fact."

"Well, if you did, I'm glad I left before they got there." She said. "I haven't heard from you in five days Solomon. I called you three times the night of Mr. Maples party and you never answered me, not once."

Solomon panicked. "Ah, I didn't hear the phone, I was sleep."

"Really," she said. "You expect me to believe that."

"I'm telling you the truth Ruby. I wouldn't lie to you. I promise." He pleaded in his lie.

"I have to go Solomon. I need to get ready for church." She said and hung up.

Ruby took a deep breath and sat still on her bed for a minute. She wanted to believe Solomon, she really did. In her mind she did, but in her heart she knew something wasn't right. She sat back in her bed, pulled her tray on her lap and finished her biscuits, bacon and her hash browns. She yawned again and placed her tray on her end table and took her shower, and got dressed for church.

Her cell rang again as she put on her lipstick. She paused, and looked, but it was Solomon and like he had done her, she ignored him. It rung again, and again, and after the fourth time she turned her cell off.

"Mama," she opened her door and called for her.

"Yeah baby, I'm in the kitchen." She said. "What do you need?"

"Can you come here for a quick minute?" She asked.

"I'm on my way." She said.

"Hat, or no hat?" She asked.

"Ah," she paused, looking at Ruby's hair. It hung way off her shoulders and it was as straight as split silk, and adorned in thick, fluffy ringlets. "No hat," her mother said. "You look beautiful." She stroked her face.

"Thanks," she said. "So do you," she placed her purse on her shoulder.

Ruby turned her cell back on and as she entered the living room she stopped to put it inside of her purse. She noticed a beautiful boutique of long stem red roses sitting on the coffee table. She paused, letting the call go to voice mail. Solomon had sent them just like he had said. Maybe he did watch a movie and fall asleep? Maybe she had misjudged him like all the others in town had done? Now, she felt bad and owed Solomon an apology.

Precious walked into the living room decked out in a red suit that showcased her toned arms; a ruffled skirt that showed off her satin red pumps and her sexy legs. In summer, she allowed herself to where sleeveless outfits and blouses to keep cool and to show her husband that in twenty years of marriage, she still had it. And, she wanted Ruby to have it, but just not with Solomon.

She watched Ruby admire the flowers and do what girls did at her age. She watched her smell the roses, pull one out of the vase and smell it again and smile like she was really in love. She stood there admiring the roses like she admired him and that bothered Precious a lot.

"Oh," her mother said. "I forgot to mention that they came shortly after you left." She said.

"How could you forget to tell me?" Ruby smelled the rose again. "Aren't they beautiful?"

"Come on," she said. "We don't want to be late for church." She placed her purse on her shoulder. "Don't forget your favorite flowers are Tulips and Morning Glories. Jake are you ready?"

Ruby didn't say a word to her mother. She chose to be silent. What was the use? He r mother didn't like Solomon, and she never would like him and nothing she could say or do would change that. Jake glanced at the roses as he went out of the door and locked it   A father's instinct told him that some boy had bought them for Ruby, and by the talking from his wife, he could only imagine who it was.

He got in his truck and looked at Ruby and the rose that sat cozy on her lap, and the smile that came from a young woman's lips when a boy she adored sent her flowers. He buckled his seatbelt, looked back at his daughter and took the rose off of her lap and grinned a father's grin. Her mother laughed at her husband's reaction and at Ruby's of course.

"Daddy," Ruby said.

"What," he sniffed the rose. "I'm the only man that has permission to buy you roses." He said and pulled off.

Ruby's cell rung again and she knew that it was Tori. Ginger had not called her since the incident and it troubled her. But, it didn't surprise her. Anyone watching her could see that she had no interest in Kameron whatsoever. She didn't know why it was so hard for Ginger to see it.

They pulled into the church parking lot and Tori and Ruby ended their conversation. Tommy shook his head at the two of them as they acted like they had not seen each other in weeks. They entered the chapel that had been in Oak Grove for as long as the town had existed. The grass had been replanted. The chapel had been repainted, and the uniqueness of the edifice restored to its original beauty.

Tommy, Tori and Ruby sat in the middle row. Tori whispered to Ruby to save Boyd a seat next to her. Boyd was always late to church, or anything that had a set time to it. It seemed Boyd had a thing against time.

It was as if there were a private battle going on between the two of them. He got teased a lot by his peers, but it didn't seem to change anything. They knew that after the first song by the choir that Boyd would come waltzing down the aisle and take his seat next to Ruby as if it belonged to him. And, that's just what he did, and they laughed.

"Never fails." Tommy said.

"Fail, never," Boyd said and smiled and took his bulletin from Ruby.

Tommy took hold of Tori's hand and held it. Tori looked up at Tommy and smiled like she wanted to kiss him. But, it was church and in their small community the world was watching and so was her mother who just happened to be sitting in back of her. Ruby witnessed their moment of tenderness and affection and of course she wished that Solomon had come so he could have held her hand in secret so her father couldn't see it. But Solomon and church didn't exactly get along.

Sometimes Mrs. Fletcher's wide brim hat partially blocked Ruby's view. Ruby was glad at times, especially when Tiffney or Daphne song in the choir. However, today of all days, Mrs. Fletcher's hat was dainty and petit and she could see Tiffney and Daphne all too well. They could see her to and they looked at her like they were still Solomon's, like nothing had changed between him and them, and it hadn't only Ruby didn't chose to listen to her heart and know that yet.

She turned from the both of them and raised her long stem

rose high enough so they could see it. Her father had left it on his dash board and when he wasn't looking she grabbed it. She took a sniff and looked toward the choir at both of them and swayed it just a little. She saw defeat in their eyes though they went out of their way not to show it. She smiled and turned away from them and looked right into the eyes of Kameron.

Mrs. Cassidy waved and blew her a kiss. She waved and kissed back. Mr. Mosely tipped his hat and smiled, and Kameron mouthed I'm sorry. Ruby shook her head as if she accepted it. She didn't but she had to pretend like she did in front of the Mosely's considering that she was so fond of them. Tori turned and smile and Ruby nicked her leg.

"Don't start." Ruby said.

"He's still staring at you." Tori lent over and whispered.

"Be quiet and listen to the sermon." Ruby said. "Besides, I got roses from Solomon." She wiggled it.

"You listen to your heart and not your head." Tori said. "He must have really messed up." She looked at Ruby.

"Don't hate." Ruby teased, seeing Ginger's parents sitting

next to the Fletcher's.

But where was Ginger. Ginger usually sat in between Boyd and Ruby and would poke fun at Mrs. Fletcher's wide hats that always nearly blocked their view. Ruby would lay her head in her lap and crack up so her parents couldn't see her. Was she really that mad? Ruby couldn't believe Ginger's silliness, then again when she remembered the look in her eyes, she knew that anger in the worse way had transformed her. Ruby's hope was that she fought it off and remembered that Kameron would be gone by summer's end.

Before she knew it, the minister had introduced visitors; the recruiter from Stanford, Kameron and others. Ruby couldn't help but smile when the preacher introduced her recruiter. In a few ticks of the clock, he and her high school counselor would be sitting at her dinner table, and her parents would be signing documents that would give her a free ticket to Stanford.

From the pews, she could see envy in the eyes of her adversaries in the choir. They envied her as much for her brains as they did for Solomon choosing her over them. Yet, they stared at Kameron like he was a piece of juicy meat, and they could not wait to get their teeth into him. What would Ginger say about them?

Ginger had picked the wrong Sunday to skip Ruby thought. Preacher had spoken on forgiveness and Ginger certainly needed to hear that. They stood, bowed their heads in prayer and church was over, and Ruby's future awaited. Ruby tapped Tori on the leg. Tori turned and Ruby whispered in her ear.

"Have you talked to Ginger?" She asked.

"A day or so ago, and she was really mad with you." Tori said.

"Yeah I figured," she whispered. "I didn't do anything. If she's gonna get mad at anyone, she needs to get mad at lover boy." Ruby said.

Tori tilted her head and they went outside. "I love Ginger like she was my own sister." Tori said. "But, let's face it Rue, Ginger is used to getting what she wants, and what she wants, wants you."

"Well, I don't want him." Ruby sat on the comfortable bench by the flower garden.

"Sorry Rue, he really likes all of you and not for just some roll in the hay."

"I resent that." Ruby said.

"Well, I don't care." She said. "You're my best friend and I don't want to see you get hurt."

"And, I don't want to see Gin get hurt no matter how mad she is at me." Ruby said.

"Me neither," Tori said. "Which is why I told her the truth?"

Ruby eyes widen. She didn't have to ask Tori what she said, she knew. But, in doing so it would only fuel Ginger's fire.

"What?" Tori said.

"You didn't need to do that." Ruby said.

"Why? And prolong the inevitable." Tori said. "We can't tell our hearts who to love. Kameron could have picked any one of us, but he picked you Rue, just like Kamari picked Ginger over me." She said. "Of course it hurt, of course I was a little disappointed, but God gave me Tommy and I'm glad that Kamari chose Ginger." Tori took a seat next to Ruby. "I just wish like you she'd open her eyes and chose him. He'd be so good for her."

"My recruiter's here." Ruby said.

"I know." Tori said. "It's what you've been dreaming about forever." Tori wrapped her arm around Ruby.

"Since the third grade," Ruby looked at Tori.

"I wish I knew what I wanted to do like you and Ginger." A sad look stood in her eyes.

"I can't believe you don't know Tori." Ruby looked at her. "You're a chef. You can cook cardboard and make it taste good. And what do you do when something's on your mind, you cook."

"Because in a crazy way, it relaxes me," she said.

"Well, why you're relaxed, start thinking about what makes you happy," Ruby faced her.

"Tommy." She said.

"Besides Tommy," Ruby smiled. "Think about it."

"Okay, I will." Tori said. "You know I'm so happy for you, but I don't want you to leave me." Tori said.

"You're my sister Tori." Ruby wrapped her arms around her. "I could never leave you."

It was a tender moment between the two girls. The two had known each other since birth practically, and they were true sisters by their souls. Ginger was one of them to, but lately she had lost her way. The life that she thought she had was crumbling. The guy that she was crazy about had chosen her best friend over her, and the guy she didn't want nor have any feelings for at all loved her. How rotten was that?

So, she stayed at home; not ready to put on that fake face amongst church folks who expected love and forgiveness no matter what. For now, she couldn't forgive those who had sworn to love her. She had waited for her father forever to return home, only to learn that he traveled so far because they were broke. And, the two chums in which she shared her life with and her inner most secrets had betrayed her. No Tori didn't make any advances towards Kameron, but she might as well have, when she revealed the truth about how Kameron felt about Ruby and took her side.

Maybe Ruby didn't intend for this to happen? So what if Kameron was attracted to Ruby. She knew how Ginger felt and she should have been trying to push him to the one who had claimed him first. In her eyes, Ruby didn't try hard enough, and Tori didn't step into help. This time she wouldn't just let it go. This time Ruby would not get what she wanted and she take the left overs. This time she would take everything she wanted including Kameron. She just had to make him see that Ruby was a girl and that she was a woman.

Tiffney and Daphne rolled their eyes at each other as they came out of church. They hated each other almost as much as they hated Ruby. They had learned through Solomon's trickery to try and do something to impress him so that he'd choose one over the other. It was a chess game between the two. Solomon liked space so Daphne would give him space. When Solomon wanted sex in his room while his mother was arguing with his father about something stupid, Tiffney was there.

It was always that sort of back and forth going on with the two of them, and though they wouldn't admit it, they had grown accustom to it. What they hadn't grown accustom to was Ruby and the flowers Solomon was sending her even though she hadn't tasted his bed yet.

Solomon needed a lesson and they were going to give it to

him. Tommy threw his hand up and Tori waved good-bye as he pulled out of the parking lot. As Ruby approached her father's truck, Daphne made her way over. Ruby turned and saw her.

"What do you want?" Ruby said.

"I guess we all want the same guy?" Daphne said.

Ruby turned and looked at Daphne who was dressed like she was going to a night club rather than church. Her dress was way too short. Her heels way too high. She looked like a street walker flashing her stuff at night. Yes, they had experience in areas that she didn't, but she had been taught by her mother's that a real lady was first courted by a man.

"Your girl made me this," she turned and modeled it as if to make Ruby jealous.

"I guess she had to design an outfit that references who you are." Ruby said.

"Don't hate." She popped her gum.

"Don't flatter yourself and do me a favor, leave." Ruby said.

"Let me leave you with something." She said. "Did Solomon tell you that he was with Tiffany the night you were at your girl's dad's party?" She popped her gum again. "Oh, "she said, "and I was just with him the other night." She smiled. "So, go home and kiss your flowers." She laughed.

Chapter 12

There was an awkward silence that could be cut with a knife. Ruby sat quietly in her father's truck not saying a word. The words of Daphne echoed inside of her head over and over again. Each time she heard it, it made her angrier. This was supposed to be her big day. It was the day that she had waited for, dreamt about even, and at times never thought it would ever arrive. But it had, and now Solomon and his Concubine's threaten to ruin it.

Her father had pulled into their driveway, and before he could take the keys out of the ignition, she had gotten out of the truck and rushed into the house. Ruby sat on her bed and tossed a pillow across the room, then another one. What if it were true? He hadn't called her in a week, and then out of the blue she received a boutique of beautiful red roses, and an excuse of him falling to sleep. So many things roamed through her mind, but only she had the power to decipher the truth.

She got out of her clothes and took a shower and put on more comfortable clothes. She sat on her bed once again and took a long deep breath. She reached for her purse and dug out her cell and hit Tori on speed dial.

"Come on Tori." She said. "Please answer."

"Now who's got perfect timing," Tori said. "I'm in the bathroom Rue." She said.

"Sorry," Ruby said. "Call me back then," her voice sounded so sad.

"Hang on." Tori said, drying her hands on a dry clean towel. "Okay," she exited out of the bathroom. "What's up?"

"Everything," she said.

"What's wrong?" Tori said.

"Are you still at Tommy's?" She asked.

"Yeah," she said.

"It's about Solomon." She said. "I don't think that I want Tommy to hear this."

"What happened?" Tori slipped past Tommy and went out back.

"Just…" Ruby's sentence was interrupted by a soft knock on

her bedroom door.

"Baby," her father opened her door. "Come on they're waiting."

"I have to go Tori." She said. "I'll call you later."

"Rue," Tori said. "I hate it when you do this."

"Meet me in Echo Park later, love you." Ruby hung up.

"Ah," Tori sighed.

Tommy surprised her and slipped up behind Tori and whispered in her ear and scared her. Tori jumped and shook like a fall leaf on a windy day. She turned, smacked his hand, only to see him smile. It was the smile she saw at Echo Park that day when he had nearly stumbled and fell, but somehow landed perfectly on his feet.

Somehow they were standing shoulder to shoulder. He tried to look at her when she wasn't looking but fate had other ideas. It was funny how just a year ago she would have done anything to have Kamari place his hands on her waist and whisper in her ear and scare her. Now, she wanted only Tommy. How funny was that and how strange was life to have her have the same feelings for Tommy that she once had for Kamari.

"No peach or apple fritters for you," she smiled when she said it. "Only your grandparents get some." She teased as she prepared to make them.

Tommy stepped in front of her and crossed his muscular arms across his chest. There was that smile again that had made her fall for him and that kindness in his eyes that always made her melt. He knew it and he used it all the time. What else was a guy supposed to do?

"Don't be thinking that, that will work on me all the time because it won't." She measured out her flour.

"Yeah it will," he kissed her and smiled again.

"Get," she said.

"No," he said. "I want to learn." He laughed.

Odette stood in the entry way of the kitchen watching them like she was watching time. At seventeen, Tommy had found the one, she could tell. It was the way he put the flour on her nose, and then his. The way they laughed in her kitchen making apple and peach fritters, and the way he scrapped flour dough off of her hands and tasted it. His parents would have been proud of their baby boy. She was certainly proud of him. Proud of the fact that at such a young age, he didn't allow tragedy to break him. Despite the dreadful car crash that took the lives of his parents, it didn't take away his joyous spirit, or his courage to live his best life.

That is what Odette loved about her grandson most, his resilience to open his young soul to the universe and allow something bigger then himself to preside over it. Her eyes watered a little at how life and God had treated him after such a rough start. She could see his future through his eyes and it was bright, so bright it made her eyes burn. She left them to their tender moments and returned to her family room to quilt.

"The key," Tori said, "is the bread. It has to be perfect, or the filling we just made doesn't matter." She washed her hands.

"Okay," Tommy said, scratching his scalp. "You gonna make a great chef." He said, washing his hands.

Tori paused from putting the filling inside of the dough. She looked at Tommy as if she had heard that before and she had. Ruby and Ginger had reminded her every time she cooked for them of how talented she was in the kitchen. How come everyone had seen her talent except her?

"It's funny you would say that." She placed a batch of apple fritters in Odette's deep fryer.

"Why?" Tommy said.

"Because, I'm struggling with trying to find out what I want to do with the rest of my life," she said.

"You're joking right?" He said.

"No, I'm not." She took a seat at their kitchen table. "I just feel like everybody knows exactly what they want except for me." She said.

"Sometimes what's for you doesn't just hop out in front of you," he joined her at the table. "Sometimes boo, you have to find it, and sometimes it finds you. It found you, so roll with it."

"I never thought about it like that." She said.

"Well, I think it's time you did." He said.

The timer went off and she took them out and put another batch in. Tommy put fresh icing on each one of them and licked it off of his fingers. The aroma of the fritters brought in both Mrs. Odette and Tommy's grandfather Clive. Tommy had his grandfather's smile and his eyes and Odette's stocky built. He pulled his Dodger baseball cap off and patted Tori's shoulder and took a seat.

"Girl, if you don't do something with this talent," he said, eating an apple fritter. "I believe that I'm going to have to put you across my lap and spank you." He took another bite of it.

"Amen to that," Odette took the milk from the refrigerator. "The scent of these fritters made me stop quilting on a dime." She laughed, and took one from the tray.

"See," Tommy poured himself a glass of milk. "I told you."

Ruby echoed the same words to her mother as they sat at the dinner table eating cubed steak with gravy, mashed potatoes, mixed vegetables, and macaroni and cheese. Briefly she had managed to forget about Solomon and his infidelity issues at present and focused on her long awaited dream. It was real now all of it; the dorm life, leaving home, leaving family and friends to introduce herself to the world and finally go after what she wanted.

She cleared her throat and took another long sip of sweet tea. She sat her fork down on her plate and as she did she could see that all eyes were on her. In Precious eyes, there were a mix of emotions; happiness as well as sadness. Ruby had been her baby for seventeen years and now it was time to let her go, spread her wings and take off. It was a new chapter for both of them, and Precious would have to readjust to the power of letting go for a mother, and Ruby the responsibility of being an adult.

Ruby's high school counselor Mr. Eborn was all smiles. He had fought vehemently for Ruby and to get her mother to see the plus size of this had been a tremendous hurdle. Her father cautious at first, but once he was assured that she would be given the best of everything, and that her college was paid for, he was ready to sign on the dotted line months ago. But, Precious was a mother and his wife, and he had to give her time, space, and the stillness that she needed to make the right decision.

Clayton Parker, the advisor in Ruby's program at Stanford had also worked tirelessly with Eborn. After seeing Ruby's grades, and her test scores, and her enthusiasm about becoming a Cardinal, he knew that Stanford would roll out the red carpet for her and they did big time. She would give them four years with good grades, and they would pay everything for her, down to her food expenses.

"Well," Clayton said, wiping his mouth. "Mama, are we ready to do this?"

"Ah," she sighed, and looked at her daughter who was as eager and ready as a squirrel climbing a tree. How could she say no? "Yes," she said. "Yes," tears arose in her eyes. "Give me the pen." She said.

"Yes!" "Yes!" Ruby jumped up from the table screaming.

She ran over to her mother and hugged and kissed her and sat cozy on her lap. "I love you." She said. "I love you. Thank you so much for doing this for me." Ruby wrapped her arms around her mother and cried.

Mr. Eborn clapped his hands profoundly at Ruby's reaction to starting her new life. It was a marathon that had finally been complete. He finished his plate and helped himself to a serving of peach cobbler, as he watched Ruby's father sign on the dotted line that had awaited him, then it was Ruby's turn. When she had finished she was given a gift from Clayton; a white Stanford sweat shirt with bold red print in front, a white mug, and another pen and journal set, similar to the one Kameron had given her.

Kameron pulled his glasses off and rubbed his eyes. He had thrown away as many sketches as he had drawn. However, the one he had recently drawn seem to have stuck with him. He worked hard to keep his mind off of Ruby, and it paid dividends for a while. But now he was tired, and he happened to see his Granny taking clothes and sheets off of her clothesline. He shook his head at her, and rushed out back to help.

"Granny," he waved his hand at her. "Granny," he said.

Cassidy turned and looked at her grandson as he so much reminded her of his grandfather. She smiled and stopped taking the clothes off of the line. "So," she said. "You finally ran out of ideas." She laughed, and kissed his cheek. "That's the only way you Mosely's ever stop working," she said.

"Is that a bad thing?" He laughed.

"Only you and your Gramps can answer that," she said.

He started helping her take the clothes and linens off of the clothesline. In fact, he made her sit underneath the bold oak tree that had engrossed her backyard with shade. A sudden breeze had come from nowhere and the scent of summer from the linens and clothes had captured his nose. He smelled the sheets and it was as if he were smelling life. He was a Mosley alright. Her husband had done the same thing when he took the clothes off the line.

"If I didn't know any better, I'd swear that you like doing this." His Granny said.

"I do actually." He smiled his Gramps smile. "In New York," he snickered. "The only way you'll find one of these is in a museum." He said, pulling off the last pin. "I guess you don't believe in dryer's Granny."

"I guess I don't baby." She crossed her legs and laughed. "If it weren't for my towels, and under ware, my dish cloths, and a few other things, I don't believe I'd have one of those things." She said. "It's just something about the good lord's sun and air when it touches your clothes and linens." She said.

"I guess you're right. But,"

"But, you young folks have to have everything at your fingertips." She tossed her hand at him.

"You're from New York Granny aren't you?" He asked, folding the sheets.

"Harlem," she said.

"And Grandpa," he asked.

"New Orleans," she smiled.

"How'd you two meet?" He said, starting on the other side of the line.

"I came here to Oak Grove one day on a mobile clinic." She said. "Wasn't nothing here than, but a few measly store fronts and a restaurant here or there, and of course your handsome granddaddy smiling that beautiful smile of his." She smiled. "I didn't tell him then, but of course I fell for him right away, and I have been falling ever since." She laughed.

Kameron smiled his Gramps smile again and lifted the wicker basket up into his arms. Sometimes he wondered how people like his grandparents found each other. It seemed to him that there were just a segregated few who did. And when they did, it was love at first sight, and a love that outlasted time. The happiness that flowed inside of his eyes had weaned somewhat. His Granny could see the abrupt change in his face, and asked him what was wrong.

"Something troubling you sweetheart," she asked.

"No," he said. "I'm good." He lied.

"Now grandson," she uncrossed her legs. "I've been around this world a heck of a lot longer than you. I'm too old to be a fool, and too wise to be stupid. Something's got your goat now tell me what it is." She said.

"It's nothing," he said. "Really," he smiled.

"Is it that Ginger Girl?" She said. "I heard how she stormed out of the shop a few days back acting a fool."

"So, you heard," He looked surprised that she knew.

"Don't nothing get past me in this small town honey." She laughed. "Well what happened?" She looked inquisitive.

"Complicated," he said.

"Boy what happened," she said.

"I really like Ruby. Ginger really likes me. Ginger and Ruby are friends and I guess I screwed things up for them." He sighed.

"How?" She said.

"Granny their best friends and Ruby made it perfectly clear that there could never be anything between us." He said. "Besides, Ruby's dating Solomon and I've seen the way she looks at him. She certainly doesn't look at me like that." He looked sad.

"Well make her than," She said.

"Make her," he laughed. "I can't do that. I thought caring about someone was mutual."

"Sometimes love doesn't come in nice pretty packages baby." She said.

"Well, what does it come in then? I'd really like to know." He shook his head again.

"You're a Mosely baby and Mosley men don't give up on nothing including women." She picked up her basket. "Solomon Garrett is a boy and you are a man. Your strength is that you want one woman. His weakness is that no one will ever satisfy him." She tossed the basket higher up on her hip. "Young girls like Ruby may fall for guys like Solomon, but deep down inside, they want a man like you." She reached over and kissed his cheek.

He returned to his loft and sat, thinking about what his Granny had said. He originally came to Oak Grove to find out where he came from. Yet, he discovered so much more, and love had shocked him when it presented him with Ruby. He didn't expect much from this little sleepy town when he arrived here. But, the quiet had done something to him.

It allowed him to appreciate the simple things that he overlooked in the big city due to the noise. And it opened his heart to a love that he would not have found in his native New York. Oak Grove definitely had an effect on him. The longer he stayed in this nostalgic town, the harder it would be for him to leave.

He returned to the loft not to work but just to think about Ruby and just how he would capture her heart. If that was possible? He watched the mellow orange sun sink behind the tall brown mountains and it relaxed him. Somehow his Gramps and all of his hard work in building his business from meager syrup, ice, and paper cones, and a beat up old van, deserved more. Suddenly an idea had begun forming in his mind, and he began sketching again. Temporarily it took his mind off of Ruby, and the mess that he had gotten himself into with Ginger.

Ruby sat in the retreat part of her room on a high. What she had dreamt about for months was now a reality, and in the fall she would attend her beloved Stanford. She couldn't way to tell Tori and Ginger that's if she weren't still mad at her. She kicked off her sandals and put her feet upon her table and just breathed. Life was great and then her cell rang.

"Hello," she said, with a smile in her voice.

"Hey, it's me." Solomon said.

"Solomon," she removed her feet from the table and sat straight up. "I don't wanna talk to you." She said.

"Ruby I'm sorry. I know I should have called. But…"

"Try telling Daphne and Tiffney that." She said.

"What?" He said. "What are you talking about?"

"Why don't you ask Tiffany since she was in your bed that night?" Ruby said. "Don't call me again." She hung up.

Chapter 13

Ginger hadn't returned any of Ruby's calls and Ruby didn't know what to make of it. She couldn't believe that Ginger would allow a perfect stranger to come in between their friendship. How silly was that when he would be gone by summer's end. She sighed and put on her slip on sneakers and her big hoop earrings. Come fall she would be attending Stanford and thankfully all of this drama would come to an end.

She grabbed hold of her purse and opened her front door. She recognized that within a few months she would be opening a new door and she was excited. She couldn't wait to tell Tori. Tori would be a little sad, but she'd be happy for her overall. Ginger, well, it would be another thing. The old Ginger would be happy and as excited as Ruby.

Ginger wanted out of Oak Grove and into a city that spilled excitement, and never ran out of things to do. She was always restless and the slow pace seemed to put a damper on her mood

Now, it was Kameron and herself that had caused her foul attitude. Despite what was going on, Ruby wanted to share the good news with Ginger, but that itself was in question. She hopped in her father's truck, pulled out of the driveway and headed for the park to meet Tori.

Tori sat underneath their favorite tree with a picnic basket full of food and goodies. She had fried chicken, cut up some melons, had a container of cold drinks, and managed to bring her warmers in which she made the dirty rice in. She had also made a surprise for Ruby for dessert.

When she sat with her she would shock her with one. While she waited for Ruby, a lot of things roamed through her head. Her life after high school for one, and the possibility of having her own restaurant outside of Oak Grove, but where?

For the first time this morning when she prepared the food for her and Ruby, she took notice of her love of doing it. She hadn't done that before. It seemed that she was always so busy doing it that she never took the time to see how much she truly enjoyed doing it. For her, it was more than just making a meal, it was the look in the

eyes of those who ate it, and the compliments afterwards. She was
learning that there was something about food, the aroma, and
gathering of people around to share it that made preparing it that
much more special. Tommy was right. It had slipped up on her, and
sadly she hadn't noticed it until now.

Ruby had driven up. Tori stood, smiled and waved. They
embraced each other as always and like Tori had planned she
surprised Ruby with a snicker doodle cookie. Ruby hugged her
again and bite into it. Ruby sat her purse down next to her on a quilt
that Odette had made for Tori and finished eating her cookie.

"Thanks," she said. "I know there's more." She looked
around for them.

"No woman," Tori laughed. "You're gonna eat some real
food first." She handed her a plate of fried chicken and dirty rice.

"Like I'm going to refuse anything that you make," Ruby
spooned up some of her rice.

"So, where are you going to be staying on campus?" Tori ate.

"I'm supposed to tell you that my mama signed for me to go first, and tell you all the details later." Ruby bit into a piece of chicken.

"Come on Rue," she said. "You had to know that she would eventually." She said.

"She just needed time is all?" Tori wiped her mouth.

"I was hoping and praying." Ruby said. "That was huge for my mama to do," She paused. "God," she said. "I just recognize how hard that must have been for her."

"Yeah," Tori said. "So, what's the dirt?"

"Well," Ruby smiled. "Because I'm starting this fall, it takes a year off of my program, and I'll finish in four years rather than five." She ate more rice.

"What about dorms and stuff?" Tori asked.

"I opted out of a crowed, stuffy cubicle with a messy roommate, and I will have my own one bedroom apartment with a loft." She got excited, and Tori got excited with her.

"That means that I can come and visit and not squeeze you out," Tori said.

"Of course," Ruby said.

"Wow Rue, I am so excited for you. But, I'm going to miss you so much." She showed a sad face with a moan behind it.

"Yeah I know." Ruby said. "We've never been separated before." She paused. "What am I gonna do without you, or Ginger?" She said.

"I am not going to start crying yet anyway." Tori said. "We've got the rest of the summer and we are not going to spoil it." Tori ate.

"You're right." Ruby said. "We gotta make this our best summer ever."

"Let's propose a toast." Tori held up a cold bottle of root beer. "Too the greatest summers we will always have together forever." She and Ruby toasted their root beer bottles and laughed. "Lots of money for your parents Rue," Tori said.

"Nope," Ruby talked with her mouth full. "I've got a full ride not a dime will come out of my parent's pocket." She said. "Maybe now my dad will help me get my truck? I've saved seven thousand dollars on it."

"Wow!" Tori said. "Have you told him?"

"Yeah, he hasn't said too much about it."

"Maybe it's gonna be a surprise?" Tori finished her plate.

"Yeah right," Ruby laughed. "Heard from Gin?"

"Nope," she said. "I don't know what's gotten into her."

"You and me both," she said. "I wanted to tell her my good news before she hears it from someone else, but," she sighed.

"I've never seen her act like this." Tori fixed bowls of melon for them. "Like it's your fault that Kameron likes you," she shook her head. "That is so dumb."

"Tell me about it." Ruby said. "I even told Kameron how much Ginger likes him, and it was like it didn't even register."

"You did what?" Tori said. "You can't make him like her Rue.

"I know that." She said. "But I tried okay, she's our friend and I just wanted her to be happy."

"You can't tell people who to love Rue." She said. "Look how Gin and I tried to tell you about Solomon, but you're with him despite his reputation and all."

"Could we not talk about Solomon," she said.

"Oh, what, there's trouble in paradise," Tori said. "Sorry, I just don't like him for you."

"Back to me telling Kameron the truth," she said. "He wasn't happy."

"I'm sure he wasn't, and I could almost imagine what you told him." Tori shook her head again.

"I told him that I was seeing Solomon." Ruby said. "And that it could never work between us even if Solomon weren't in the picture because…"

"Ginger is your best friend." Tori stopped eating her fruit. "Look how she's acting. Did she ever once consider you? She hasn't even called to say that she's sorry. All she wants to do is blame you for Kameron not liking her." She took a deep breath, and swung at a fly.

"I would have done the same thing for you." Ruby said.

"You wouldn't have had to, and neither did she when Kamari chose her. It's a part of life Rue everyone goes through it."

Ruby didn't say a word. In her heart, she knew Tori was right. This experience with rejection had changed Ginger somehow. Ruby wondered if through the hurt of it all, if she somehow would find her way back. She didn't want to leave and go off to college without having Ginger's friendship and forgiveness. But that was not up to her, it was up to Ginger and in a way that's what hurt Ruby.

As they sat eating their melon, silence had struck the both of them. They didn't try to fight it like they normally would have. They didn't try and come up with something to say just to force the silence away from them. They welcomed it and for some reason neither of them mind it speaking to them. Ruby thought a lot about Stanford and how Solomon would fit in. Tori about what colleges to pursue, and if she should take an early exit out of high school since she too had finished all of her credits in her junior year.

She needed a program that gave her both the business and the hospitality side. But, what college did that, and where would such a program be if it existed at all, and would she be willing to go there? And what about Tommy, several colleges had come calling after him, but as far as she could tell, UCLA had seemed to be the one that he would choose. In the stillness of the moment, somehow, she knew what she needed to do.

Ruby in silence suddenly found the courage to listen to the truth that she had avoided for way too long. As much as it hurt her to admit it, Solomon was his reputation, and he was not the guy that she had wasted so much time waiting on. He was merely a figment of her imagination of her knight on the white horse, and the truth was he never quite measured up.

Good-bye was in order. The moment her mother had said give me the pen, their fling had ended and her dream had begun. Now, what was telling him, or maybe he had already told her when he chose not to return her phone calls after being with both Daphne and Tiffney.

They both looked at each other and in both of their eyes; it was obvious that they had something very real and very new to say to each other. In a scared moment of silence they had grown. The quiet that they once feared, they were now open to it. At the same time, they both tried to speak.

"You first," Ruby said.

"I believe I know what I want to do." Tori said.

"I hope it's building your own restaurant." Ruby said.

"After college first," Tori said. "Wherever that is?"

"Are you serious? What happened?" Ruby got excited.

"I don't know?" She hunched her shoulders. "I guess I just finally got it." She laughed. "It took long enough."

"Better late than never," she said.

"Your turn," Tori stole one of her snicker doodle cookies and ate it.

"It's over between me and Solomon." Ruby said. "So, I'm going to tell him, and he can go back to business as usual." She took a snicker doodle from the bag.

"What!" Tori screamed. "What brought this on?"

"The truth I guess." She looked at Tori. "And, Daphne telling me at Church on Sunday that Tiffney slept with him on the night of Gin's dad's party, and she the next night."

"Dog," Tori said.

"Yeah," Ruby sighed, "which explains why he didn't call me that night, and why he sent me the roses."

"Which aren't your favorite, by the way?" Tori pointed to Ruby. "I bet Kameron would have gotten it right." She said.

"Don't start." Ruby laughed. "It was the thought that counted, or should I say the guilt."

"My thoughts exactly," Tori said.

"So, was it worth it waiting on him?" Tori asked.

"I honestly can't answer that now. Maybe when I find my knight I can tell you." She said.

"What if you've found him but you don't know it yet?" Tori said.

"I haven't. I would know, and for sure it is not Kameron." She said. "Besides, in two months he's gone, and so am I."

"Don't mention that," Tori said.

"Oh, you'll be gone to." Ruby said. "Fate was just waiting, now watch and see what happens."

"I wouldn't know where to start." She lay back on the quilt.

"Where would you want to live, and where do you see yourself building your restaurant?" Ruby stretched back on the quilt with Tori.

"San Francisco." Tori said. "LA would be nice too."

"Nah," Ruby looked over towards Tori. "I don't see you in LA. San Francisco suits you," Ruby smiled. "But, then again I'm partial," she said.

"Of course you are." Tori laughed.

Ginger had sewed herself into a frenzy. It was her way of dealing with all the craziness in her life, and all the bickering going on between her parents. Her mother spent less time at home. There were times that she didn't come home at all and when she did, all they did was fight. It drove Ginger crazy. All she did was stay in her room and sew, and it drove her nuts, but Ginger didn't care.

On top of all of that, Ginger hadn't gotten over Kameron. She had only buried her feelings and tricked herself into believing that she could move on without so much as a scratch. For her, just the opposite was true.

Her own anger had caught her in a web and she was missing out on Ruby's new chapter, Tori's and even hers. Confusion had her not seeing straight. If she had of welcomed the stillness and not chased it away, it would of revealed the truth, and she would have never pursued Kameron in the first place.

Ginger was through with men who pretended that they were a step ahead of the boys who were full of the same old tricks and lines that nearly bored her to tears. Kameron was no different. In her opinion he was a charlatan, who had no idea who he was or what was good for him. She showered and changed into a pair of spicy jean shorts and a crisscross blouse that she had designed, but hadn't worn. Two days without food had made her hungry and had also given her a splitting headache.

Ginger was surprised to see her mother in the kitchen making sandwiches. If she were going get into another confrontation with her father, then she'd rather she stay wherever she was. She worried about a lot of things: her mother's odd behavior, her parents' divorcing, Kameron, though she lied to herself about it. Her head was throbbing and she was striving. The moment her stomach had tasted food, it sent signals to her head that more was coming. The more she ate, the less her head hurt. Suddenly, she was beginning to feel relief, and it felt good.

"Somebodies hungry," her mother said.

"Yeah," she talked with her mouth full. "I feel like I haven't eaten in ten days."

"Close," her mother said, biting into her sandwich. "You scared me" She said.

"I'm surprised you even paid attention." Ginger said.

"Ginger," she said. "How could you say that?"

"Mama please," she said. "You're hardly ever here. You think I don't notice."

"Your father and I are just going through a rough time." She said. "But, everything is going to be okay…"

"Mama stop it." She said. "I'm not a kid anymore." She placed her plate into the sink. "I finally get to have my dad home, and what do you do, ruin it."

"That is not fair," Jasmin said. "I am doing everything I can to make this work out."

said.

"Oh really," Ginger said. "Well, try staying at home for a while." She said and left out of the back door.

Chapter 14

Everyone in Oak Grove knew about Ruby's good news. The old men at Ben Nelson's barber shop made it their lunch hour conversation. Solomon's grandfather Ben was extremely proud of Ruby, and even prouder that his grandson was dating her. It looked like he had finally picked a winner. Ruby was the first to head to a university such as Stanford from a little sleepy town like Oak Grove. She had impressed them and they had come looking for her and the people in Oak Grove couldn't stop talking about it.

"Yeah," Mr. Fletcher said. "For that man to have come here for that little girl," he shook his bald head. "Nelson," he said. "She was handling her business let me tell you." He said.

"I know it." Ben turned his clippers off. "Like I was telling my daughter," he said. "Them folks don't got time to be traveling down the hall to get lunch let alone coming here to recruit somebody to go to their school." He said. "She had it and they knew, or they would have never sent that man down here."

"I'm trying to tell you." Mr. Fletcher said.

"Hear she got a free ride," Boyd's father said.

"That's what my wife say." Mr. Fletcher munched on his potato chips.

"Um-hum," Ben talked over his clippers. "Big Jake told me that his son and his daughter-in-law ain't got to pay for as much as a sandwich for her." He said. "That's how much they're taking care of that little girl."

"Well, like I was telling my wife." He said. "The Wells is some good hearted people."

"You right about that," Big Boyd said. "Big Jake will give you the shirt off his back, and his son is the same way."

"That's the truth." Ben Nelson said.

"And, let's face it," Mr. Fletcher said. "When you that good to somebody else, the good lord is better to you."

"Amen." Ben said.

"That's it," Big Boyd said. "I'm happy for them." He put his magazine down. "Hell," he said. "It sure makes our town look good don't it." He laughed.

"Damn straight it does." Mr. Fletcher said.

"Solomon know yet?" Big Boyd said.

"I'm sure he does." Ben said. "What don't these young folks know?"

Precious Shop was no different. The usual shop gossip had taken a back seat to Ruby's grand news. The look in the eyes of the older woman was a look of pride and accomplishment. Ruby was their daughter and they had mentored her and spoke genuinely to her about life. She had responded and made them proud.

They had given her a part of each of them and she had taken it and bloomed. Now, they would watch and wait for her new chapters to be written and to see how her future would unfold as if they didn't know. Thankfully she had escaped the web Solomon had spun for her. But, that's what they had taught her. And, though she had stumbled just a bit, they had risen up inside of her and when Stanford came calling along with the truth, she responded like a woman and not like an immature youth.

They showered her with love, gifts, food, and more advice. And Ruby sat there like she always had, eating their food, drinking their sweet tea and lemon aid, and listening to their stories as if she were one of them. But, that's what they loved about her. She listened regardless of whether she agreed with them or not. She laughed at their jokes and naughtiness, and she took to heart what they were trying to teach her, and on top of that she made them look and feel like royalty. She may have been seventeen, but she was one of them.

Through all the adorning of Ruby, Mrs. Fletcher sat unpleased wishing all that would have befell on Ginger. Not to stand out, or to appear jealous, Mrs. Fletcher put on her fake face, fake smile, fake laugh, and even started a fake conversation to appear happy for Ruby. In a sense, she was happy for Ruby. Happy that she had gotten into the school of her choice, but unhappy by the way that the towns people rambled on about it.

Ginger would show them. It was going to be her turn next and unlike Ruby who needed that scholarship to fund her schooling, Ginger wouldn't have need for such a thing. Her Godson had managed his finances well, and despite rumors, Ginger's college fund was safe as long as Jasmin's hands were off of it. When Ginger would announce that she had gotten accepted in NYU, would there be this much celebration? And when her lines of clothing hit the runways and hung in the Macy's, Nordstrom's, and Bloomingdales' would they brag on Ruby then?

A sneaky grin came across her face as she could live a little bit longer to see her shop buddies have egg on their face. There was a fierce knock at the screen door that captured the ladies attention. Beyond the screen door was a tall man with a sky blue shirt on and black pants with a square box attached and a digital pen in his hand. Precious paused from wet setting Mrs. Amy's hair.

"Can I help you," she said. She looked down and saw the most beautiful bouquet of forty-eight yellow tulips beside him.

"I've got a delivery of flowers for a Ruby Wells." He said. "Are you Ruby?"

"No, that's my daughter." She signed for the flowers. "They're beautiful." She said.

"I should say." He said. "Do you need me to take them in ma'am?"

"Yeah," Precious said. "Right this way." She pointed to Ruby's station.

The shop was still and all of the women watched the gentlemen bring in the gorgeous bouquet. Odette stood and stretched her neck over towards Ruby's station and a smiled flashed across her face. Mrs. Amy turned her chair and tried to see from the tiny card attached who had sent them, but the tall man had blocked the way, and she smacked her lips. As if she knew, her phony demeanor had changed. Unexpectedly, she had become stiff and cold. And, before she lost her breath, she took to the outside and sat gingerly on the porch swing. The ladies looked and snickered as if they knew.

"Have a blessed day ladies." He said exiting the screen door. "Have a nice day ma'am." He tipped his hat to Mrs. Fletcher.

"Yeah," she frowned. "You do the same."

"You okay out there Fletcher?" Mrs. Amy couldn't help herself.

"Just getting air is all," she said.

"Wonder what she gonna do when they start dating?" Odette said.

"Get more air." Mrs. Amy burst out laughing.

Ruby trotted up the front steps. She stopped and saw Mrs. Fletcher sitting alone on the porch swing, and she sat next to her.

"You okay Mrs. Fletcher." She asked.

"Yeah child," she said. "Just enjoying the good lord's air is all," she said.

"Want an orange soda?" Ruby said.

"You know what the old girl likes." Mrs. Fletcher patted Ruby's hand.

"Hey mama," Ruby opened the screen door, and the bouquet of forty-eight golden tulips nearly took her breath away. "Oh my God," she stood before them. "Daddy bought me these." She was moved.

"Your daddy didn't buy those baby." Precious set Mrs. Amy's dryer.

"He didn't." She looked surprise. "Well, then who did?"

"Look," they all said in unison.

Ruby looked at all of them strange, then she opened the card; stunned she read. "Congrats on getting admitted to Stanford. I know that you will supersede all of your expectations. I am so proud of you. Go Cardinals. Love Kameron."

The expression on her face was priceless. She didn't know what to think or what to say. The bouquet had nearly covered her entire station. How did he know that tulips were her favorite flowers? And how did he know that the golden ones were her preferred color? He had known her a minute and Solomon had known her for years and had sent her red roses. She was positive that she had never told him that gold tulips were her favorite flowers, so how could he have known?

She turned and found all of the women's eyes on her including her mother's, and she could read every single one of them. "They're beautiful." She said. "I don't know what to say."

"Well tell him that, not us," Mrs. Amy said.

"Little girl," Odette said. "You need to call that boy."

"Like in now," her mother said.

Ruby walked outside. Mrs. Fletcher came back in. What would she say to Kameron? They hadn't exactly left as friends, and yet he had enough compassion inside of his heart to set aside any differences and send her flowers, and she loved them. She dialed

Mrs. Cassidy's number and it rang a few times, then she answered.

"Mosely residents, this is Cassidy." She said.

"Mrs. Cassidy," Ruby said. "It's Ruby. How are you?"

"Ruby," she smiled. "How are you doing baby and

congratulations?" She said.

"Thank you."

"So, when are you leaving?" She asked.

"In about two and a half months," she said.

"I know you're excited, and when you do I have something

special for you." She said.

"Thank you, but you don't have to you…"

"I am not hearing that." She said.

"Okay, "she laughed. "Is Kameron there?" She asked.

"You know baby, I believe that he is." She stood. "He's

probably in his little hole is what I call it. Let me see." She said.

She hit the star button on her phone and the phone in the loft rang.

"Hello," Kameron said.

"Baby, its Granny. Ruby's on the other line and I think she's calling about those beautiful flowers that you sent. I'm gonna switch you over okay."

"Okay," he said.

"Ruby, I'm switching you over to the loft okay." She said. "Love you."

"You too," Ruby said.

"Ruby," Kameron said.

"Yeah, how are you?" She said.

"Good," he said, "and you?"

"Fine," she said. "I just wanted call and thank you for the flowers."

"You're welcome." He leaned back in his chair. "I'm glad you liked them."

"I love them." She said. "By the way, how did you know they were my favorite flowers?"

"Lucky guess," he laughed.

"Luck had nothing to do with that." She said. "Someone had tell you. So who was it?"

"I'm not revealing my sources." He teased.

"Sources," she smiled. "So, someone did tell you."

"I plead the fifth." He snickered.

"You know I'm going to find out." She said. "This is a small town. Secrets don't have a chance here."

"So far so good," he teased.

"For now," she said.

"Listen," he leaned his body forward and rested his elbows on his desk. "I just want to say I'm sorry again about Ginger. I'm not trying to come in between your friendship."

"You don't have to apologize again Kameron." She said. "I read your lips in church, and you're not coming in between Ginger and me." She sighed. "I'm sorry for making you feel that you were."

Kameron was stunned. He couldn't believe what he was hearing. A week or so ago Ruby was all over him. Now, her attitude was totally different and he wondered why. But, he didn't want to pry. This was the crack that he needed and wanted, and he needed to think fast.

"My Grannies making a surprise lunch for you by the lake and…" He stopped himself. "I can't believe I just did that." He pretended to laugh.

"Well you did," she laughed. "I'll just pretend like I don't know." She laughed again. "What day is it?"

He paused in thought thinking what he should say. He scratched his scalp and blurted out "next Friday, and feel free to bring your friends." He said. "But, just…"

"Don't let Mrs. Cassidy know." She finished his sentence, or at least she thought she had.

Ruby thanked Kameron for the flowers again and hung up. Kameron took a long deep breath. What had he gotten himself into? The great thing about his lie if there were anything great about it, was that Ruby loved his Granny and the feeling from his Granny was mutual. He knew that his Granny would go along with his lie and make it look all official and that Ruby would never know that it wasn't.

How else was he supposed to get to know her and turn her heart from Solomon? He stood, stretched his long body and left the

loft headed to the main house to tell his Granny what he had done
and ask for her help.

Solomon definitely needed help with Ruby, something he
had never anticipated. Tommy was right though he hated to admit it.
Daphne had gotten mad at him for sending Ruby roses and for
crowning her his new princess when she had done the things that she
had done for him, and she ratted him out. He would have thought it
would have been Tiffney, but it wasn't. Tiffney was the clinging
vine. Daphne pretended to let him sow his seeds and be Solomon.
But, obviously, she had an agenda.

He was done with her no matter how much she fulfilled his
needs, and he had told her so. She reacted the way he thought that
she would, crying and pleading with him not to dump her. He had to
turn his cell off. His Papa had to tell her not to come back to his
shop anymore, and his mother God forbid talked about laying her
hands on her if she came back to her house again.

It's what they all did when he was through with them.
However, he never anticipated acting out when a girl like Ruby was

done with him. He had blown up her cell but she wouldn't answer it. He left messages, but she didn't return his calls. Talk about punishment, hers was grueling, and like Daphne, he would do anything to get her back.

He needed help he had to admit. But, he knew that as much as he loved his boys, they had made it perfectly clear at Berries of what they thought of his cheating. Maybe it was time for him to call on the old men at the shop? He'd hear a lecturer he was sure and probably secrets from their past that only the men knew about. But, because they had adopted him as one of theirs, they'd be willing to share their stories, and at the end of it all, show some love. It would be more than what his so called boys had done.

The doorbell rang as he chilled in his bedroom thinking. It rang again, and he called out to his mother but she obviously didn't hear it. He sighed, left his bedroom, called his mother once more, but she didn't answer. He smacked his lips and answered the door.

"Is your mom here?" Ginger asked.

"Yeah," he said. "She must be out back or something."

"Well, are you going to let me in?" She rolled her eyes.

"I guess I have to." He said. "Not that I want to," he called out to his mother again. This time she heard him and came in from the back door.

"Yes Solomon," she said. "What is all the commotion?"

"Ginger's got your stuff." He said.

"Oh, thank the lord," she sat at her kitchen table. "I can't wait to see it. Sit down baby."

"Thanks." She sat.

"Solomon, offer the girl something to drink." She said. "You know I taught you better than that."

"Reptiles don't drink mama, they devour." He placed a jug of sweet tea on the table with a glass.

"True," she starred at him, handing his mother her garments. "And you better be glad your mama is sitting here at this table."

"Girl," his mother looked at her two dresses and her suit. "You are good." She starred at her garments.

"Thanks, I try." Ginger said.

"Honey, you more than try." Yolanda said. "You are gonna make a fortune baby."

"That's the plan." She said.

"How much I owe you baby," she said.

"One hundred and forty dollars," Ginger said.

"Solomon bring my check book baby." She said. "You must be so proud of Ruby."

"Here mama," he said.

Ginger looked clueless. She hadn't spoken to Ruby in a while, nor had she returned any of her calls. Whatever it was, Ruby had probably left her a voice mail or an urgent message, but out of anger she ignored it. Now she was about to discover something grand from Solomon's mother, that she should have found out from Ruby. Now, she had to fake it.

"Rue was blowing up my phone, but I had gotten behind on orders." She wrote Yolanda out a receipt.

"Solomon," she turned to face him. "Don't tell me you haven't heard."

"Heard what?" He looked ill-informed.

"Did you and that girl get into a fight?" She said. "If you so, you need to fix it because she's going to Stanford come fall."

Chapter 15

Ginger's eyes lit up like light bulbs. Solomon's mouth nearly dropped to the floor, and he nearly fell into his mother's lap. His mother could tell by their reactions that neither of them had heard and she found that to be awfully strange. Yolanda looked at Ginger first, than her son, and stood with her garments in her hand.

"Don't tell me that neither one of you knew." She said.

Ginger paused, her eyes giving it all away no matter how non-surprised she tried to look. She looked at her cell to play things off, and to her surprise Ruby had left a message on her cell and she could almost say that, that's what it was. "See," she showed the message. "I bet it's probably on the day that she got the news." She placed her cell in her purse.

Yolanda looked at Solomon as if she knew that Ruby hadn't contacted him. "Well," she said.

"It's probably a hit on my phone." He said, looking unsure.

"I hope so." She said. "Because this girl is going places," she took her garments into her room. "You need to call that girl Solomon." She said, as her voice trailed off from her room.

There was a weird silence that hovered over the kitchen table at Solomon's house that day. Solomon was not one to be in panic when it came to girls. He had always been in control and they were the one's always in panic. Ruby had not contacted him since she had told him what she felt that Sunday, and she had not returned any of his phone calls; now he knew why. He had Tiffney and Daphne to thank for that, and he was through with them.

Lots of things roamed through Ginger's head. How could she have been so stupid? How could she have let anger get in the way of knowing Ruby's big news? Not, that she had forgiven Ruby especially for taking Kameron or Tori for knowing about it and not telling. But, it was an opening, and maybe if she played her cards right, she could move back into Kameron's heart and it would be like Ruby never existed.

Without warning, they're eyes connected. Neither of them was found of each other but both had an agenda; a motive, and both of them needed each other's help. As if they knew what they were going to ask each other, they giggled a devious laugh. Solomon finished his milk and she placed the check in her purse and finished her sweet tea. They asked each other no questions.

Neither of them past blame, or got into an immature cat fight that would get them nowhere. Solomon got up from his seat, tilted his head towards the front door, and without question, she followed. She paused at the table and raised her voice to reach Solomon's mother's room. "Good-bye Mrs. Garrett, and thanks so much for your business."

"Oh no baby," she said. "Thank you."

"You're welcome." She said, and followed Solomon to the door.

Solomon walked Ginger to her car and stood on the edge of the sidewalk. She placed her belongings in her father's Benz, and walked back around standing in front of him. She leaned her body back on the car and folded her arms across her chest.

"Honestly," he said. "You didn't know?"

"No," she said. "Apparently you didn't either."

"Long story," he said.

"I bet." She said.

"You're her girl and you didn't know?" He shook his head.

"So, she's not coming back to King."

"Obviously not," she sighed. "She always gets what she wants." She sighed again.

"Excuse me," he said. "Are you hating on her?"

"For going to Stanford," she leaned back further on the car. "No," she said. "I'm hating on her for taking Kameron."

Solomon nearly fell back. But, learning from Tommy first, than football, he had learned how to balance himself in awkward situations. He moved his arms in tiny circles to balance and he stood perfectly on the edge of the curb. He had heard that before about Kameron checking out Ruby from Kamari first, and then Tommy. He didn't think twice about it until he heard Ginger say it. He never guessed that Ruby would ever be interested in him. But now, it all made since. Ruby was headed for Stanford and she wanted an upgrade.

"So," he could barely get his words straight. "She's really into this dude, and seeing him behind my back." He sounded angry.

"Karma is a mother isn't it?" She laughed.

"Yeah, I guess." He said. "Weren't you after that dude?"

"Funny," she rolled her eyes. "It's obvious we both want something here."

"I never thought in a million years that I'd be needing help from you." He shook his head. "Talk about Karma."

"Please," she said.

"I want Kameron." She said.

"I want Ruby." He said.

"Correction, you want something from her," she said.

"And you want old boy because your pops is broke, and the Mosely's are a gold mind." He said. "So, let's cut to the chase and devise a plan."

"First things first," she said. "I have to pretend to swallow my pride, ask for forgiveness, and get back into the loop so I can find out what's going on." She said.

"I have to act like it's cool with this Kameron guy, when I want to punch this fools lights out for messing around with my girl."

"I'm gonna act just like I didn't hear that." She said.

"Just hit me up when you hear something." He said.

"I will." She said, and drove off.

Solomon entered back into his door with a million frowns in his face. Kameron entered his Grannies kitchen with a smile. He kissed her cheek as he always did, and bit into a juicy ripe tomato and then put salt and pepper on it. His Grannie couldn't help but smile. He was his grandfather's child, and he reminded her so much of him.

"You mean you are not working in that loft today?" She asked.

"Yeah, actually, I just came down for a little snack." He smiled. "And bingo," he finished the tomato.

"I should have known." She shook her head, making a fresh garden salad with vegetables picked from her garden.

"Mosely trait I guess." He helped himself to sandwiches that his Granny had made.

"You got that right." She said.

"Come on Granny." He bit into his sandwich. "Doing what you love isn't so bad is it?"

"Not as long as you make time for the ones you love baby," she said and placed the salad in the refrigerator. "How'd she like the flowers?" She asked.

"She loved them." He talked with his mouth full.

"So when are you going to ask that sweet girl out on a date?" She paused from going into the cupboard. He finished his sandwich, wiped his mouth and laughed. "I sort of did in an unconventional way."

"What do you mean sort of did?" She filled her stock pot up with cold water.

"I told her that you were giving her a surprise lunch next Friday, and I pretended like I wasn't supposed to tell." He laughed.

Cassidy couldn't help but laugh. "Why didn't you just ask her out like…?"

"Like normal," he took another sandwich off the tray. "Because I know she adores you, and she wouldn't come up with an excuse."

"So," she looked at him and laughed again. "She agreed to it?"

"Yes she did, and I told her that she could bring her friends if she wanted because I didn't want to scare her." He wiped his mouth.

"Lord have mercy." She shook her head. "Young people," she laughed. "So, what do you want me to prepare?" She asked.

"I have no idea. But, I will find out, promise." He said.

"You had better." She said.

"I will." He said," Gotta go catch up with Gramps, it's about that time." He kissed her cheek again and went back to the loft.

Ginger could smell her mother's cabbage and cornbread before she walked into the door. She was surprised that she was home. Lately due to the bickering, her mother had left the nest, but thankfully she had returned. Maybe what Ginger had said had a profound effect on her? Beyond the cabbage and cornbread, she smelled oven fried pork chops, and she could see Mrs. Fletcher's old lady purse on the coffee table. Certainly, news was in order, what was it this time?

"Ginger is that you?" Her mother said.

"Yeah mama, it's me." She went upstairs to her room and placed her purse on her dresser. "Dinner smells good." She yelled from upstairs. "Hi Mrs. Fletcher."

"Hi baby." She said.

"It will be ready in another five to seven minutes so freshen up and come down to eat." Her mother said.

"Be down in a few," she said.

"Does she know?" Mrs. Fletcher asked.

"About Ruby going to Stanford," Jasmin crossed her legs. "I'm positive she does."

"Oh not that," Mrs. Fletcher waved a hand at her. "I'm talking about that boy sending Ruby flowers."

"What?" Jasmin looked surprised.

"Forty-eight beautiful golden yellow tulips," she said. "Damn near covered her station," she said, "made me sick to my stomach."

"Why would he do that?" Jasmin said.

"Why do you think?" She said.

"Well, I don't know what to think?" She checked on her pork chops and returned to the family room.

"He likes that girl a lot." He shook her head. "It hurts me to say it, but he does, and we've got to figure out a way to turn him towards our Ginger." She said.

Ginger nearly fell on the living room couch. What was it about Ruby that Kameron went for? What was she doing so wrong? She should have known he'd pull something like that. First it was trying to get Ruby to go out to lunch, now he was sending her favorite flowers and forty-eight of them at that. She couldn't lie to herself at the moment she felt discouraged. However, there had to be a way to make Kameron love her. But how?

Ginger took a deep breath and closed her eyes. She had to call Ruby despite how she felt and she had to be good. Ruby could sense things, and she could smell a lie even if she didn't confront you right away. She paused thinking about it. Maybe she should go through Tori first. But, then it wouldn't seem sincere and Ruby would feel it. She moaned and dialed her cell knowing that she would answer and she did.

"Gin," she stopped looking at her Stanford catalog.

"Yeah, congrats on Stanford," she said. "You know that I'm so happy for you." She lied.

"Thanks," Ruby said. "I was hoping you'd call so I could have told you first, but…"

"But, I was acting a fool, and I'm sorry." She said. "I hope you and Tori can forgive me." She pretended to get all choked up.

"I forgive you Gin." Ruby said. "But, if you ever do something so stupid again, I will disown you for life." Ruby scolded her. "We're friends Gin, best friends and why would you let some guy come in between us." She said. "Besides, he's leaving by the end of summer."

"True," Ginger resented what Ruby said. "Again, I'm very sorry, and it won't happen again." She lied.

"It better not." Ruby said. "Oh," Ruby said. "I'm sure you will be thrilled to hear this." She sat up in her bed. "I'm breaking up with Solomon." She said.

Ginger got stone quiet. Her silence had given her away. This was not what she was expecting to hear, and Ruby began to get suspicious.

"Gin," Ruby said. "Say something," she said. "I thought that you'd be jumping up and down, and doing cartwheels or something."

"Ah, ah, I'm shocked." She tried to fake it. "I'm thrilled.

I'm elated." She said, but her voice didn't show it. "I guess I'm shocked because I know how much you like that idiot." She tried to recover.

Ruby paused. Something didn't feel right, and Gin didn't sound all that happy about her wanting to break up with Solomon. Ginger deplored Solomon. In fact, she cursed the ground that he walked on and now in a subtle way, or at least that's how it came across to Ruby, it was as if she wanted them to be together. But, that couldn't be, maybe she was just reading too much into things.

"Gin," Ruby said. "Mrs. Cassidy is giving a surprise luncheon for me next Friday. Kameron told me by accident. He wasn't supposed to tell, but it slipped somehow." She said. "You're coming aren't you?"

Ginger paused again, longer than what she wanted to. What was Kameron doing talking to Ruby, and what was Ruby doing talking to him. Something had to be going on between those two and Ruby was hiding it. But, maybe she and Solomon could turn it around? Maybe she could make Ruby wish that she would have never invited her and him. The catch was, she wouldn't let her know that she was inviting Solomon. He would just show up and that would be the end of Kameron's crush.

"Gin," Ruby said.

"Yeah, yeah, sure I'll come. I'd love to." She smiled a devious smile.

"Good, good," Ruby said. But, in her gut, she sensed something was wrong. "Gin, are you okay? You seem sort of out of it."

"No, I'm good." She said. "My parents were really getting on my nerves fighting, but now they're all lovey with each other." She said. "You know how that goes?" She pretended to laugh. "Listen, I have to go dinner is ready, and my dad just walked into the door." She said.

"Okay," Ruby said.

"Again, congrats Stanford brat, I want all the details later; love you." She said and hung up.

Ginger breathed a sigh of relief. If she could go back and edit that conversation she would. But, she couldn't. She would just have to convenience Ruby that nothing had changed between the two of them and that she just had an off day.

Ruby sighed and picked back up her Stanford catalog. In a few months she would be going through some of the same doors that she starred at on her catalog. It seemed like a crazy dream. Sometimes she felt as if she would wake up and be disappointed, but this was real and sometimes she had to pinch herself to believe it.

However, what was crazy was Ginger's behavior. Maybe she was making too much of it, but she seemed distant and bothered. Something was wrong and no matter how much she tried to tell herself that it wasn't, a yearning inside her stomach would nearly burst. She hated when she got those feelings and it seemed that the feelings disliked when she tried to ignore them. Ruby was troubled by Ginger's attitude but her mother couldn't sense it.

"Hey Stanford girl," Precious had the look of a proud mother.

"Hey mama," Ruby said, and put down her catalog again.

"So, how's it feel," she asked.

"Like a dream, and like I haven't waken up yet," she said.

"Well," her mother climbed into her bed and wrapped her arms around her. "You had better wake up baby because this is real." She kissed her cheek. "I'm so proud of you. God, I am so proud of you."

"Thanks," Ruby said. "I'm proud of you to. I know it wasn't easy for you to make that decision, but you did."

"It was time baby." She looked into her daughter's eyes. "What am I gonna do without my baby at the shop?"

"What am I going to do without you?" Ruby looked at her mother. "It will be different for both of us, but I promise to come back to the shop during spring break, and during summers." Ruby smiled at her mother.

"Deal," she kissed her forehead.

"Mama," she said.

"Yeah," Precious said.

"I guess you should know that it's over between me and Solomon." She said.

"Really," Precious rose up. "So, what happened?"

"Let's just say he wasn't what I thought he was," she looked sad.

"A frog instead of a prince huh," Precious stroked her face.

"You were right." Ruby said.

"Baby I didn't want to be right," Precious said.

"You didn't," Ruby looked confused.

"No," she said. "I just didn't want you to get hurt."

"You okay?" Her mother asked.

"Yeah," Ruby looked at her mother. "The right guy is out there. It's just not time yet." She said. "And, thank God," Ruby snuggled in her mother's chest. "I think I just want to concentrate on Stanford."

"I think that I would like that." Her mother laughed. "But Kameron may not," she said.

"It doesn't matter what he likes." She said. "Besides, I'm not interested in him." She yawned. "Guess what?" Ruby said.

"What?" Precious rubbed her shoulder.

"Gin called me." Ruby said.

"So, she's gotten over her madness," Precious laughed.

"Yeah," Ruby sat up. "At least that's what she says, but something just doesn't feel right." She looked at her mother.

"I can't put my hand on it." She said.

"It has been a while since she's called you." Her mother said.

"Two weeks," Ruby said.

"Woo! She was mad at you," her mother laughed.

"Yeah, I know." She said. "Stupid."

"Maybe she didn't know how you'd respond to her?"

"Maybe, but when I told her that I was breaking it off with Solomon, she paused. "It was strange. I can't explain it, but for about a minute it was a silence in the phone. Gin hates Solomon and I would have thought that she would have been thrilled, but she wasn't." She said. "She tried to pretend like she was but she wasn't. I don't know?" Ruby hunched her shoulders.

"Really," Precious was surprised.

"Yeah," Ruby said. "I was surprised to."

"Well, I wouldn't worry about it." Her mother said.

Ruby didn't say a word, but there was a troubled look in her eyes.

Chapter 16

Echo Park was still. The only sound that penetrated the park was the breeze of the wind, shaking the branches and the leaves on the tree. Ruby and Tori lay relaxed underneath a huge sweet gum tree on top of an oversized quilt that Ruby's Big Mama had made for her. Ruby folded her arms back behind her head staring into the deep blue sky as if her eyes were supposed to be focused there.

Tori raised her body up and let the wind sweep softly across her face. She too stared into empty space; eyes as focused as Ruby, except the colleges she now would choose had her complete attention. A few leaves had blown on their quilt, landing on Ruby's shoulder and one on Tori's thigh. Ruby took the leaf from her shoulder and sat up, twirling the stem of the leaf in her hand.

"Can you believe it?" Ruby said.

"What, that Ginger Called?" Tori said.

Ruby shook her head and looked at Tori, and twirled the leaf some more. "Yea, and the oddest thing was her tonality." Ruby watched the leaf. "When I mentioned that I was breaking it off with Solomon, she just got real quiet like she didn't want me to.

It was strange knowing how she feels about him."

"Really," Tori looked surprised. "Yeah, that is strange." She said. "You would think that she would have been celebrating."

"Tell me about it." Ruby said. "I don't know Tori something just doesn't feel right."

"So, what are you saying?" Tori looked at Ruby.

"I don't know?" Ruby hunched her shoulders. "The call out of the blue after two weeks of nothing, and just the distance in her voice, I don' know?" She sighed.

"Well," Tori said. "Only time will tell," she twirled a leaf.

"You know it's funny," Ruby said. "I've waited so long for Solomon, and just when we finally got together Crazy stuff started to happen."

"Obvious it wasn't meant to be?" Tori handed her a cold bottle of water.

Ruby turned and looked at Tori. For a moment, she stopped twirling her leaf. She had heard that before. Before, it would have bothered her but this time it didn't. She didn't know why. Obviously she had opened her heart and mind, and finally saw

Solomon for what he was? Maybe she was learning to welcome the truth rather be a victim to a pretty lie? Or, maybe she discovered that she was entitled to better and didn't have to settle for the left overs?

"It's funny." She almost laughed. "I didn't ask for any of this." Ruby opened her water and took a sip.

"I didn't ask to be with Tommy either." Tori opened her bottle of water and drunk some. "But I'm finding out that life doesn't always give us what we want." She snickered. "I had a mad crush on Kamari, but look who I ended up with." She smiled.

"I remember that." Ruby laughed. "You were so in like with him." She smiled.

"It only lasted for a minute." Tori drank more of her water. "Besides, when I saw the way that he looked at Ginger verses me, I was done." She said. "I happily moved on. "His eyes told me all what his mouth couldn't."

Ruby capped up her water and laid it down on the quilt beside her. "Did you ever tell Gin about it?" Ruby crossed her legs and picked up her water again.

"It went out of one ear to the next." She said. "She wanted a man not a boy, and she would wait until her chances came." Tori shook her head. "I thought Kamari would have been good for her." She said. "What about you?"

Ruby sipped some of her water and thought it over for a minute or two. "Yeah," she said. Ginger was the wild cat that needed to be house broken. She was strong in certain areas and deficient in others that even she would never admit. She was everything that Kamari wasn't.

He was everything that she needed, but would never admit that she wanted. Ginger was sort of silly like that. Sometimes, Ruby and Tori both wondered if Ginger truly knew what was good for her. Kamari was smart, mature beyond his seventeen years, and unlike Boyd and even Solomon, he knew what he wanted out of life.

Through all of Ginger's list of important criteria's, she hadn't a clue of what she truly wanted in a relationship. She had a meager sketch of her own carefully crafted fairy tale; white pony and the prince that rode on top of it. She had drafted that story. But, she forgot the most important element; love. Ginger was the pup chasing her own tail and thinking if she ran harder that one day she would eventually catch it off guard and fool everyone who said she couldn't do it. She was hell bent on proving that she could do anything, and her stubborn spirit had cost her.

Ruby took a deep breath and rose back up again. Everything had happened so fast and still summer was tip-toeing by as if it had its own purpose and specific agenda. Except for Stanford, it seemed in Ruby's eyes that she had struck out this summer in finding love. However, Tori had nailed it.

"What?" Tori swallowed her last drops of water.

"I don't know?" Ruby said. "I was just thinking how you found what I was hoping I'd find with Solomon this summer." She shook her head.

"And, what was that," Tori said, handing her a bowl of fresh cut melons.

"Love," Ruby said.

Tori put her empty water bottle down. She looked at Ruby as though she was baffled. Here she was trying to discover what she would do with the rest of her life, and here was Ruby just trying to

find love. If she could only manage to open her eyes wide enough,
she would see that in Kameron she had found it.

"I never knew it meant that much to you." Tori said.

"Well, it does, but its okay if I didn't find it this time." She
said. "I'm sure it'll come when I least expect it to."

"What if it already has?" Tori talked with her mouth full.

"I think I would know that." Ruby said. "Don't you?"

"No, I do not." Tori said.

"Come on," Ruby talked with her mouth full. "I would
know."

"I hate to keep repeating myself." She turned to face Ruby.
"Kameron Rue, he sent you favorite flowers. He cares about what's
important to you, and he bought you a journal which was a good
omen because a day later you were headed to Stanford. Wake up."
She said. "He seems like a really nice guy. You gave Solomon a
chance why not him?" She finished her melon. "And please don't
start with Ginger, please," she said.

"I don't know anything about him." She said.

"You thought you knew Solomon and what happened?" Tori fired back.

"He's going back to New York around the same time that I'll be starting Stanford and…"

"Excuses, excuses, and I'll say the last one for you, our lovely friend Ginger." Tori said.

Ruby shook her head. "Speaking of Kameron," she said. "I called yesterday to thank him for the beautiful tulips that he sent me."

"You mean you actually called him?" Tori got excited.

"Come on Tori, it would have been rude not to." She said. "Anyway, by mistake he happened to mention that Mrs. Cassidy is giving me a surprise luncheon next Friday at the lake, and that I could bring my friends if I wanted so,"

"Slip my butt," she said. "I'm there. Can I bring Tommy?"

"Yeah," Ruby said.

"Please don't tell me that you told Ginger?" Tori said.

"I did." She said. "I didn't know what I know now when I invited her, and I can't un-invite her." Ruby bit into a turkey sandwich.

"Rue," Tori said.

"Well, she's still our friend." Ruby wiped her mouth.

"True," Tori unwrapped a ham sandwich. "And, on top of all of that, her parents aren't getting along, and I hear that they're broke."

"What," Ruby stopped eating her sandwich. "You're kidding right."

"Nope," she swallowed. "Those were her words, not minds."

"Funny, she never mentioned it to me." Ruby said.

"No," Tori said. "Now that is weird." She paused. "Maybe, whatever was wrong, they fixed it?"

"Maybe," Ruby said. "Maybe that's why Gin was acting so strange when I talked to her."

"Could be," Tori said. "You know, I did see Mrs. Maples at Tommy's place buying veggies and fruit, and," she paused from eating.

"Her skirt was way too short for a woman her age; even Mrs. Odette noticed it." Tori said.

"What," Ruby said. "So, what are you saying?"

"I don't know. It just seemed a little too short for me." She took another bite of her sandwich. "Your mama nor mines would ever wear their skirts or dresses that short."

"True," she said. "Now, we know where Gin gets it from."

"Gin is young." Tori said.

"Well," Ruby said. "Mr. Maple's is home." She smiled.

For a moment between them it was quiet. Tori sat tracing a leaf and she stared at its deep green color and its pointed but tender spikes that held the shape of the leaf. In an odd way, the leaf reminded her of Tommy; thick, but simple with lots of love in between. Tommy was all she thought about now besides applying for places to go to college. She hadn't told Ruby but she had applied to a couple of college's; one back east, Cal Poly Pomona, and San Francisco State, her first choice.

All of them were taking applications for the upcoming fall term. She didn't want to jinx her chances, so she sealed her lips and forced herself not to tell Ruby. She wanted to surprise her if she got in. Tommy had met with scots at Berkley, and Stanford, but his dream school had always been UCLA. He didn't want a long distance relationship. In his own words to Tori, he could play baseball anywhere as long as she was near. She was tempted to tell Ruby, but she stalled hoping in a few weeks that both of them would be celebrating. Ruby on the other hand was thinking about what Tori had said about Kameron, and if Ginger would ever come to her senses.

A New day and eight hours of sleep had Ginger in a good mood. Her father had left a yellow rose on the opposite side of her pillow. She reached for it, smiled and sniffed it. He always knew how to make her smile; always knew how to help her start her day on a perfect note, and she loved him for it. She lifted her body up and sat. On her end table, underneath her lamp was a note from her mother telling her, she would be out for a while, but that she'd be home by noon.

At least it was noon, and not overnight, and at least she felt her mother was listening. She yawned and rubbed her eyes. She felt rested and new. She had to contact Solomon, but how? She certainly couldn't ask Ruby for it. What was she to do? Suddenly

Kamari came to mind, and she called him with a good lie.

"Hello," he said, not recognizing that it was Ginger.

"Hey you," she said.

"Ginger!" He sounded shock. "What's up?"

"Nothing much," she said at first. "Mrs. Cassidy is giving Ruby a luncheon by lake on Friday." She said. "You know she's going to Stanford come fall."

"Yeah, I heard." He smiled. "Sweet."

"Yeah, I know." She said. "Anyway, I was wondering if you wanted to come with me." She said. "Rue said I could bring someone."

"Ah, ah, yeah," he was stunned. "I'm down."

"Perfect," she said. "One more thing," she said.

"Yeah," he said, still numb.

"Solomon's wants me to make his mother a jacket but he doesn't want her to know about it. Do you think you could give me his cell?"

"Yeah, yeah, no problem," he said. "Ready, I'll text it to you right now." He said.

She sat with her legs folded underneath her covers, then the text came. "Got it," she said.

"Cool," he said. "Can I ask you something?" He said.

"Yeah," she acted like she didn't know what he was going to say, but she did.

"What made you ask me to go with you? I mean you haven't given me the time of day."

"My mistake huh," she said. "Don't you dare skip out on me," she said.

"Please," he said. "So, you wanna hang out later," he finally got the courage to ask.

"Sure," she said, dinner and a movie."

"Cool," he said," see you around six."

"I'll be here." She said and hung up. "Ginger girl, you are good." She dialed Solomon's cell.

Ginger yawned again and sat straight up on her bed. This time she couldn't but help smile when she dialed Solomon's cell. She just knew that Kamari would have a million and one questions when she asked for Solomon's cell, but he didn't. This was easier than she thought. Had she would of known that he was going to be this easy, she would of done it before storming out of the shop and making a display of herself.

"Hello," Solomon answered.

"It's me, Ginger," she said.

"Oh, hey, what's up?" He said.

"Great news," she smiled.

"What," he said, almost hearing the smile in her voice.

"Mrs. Cassidy is giving Ruby a luncheon next Friday by the lake, and all of her cronies are invited." She said.

"And that's your great news," he said.

"Solomon," she said. "Do I have to spell it out?"

"Yeah," he said. "Because, I don't see what's so great about it," he opened the refrigerator and got out the picture of orange juice.

"Ruby would never expect you to show up there; especially uninvited. And of course, Kameron would never expect me to show up there either." She shook her head.

"Yeah," he said, as it suddenly became clear. "That's good looking out. I still can believe that she's into this fool." He said.

"I think he's more into her for now than she is in him, but I'm sure the way he's pursing her that will all change." She said. "Just so you know, he sent her 48 beautiful golden tulips," she stood.

"Are you serious?" He said; his eyes displaying shock. "I know she didn't take them."

"Yeah, she did. And just so you know, her favorite flowers are tulips, the gold ones." She was almost laughing.

Solomon was embarrassed of course. He never once stopped to try and find out what Ruby's favorite flowers were. He was in trouble and he was desperate. All he knew was that most women loved flowers and that red roses were a favorite. Now, he really hated Kameron trying to show him up. And, he loathed Ginger for making a fool out of him. Somehow, he would make sure that she got hers.

Ginger was on a high. She sung in the shower. She danced in her room as she put on her clothes. When she sat to eat breakfast, she swayed and turned as she sprinkled brown sugar and cinnamon over her oatmeal. She usually hated eating breakfast and dinner a lone but, right now she didn't. She actually enjoyed having the table all to herself with no one to disturb her thoughts.

Ginger hadn't smiled this much in weeks. Mrs. Cassidy hadn't laughed that much in months. Every time she looked at Ruby's grandmother, Pauline she would wallow in laughter. It was Mrs. Fletcher who became their topic of conversation with Pauline feeling Cassidy in on her sad behavior in Precious' shop. From her old lady frowns, to her angry silence, Pauline seemed to capture the ambience of the shop that day. She even laughed at herself as she reiterated the tale.

"I tell you girl. It was a sight." She said.

"Was it?" Mrs. Cassidy wiped her eyes.

"I mean she was actually mad at the young man who delivered Ruby's flowers." Pauline shook her head. "I don't know if she were more upset with him or with Kameron."

"Now you know, that's a shame," Mrs. Cassidy said.

"I know it." Pauline sipped on sweet tea.

"To be honest," Cassidy said. "I wouldn't want my grand baby with that Maples girl." She reached for a tea cake that Pauline had made. "I know that she's your granddaughter's friend, but she's a bit on the loud side for me." She bit into a teacake. "Girl can't nobody; I mean nobody make teacakes like you." She placed the rest of it in her mouth and ate.

"Thanks girl," she said. "I appreciate that. I make them out of love." She said.

"Something," Cassidy took another one. "And, another thing about that Maples girl," she said. "She wears them dog gone skirts, dresses, and shorts, way too short." She said. "I'm mean leaving nothing for the men to imagine about."

"Well, who you think she got it from." Pauline said, and helped herself to a teacake.

Cassidy burst out laughing. "That's the truth," she said. "I'm sure you heard the rumors." She said.

"Um-hum," Pauline said. "Heard that husband of hers had to get a transfer to San Francisco cause she couldn't control her spending."

"Humph!" Cassidy shook her head. "I heard that wasn't all she couldn't control." Cassidy said.

"Girl shut your mouth." Pauline said.

"Just think about it honey," she said. "That man was making six digit figures, he ain't just leaving that life or that career with them big bonuses cause she can't control her spending." She looked at Pauline the way older women looked at each other and giggled. "She's got needs, and I'm sure she's been getting them met."

"What did you say," Pauline didn't know how to take that. "I don't believe it." She shook her head. "She loves that man, and besides we would have seen something."

"Girl, do you think that she would creep here in Oak Grove?" She said. "Child please."

"Well, where would she go?" She said.

"How the hell would I know?" She laughed. "But she's creeping, and the truth will come out."

"I'll have to see it." Pauline said.

"Well," Cassidy said. "You will. Anyway," she said. "My grandson asked your granddaughter out on a date, if you can call it that," she laughed.

"Oh really," Pauline sipped more of her tea.

"I don't know why the boy just couldn't come right out and ask her instead of having this luncheon, which I don't mind cooking for it, and having her friends come either, but…"

"Leave the boy alone." Pauline said. "My grand baby hasn't been the easiest to pursue. I just hope she accepted it."

"She did." Cassidy said. "And now, I've got to figure out what to prepare."

"No you don't." Pauline said. "I'm right here. The girl loves fish, and chicken, and her favorite way to eat chicken is barbecued." She said. "I'll help you cook."

"Well barbecued chicken it is with all the fixings." She said. "And don't forget a batch of these teacakes for us." She laughed.

"And a peach cobbler for Ruby," Pauline said.

"You must be so proud of her." Cassidy said.

"Oh I am." She said. "Maybe now that she knows that she's going to Stanford, she'll get rid of that dog gone Solomon?"

"Yolanda's boy," Her eyebrow rose a bit. "I thought that

was just a rumor."

"Nah honey it ain't, but…"

"If we have anything to do with it, it's gonna be my grandson let me tell you." Cassidy said. "I think they make such a nice couple."

"Ditto," Pauline said. "You know we got old lady Fletcher trying to get that Maples girl on your grandson's arm." She said.

"Wanting ain't getting," Cassidy said. "Let her go get Solomon girl, they're more compatible."

"My sentiments exactly," Pauline said, and reached for another teacake.

"If anybody's getting into this family, it's going to be Ruby." Cassidy said with a smile. "That granddaughter of yours is something special, and my Kameron sees it to."

"Speaking of that grandson of yours, where's he at by the way." Pauline asked.

"With his Gramps at the Lowes store," she said.

Ruby to was with her Papa and like always, she had her clip board with her with his list on top; a pen to cross out each item. It was what they did every third Saturday of the month, and afterwards they'd go to lunch and talk like time waited on them. He had taken Ruby on that venture before she could walk and she had grown accustom to it.

Her stomach growled almost yelling at her. She poked it lightly thinking that it would stop like it always did, but this time it didn't. Her Papa stopped cold down isle ten where his drill bits, screws, and chair pins for Mrs. Fletcher's antique chair were. The look in his eyes was priceless; the caring papa bear rushing to finish so he could feed his cub. It made her laugh all the time.

"Papa," she looked up from the clipboard. "We have two more items to get and then, we can check out." She patted her stomach as if it were going to do some good.

"I'm hurrying peanut." He hurried down the aisle old man style. "I hear that tummy of yours way over here."

Ruby just laughed and shook her head. In rushing to try and feed his granddaughter, Big Jake had passed the drill bits he needed and his pins to put in Mrs. Fletcher's chair. Ruby sighed in frustration as the drill bits always sat up top where she couldn't reach them, and she'd have to go find a Lowes employee to get them down.

"Darn it." She said.

"Is this what you needed?" Kameron reached over her and grabbed the bits.

"Kameron," she seemed surprised. "Thanks," she said. "They act like only tall people purchase these things."

"Ah, yeah," he caught himself staring at her. "I suppose they need to fix that." He said, looking at her again. "So, you're with your grandpa?" He asked.

"Yeah, yeah," she scratched off the drill bits and the pins. "We do this every third Saturday of the month." She looked at her Papa talking with Kameron's grandfather.

"Cool," he said, gazing at her. "Yeah," he said. "I wanted to hang out with my Gramps so…"

"Here you are." She said, her stomach growled loud again, and she couldn't help but laugh.

"Somebodies hungry," Kameron laughed.

"Yeah, embarrassing," she laughed again. "Papa,

we're done." She beckoned for him.

"My Gramps and I are gonna stop and have lunch." He said. "Why don't you and your grandfather come and join us." He said, seems like they have a lot to catch up on."

Her Stomach growled again as if it were preventing her from saying no. "Ah, are you sure?"

"Of course I'm sure," he said. "I'll even buy this time."

"No you won't," she said as she went and got her grandfather's basket, and hugged and kissed Mr. Mosely.

"You have something against me buying you lunch?" He laughed and followed her.

Big Jake did nothing but laugh when he saw Ruby come and hijack his shopping cart. It was a ritual of some sort; for him every time he took a shopping trip to Lowes there seemed to always be somebody there that he would run into, and have an extended conversation with. In all honesty, if Ruby didn't come and take his basket, he would stand nearly forever, or until his old back had given out.

He and Mosely sat in the comfortable chairs talking and watching both their grandkids check out for the both of them. They didn't get the chance to see each other often, but when they did they made up for it. Before they knew it, Ruby and Kameron had placed all of their items in both trucks and they left their comfortable seats to join them. Kameron and Ruby stood shoulder to shoulder making small talk. And, as both grandfathers walked gingerly to their trucks, they noticed the two chatting and they smiled at each other as if their smiles meant something and they did. They could finally see what the women had seen all along. The two of them looked good together, Big Jake wondered if Ruby felt it since she was so into that Garrett boy.

"Say Wells," Mr. Mosely said. "My grandson and I are going to lunch, why don't y'all come and join us." He said.

"See," Kameron nudged Ruby's shoulder. "I was just thinking the same thing." He snuck in a stare.

"I bet you were." His Gramps mumbled underneath his breath. Somehow Big Jake had managed to hear him, and he laughed.

"I don't have a problem with it if my granddaughter doesn't."
He said.

"No, I'm down." She said.

"Where to," Mr. Mosely asked.

"Fat Cats," Ruby said.

"Fat Cats it is." Mr. Mosely said, as Kameron started up the
truck and followed Ruby.

"So," Ruby stopped her speech at the look in her Grandpa's
eyes.

She had seen that look before from the women at the shop
and she had seen it from her father when Solomon had sent her the
flowers. Now, her Papa had the same look in his and she could
almost tell what it meant. What was it about Kameron that made
everyone who observed her in his presences feel as if they belonged
together? Was there something that she was missing?

Okay, so he appeared to be a nice guy? He bought her a
journal and pen set with the College she would now be attending
come fall. And, he congratulated her with forty-eight of her favorite
flowers upon getting in Stanford. How he knew that tulips were her

favorite flowers still bugged her.

She didn't get it. But somehow everyone else did, that is except for Ginger. She stopped at the light, patting her hands to the music.

"That boy likes you," her Papa said out of the blue.

"How come I knew that you were going to say that?" She pulled away on green.

"Probably because you already know that, but you've got that hard head of yours stuck on that Garrett boy." He said.

"Papa," she laughed. "So, now your true feelings come out about Solomon after I cut him loose."

The look in his eyes was hilarious. Ruby couldn't help but laugh as she helped her Papa out of the truck. Kameron watched starry-eyed. He loved how caring she was and he was determined to get her to care that way for him.

"I don't believe it." He said.

"Don't believe what Mr. Wells?" Kameron opened the door for everyone.

"That my grand baby here has cut that Garrett boy loose."

Chapter 17

Kameron's eyes spoke long before his mouth could react. It was a look of relief and shock at the same time. He had seen how Ruby had looked at Solomon and he had wished for her to gaze at him like that. He knew something must have gone terribly wrong. But, in all honesty, he could care less. It was his opening and he knew it.

Ruby looked at her Papa briefly, but somehow her eyes fell prey to Kameron's. There was a joy in his eyes that she had not seen before; a determination from his demeanor that frighten her. In his eyes, he was telling her all that she needed to know, and he was stepping in to what he termed his rightful place.

Mr. Mosely removed his hat as he sat at the corner booth in the back towards the big picture window. Big Jake followed by removing his hat as well, and smiling at his granddaughter as if he were so proud, and he was. Kameron wasted no time sitting next to Ruby. Both smiled at his actions. Both waited to see what Ruby would do. Ruby scooted over to the far end. Kameron scooted over next to her. They sat shoulder to shoulder as if they were a couple.

"So," he looked at the menu, and then at her. "What are going to order?"

"Catfish and chips with a side order of rice pilaf." She said. "You," she looked at him.

"What you said," he closed the menu. "It sounds good to me." He looked at her.

"Papa's gonna order the mixed platter." She smiled like she knew, and she did.

"That's my peanut," he reached across the table and kissed her hand. "Always know what the old man likes," he said.

Kameron smiled and his Gramps smiled at Ruby and her Grandfathers' moment. It was special and anyone looking at the both of them could tell. They were like two peas in a pod and though they were from two different era's, their souls were connected in ways that she wasn't connected to anyone else.

Kameron loved that about her. He had seen it at Echo Park that day. He had seen it in the sway of her hips which kept him up late at night dreaming. He'd seen it in her smile, and even though she pushed him away, he couldn't help himself. His thoughts always found a way to come back to her.

"So, Gramps," Kameron said. "What are you going to order?"

"Same thing the old man's having." He smiled. "Man," he looked at Big Jake, "It's been a minute since I've been in this place."

"Oh, I hear you." Big Jake said. "But hey," he said. "Thank God we are here now." He chuckled.

"I'm with you with that man." Mr. Mosely said.

He cleared his throat and looked at Ruby and instantly he smiled. "Miss Ruby," he said. "I am so proud of you." He shook his head. "Stanford, Girl, you know that's pretty big time around here." He said. "You go down there and make us little folks down the hill proud." He laughed at himself.

"I will." She said.

"Man you gotta to be proud of her," Mr. Mosely said.

"Very," Big Jake said. "Just like you've got to be proud of this grandson of yours," he looked at Kameron.

"Oh yeah, this cat here is sharp. Now Mrs. Ruby, you might want to latch on to this dude cause, he's going places just like you."

He winked at his Grandson.

"I'm in firm agreement with that." Her grandfather said. "And Kameron might want to latch on to Peanut to." Big Jake winked at Ruby.

Kameron cleared his throat and Ruby playfully punched him in the arm. He moaned and rubbed his arm, pretending that it hurt when it didn't. It was a step in the right direction for him. For once, he felt as if he had gotten to first base with her. However, his goal was to hit a home run with her.

The waitress had come and took all of their orders. They sipped on sweet tea, lemon aid, and munched on cracklings. Big Jake and Mr. Mosely had soon forgotten the two of them were there and struck out on their own conversation. Kameron turned towards Ruby and nicked her on her thigh as if he owned it.

"So," he said. "If you don't mind me asking, what happened between you and lover boy?" He asked.

"He was just being Solomon." She said.

"What does that mean?" He looked confused.

"He cheated on me." She munched on a crackling.

"What," he said. "I'm so sorry. I do not understand how he could do that to you."

"Me neither, but he did." She said. "I guess he can't just be satisfied with one girl." She looked at him and hunched her shoulders.

"I could." He gazed into her eyes, and stroked her arm softly. "I could definitely be so satisfied with you." He pulled her bang away from her eyes.

Their plates had arrived and she breathed a sigh of relief. She could tell by the way that he looked in them that he meant what he said. They bowed their heads as Big Jake said grace over the meals. He placed his strong hand in hers and held it and she liked it though she told herself that she didn't.

His touch was warm and caring. His stroke was easy and loving, and the way that he held her hand made her not want to let it go. She knew right now that she should be thinking of Ginger, but she didn't. At the moment, all she could think of was herself. Half of her felt selfish, the other half wanting to get to know this man that was the exact opposite of Solomon.

What was happening to her now that hid from her before?
His feelings hadn't changed towards her. If anything they had
grown, could it be that truth had opened her eyes, or was it that she
was falling for a guy that had caused her friendship with Ginger to
grow cold?

Kameron found little ways to touch her again. If she reached
for a napkin he'd reach to and stroke her hand. If she reached for the
salt, he handed it to her and made sure her hand fell softly into his.
His hands were like a warm bath every time he touched her, so
unlike Solomon when they held hands.

"This is good stuff." He nicked her thigh again.

"Yeah," she said. "I love this place."

"Oh me to," he talked with his mouth full. "We need to
come back here." He looked at her. "But we can't," he said, turning
to face her, "because of Ginger." He looked at her with question
marks in his eyes.

The two Grandfather's saw that as a cue to leave and they
did. And as they moved across the way, Tommy's Grandfather
waved at them as he walked into the door. They waved and

Beckoned him over. Ruby sighed. What was she to say? She was trying to do what a best friend would do, but Ginger didn't appreciate it. She saw Ruby's efforts to try and get her and Kameron together as an act of betrayal, and even when she had called and apologized there was something about it that was fake.

"I'm sorry Kameron. It was a bad time, and Ginger, is or use to be, I don't know, my friend." She sat her fork down on her plate. "I never been in that situation before, and I don't know what you expected me to do? Then, there was Solomon, and drama, and…I'm sorry. I don't know what else to say." She sighed.

"Hey," he scooted even closer to her and placed his strong hand on the side of her face. "I'm sorry. I shouldn't have brought that up." He said. "But, I want you to know something, there is nothing you could have done to make me feel for Ginger what I feel for you, nothing."

"I know that now." She said.

"I came here to relax, to hang out with my grandparents', and learn more about my Gramps incredible business and I'm still learning." He laughed. "I don't know how he does it. I don't know how he ever done it all these years by himself?" He hunched his shoulders. "I never thought in a million years that I would come down here and see someone as beautiful as you, and fall in love. But, I have, and I don't know what to do about it." He gazed into her eyes wanting badly to kiss her.

Ruby eyes widen. She wanted to say something but her tongue wouldn't move. She wrestled with her brain. She got nervous, cleared her throat, and took a deep breath.

"Tell me what to do about it." He stroked her face, and then kissed her forehead.

"What do you want to do about it?" She turned to face him.

Kameron kissed her and she didn't fight it. And, it was the way that he kissed her that told her that his earlier words of being in love with her was not a lie. Not even Solomon had kissed her like that; soft, feeling the tip of his tongue merging his with hers. She didn't want him to stop and he didn't want to. Time seemed to have stopped just for them.

At Fat Cats that day, she had forgotten about Ginger, and her crazy attempt to make something hers that wasn't. When their kissing had slowed and began to wean, Kameron stole sweet soft kisses from her luscious lips, and their stood Ginger with her mouth wide open. Kamari couldn't believe what he was seeing. He stood at the entry way at Fat Cats with his mouth to the floor, and his eyes glued on Ruby and Kameron.

He had warned Solomon about Kameron, but Solomon had an ego. He was used to having his way with women and he didn't take Kameron's interest in Ruby seriously. His ego had fooled him. And he thought that because Ruby had waited on him for so long that nothing could sweep her away from him. He was fooled by her puppy love and he thought that he had command over her heart.

Ruby's and Ginger's eyes connected and she saw a nasty revenge in them. The Ginger she once knew was gone. Ginger yanked Kamari by the arm and gave Ruby a vicious glare. Ruby and Kameron looked at each other. Kameron was clueless; Ruby an "oh my God" expression stood idled on her face. Kameron placed an arm around Ruby and rubbed her back softly.

"Are we okay?" He asked.

"Yeah," she looked at him, but her mind was on how Ginger looked at her.

Reality had hit Ginger; a cold slap in the face. The man she had dreamed about never was hers. That hot summer day in Echo Park had sealed her fate, sadly it had slipped under her nose and she didn't know it. She felt betrayed and foolish. And it was time to give Ruby a taste of her own medicine. Anyone who came into her pathway was subjected to her wrath and that included Kamari, who just genuinely loved Ginger for who she was. He too was fooled by Ginger's pretense feelings for him as she was fooled by her fantasy with Kameron.

When Ginger had fed him, had cuddled with him, got him feeling manly, she knew that it wouldn't take much to get him in bed. It didn't and this was where her master plot to destroy Ruby had begun. Ginger's father had called out to her, but she was too busy calling out to Kamari in his bedroom. He trotted downstairs and ran into his wife Jasmin.

"Have you seen our daughter?" He asked.

"No, why," she said and headed to what use to be the room where she once painted.

"I just wanted to see my baby girl is all?" He bit into a green apple.

"She's probably out with her friends, or making deliveries." She sat the framed paintings aside. "To be honest, I don't know what the girl does on a regular basis." She took out more paintings.

"Really," he took another bit of his apple.

"Marcus she is seventeen years old. She almost grown." She said. "Besides, we haven't been seeing eye to eye lately, and soon she'll be going to college somewhere, if we have the money?"

"Is it just me or is my wife not happy?" He massaged her shoulders.

"How could I be when you made too hasty of a decision to just up and leave your job?" She said.

"Oh, so we're still on the career thing," he said. "Baby, I missed my little girl growing up. I missed being with my wife. I missed taking you to nice restaurants on weekends, having picnics in the park, and fixing you breakfast in bed on a Sunday morning."

He sighed. "Money is not everything." He raised his voice. "I know. I've lived it from country to country, and bad connections, sleeping on planes, was giving up some of that so bad?" He said.

"Yes," she said. "Yes it was, because we're over extended, and your daughter doesn't have a college fund."

"What?" He said. "You dipped into my baby's college fund?"

"I didn't want to." She said.

"But, you did, when I said, that no matter what neither of us touches that," he raised his voice again.

"It was either that, or we lose this house." She yelled back.

"You get out of my house." He said. "Now!"

She stood their looking dumbfounded. For a moment, she couldn't move, and it was as if her brain didn't comprehend what her husband had just said to her. Tears mounted in her eyes and now she felt bad. The look in her eyes said all that she wanted to say, but would bring to reality at how horrible of a mom she was to squander her daughter's college fund over loneliness and a false image that she couldn't possibly live up to.

She gathered her paintings, placed them in the back of her Mercedes. She grabbed her purse and sped out of the driveway. Now, she worried about Ginger, and she worried about what she would think and how much she would hate her. So many things roamed through her mind as she drove her Mercedes with no direction in mind.

Night had fell upon her and her cell rang. She knew by the sound of it that it was Ginger, and she let it go to voice mail, fearing that she would lose it. She had driven for hours and had parked into the Regency Gardens in Berkley, California. Her eyes were swollen from crying. She blew her nose and entered the hotel, checked in and went directly to her room and fell on her bed crying profusely.

Her cell rang again, it was Ginger, but again, she didn't answer. Not answering made her cry even more. She was miserable and in a horrible funk and she hated feeling that way. Perhaps a drink would loosen her up, and help her think, and make up something when she returned her daughter's call. She dried her tears, showered and replaced her make up and went downstairs to the bar.

She sat decked out in a yellow wrapped dressed that showcased her figure, and showed off her sexy yellow thighs. She sat her clutch on the table of the bar and ordered a glass of Merlot. She tossed her hair back from her face and thanked the bartender. He tilted his head and smiled.

"Jasmin Maples, how long has it been." Bobby Garrett said.

"Bobby," she said, looking surprised to see him. "It's been a while." She said, taking a sip of her wine. "So, is this where you've been hiding yourself?"

"Now, you're starting to sound like my ex," he looked at her legs. "I've been here for a little while." He ordered a drink.

"My question is what brings you here?" He said.

"Ah," she took another sip of wine. "You don't want to know." She said.

"Try me." He lowered his eyes down to her legs, then back up to her breast.

"I'd rather not talk about it." She said.

"Trouble in paradise," he took a sip of his scotch.

She looked at him and finished her glass of wine and ordered another one. "You would know about that wouldn't you?"

"Oh," he snickered. "I see that there's still some hateration for me in Oak Grove." He gazed at her. "You are wearing that dress." He stole another look at her legs.

"Same old Bobby," she took a sip of her wine.

"Bartender is this woman not beautiful" He said. "Is she not wearing that dress?" He finished his scotch and ordered another.

"I can't disagree with you there man." He winked at Jasmin.

"You are bad." She sipped more wine and she began to feel a little giddy.

"So, Marcus hasn't been home a minute and you're already giving the man trouble." He said.

Her eyes widen and a curious look came across her face. "How'd you know he was back in the states?"

"Word gets around in a small town." He said. "Even up here," he took a drink.

"Secrets in Oak Grove don't have a shelf life," she said, and sipped more of her wine.

"I didn't know it was a secret." He said, focusing on her

legs.

"Doesn't matter," she said. "When's the last time you saw your son?"

Marcus paused, and frowned somewhat. "He doesn't want to see me. What can I do?"

"Try harder." She said. "He's your son."

"Yeah," he drank. "I've been doing that."

"Really," she said.

"Really, but can we talk about something else." He said.

"Um-hum," she said. "Say," she was starting to feel the wine inside of her head. "You know of anyone who would want to buy some art work?"

"Depends on who's selling it?" He starred at her.

"I am." She said. "I'm trying to fix something, and don't you dare ask me what." She laughed giddy.

"I may know some people." He said.

"I need assurance. Can you help me?"

"You need money?" He asked. "Cause, I got money," he gazed at her.

"I need to sell my work. Can you help me, or not." She took another drink of her wine.

"Can you help me?" He placed his hand on her leg.

She was drunk and the touch of his hand on her thigh made her hot in places she shouldn't have been. She pushed his hand away at first, but Bobby was charming and persistent and he found a way to put it up just a little higher underneath her dress, and it was getting to her. Before she knew it he had his fingers in a spot where only Marcus' had been. His fingers were highly skilled and he was turning her on to the point of where she accidently knocked over her empty wine glass. And as if the glass that fell had suddenly jarred some sense into her, she leaped up from the bar stool and ran off to her hotel room.

Chapter 18

Kameron barley slept a wink last night. All he could do was think about the taste of Ruby's lips and how she made him feel. It was better than even he had imagined. He wanted more. And now that the window of opportunity was wide open, he would leap through it and take her with him.

He was all smiles at the breakfast table. He hummed and he stirred his coffee with a fork rather than a spoon, and he didn't even pay it attention. He buttered his pancakes with a spoon and even tried cutting them with a spoon. His Granny watched knowing what it was, and who it was. And, she enjoyed seeing him love struck, and she watched him like she watched a movie at the dollar theater.

"You might want to use the knife and the fork to cut your pancakes, and the spoon to stir your coffee." She giggled. He looked embarrassed at first, but somehow it passed through him. He tasted his pancakes and syrup and it reminded him of Ruby's lips. He blew on his coffee and sipped.

"You know I heard about you and Miss Ruby yesterday."
She sat across from him. "Honey, come get your breakfast." She
called out to her husband.

"Coming," Mr. Mosely said.

"Gramps I know." He nearly laughed. "What can I say?"
He said. "It just happened."

"I told you baby. Girls like Ruby want men, not boys." She
ate. "Solomon was just a stepping stone to get to you." She winked.

"Oh," his Gramps took a seat at the table. "You mean you
can eat this morning?" He teased as he seasoned his coffee first, and
then buttered his pancakes.

"Gramps," he smiled again and chewed on his bacon. "She's
beautiful come on, and it just happened…it just did." He sipped
more coffee.

"Everybody in Fats' could see that." He pulled off his
baseball cap, said grace and went back to teasing his Grandson.
"Only love could make you kiss a woman like that."

"Jesus," he said with a smile as he put his plate into the sink.
"Gramps, I'll be in the loft working on my project." He said. "Let

me know when you're ready to go out on the truck."

"Grandson," he looked up at him. "You can have a day or whatever you need." He wiped his mouth. "I know you want to spend time with that girl." He munched on Bacon. "Hell, I would too."

"Just let me know when you're going out," he smiled. "And don't you dare leave without me," he left out of the door.

The Mosely's smiled at each other the way older people beamed when they witnessed old fashion love the way they had experienced it. It was all over Kameron's face anyone looking could tell. And, it was starting to show up in Ruby's face to. If her mother hadn't of gotten the news from her mother-in-law, she would have known it anyway.

Her entire demeanor was different, more distinctive than it was with Solomon. Ruby's eyes looked like they were in a dreamlike state. She sang love songs softly. She barely touched her breakfast, and she wiped down the kitchen counters over and over. Precious couldn't help but laugh. She was once there to.

She couldn't help herself. She thought more about Kameron

and she hadn't thought about Solomon once. She relived the kiss over and over and the more she did, the more she wanted to be in his presence so he could kiss her again. It was something about the way he did it. The way he held her face in the palm of his hand; and the way he kissed her lips. It made it all so special and it made her change the way she thought of him. In a way she never imagined, it made her connect to him the way he had already bonded with her. Finally, she was able to see what Tori and the other's saw about them.

Her phone rang as she was about to exit her front door. She stopped at the door to answer it. "Hold on Tori." She said. "Mama, I'm going to pick up Tori and then we're going to Papa's house." She said. "He needs us to paint some chairs he's refurbished."

"Alright," she kissed Ruby on the cheek. "And after that, it's Kameron's right," she smiled.

"Mama," she couldn't help but smile. "No," she said. "He hasn't asked yet."

"Oh, he will according to your Papa." She teased.

"Papa's exaggerating," she grinned. "Love you, gotta go."
She said. "Tori," another call came in. "Sorry, hold on a minute,"
she said.

"Alright," she said.

"Kameron," she sounded surprised. "Could you hold on for a
second?"

"Sure." He said.

"Tori, I'm on my way." She tossed her purse and her
belongings in the back of her father's truck. "It's Kameron…"

"It's who?" Tori's eyes widen. "Are you seeing him?"

"He's waiting. I have to go." She smiled. "Love you."

"Rue, damn it!" She heard a dial tone.

"Hey," she said. "I'm sorry about that. It was Tori."

"Oh," he said. "Did you need to talk to her?"

"I'm actually on my way to pick her up. My Papa needs us
to paint chairs that he's refurbished." She started her father's truck.

"Cool," he said. "Ah," he paused. "Are you going to be free
for dinner later on?" He asked.

"Sure," she said. "What did you have in mind?"

"Ah," he scratched his scalp. "Actually, I was going to make you dinner tonight. I know this quiet little spot." He turned around in his chair.

"You cook." She stopped at the stop light.

"All Mosely men cook," he grinned. "What," he said. "You don't believe me?"

"I guess I'll just have to see won't I?" She said.

"What time shall I pick you up?" He asked.

"No need, I have my daddy's truck." She made a left and went further down the block.

"But, what if I want to pick you up," he said.

"Well, if you want to, but…"

"But, it's solved," he said. "7 O'clock sound okay?"

"Perfect." She said. "Should I bring anything?" She turned into Tori's driveway.

"Just yourself," he said, leaning on his desk. "You know I couldn't sleep for thinking about you." He said.

"Me too," she placed the truck in park. "I'm at Tori's so…"

"Yeah, yeah," he knocked over his pencil dish. "Ah, I'll see you at seven." He said.

"See you." She said and hung up and screamed.

Tori rushed out of the door before Ruby could even blow. She practically leaped into Ruby's father's truck with a huge smile on her face. The look in Ruby's eyes suggested that something was going on between Kameron and her. It was all in Ruby's voice when she placed a dial tone in her ear. Something had happened between the two of them, or maybe Ruby was beginning to see the light. Tori was tired of guessing.

"Okay Rue, what's going on between you and Kameron?" She said.

"Well, for one, we're having dinner tonight at seven, and he's cooking." Ruby smiled. "I don't know how to say this…"

"Just say it Rue, say it." Tori was anxious.

"Long story short, we kissed yesterday at Fat Cats…"

Tori screamed and nearly blew Ruby's ears out in the truck. "What," she said. "What happened?"

"I don't know?" She said. "Maybe it was the way he opened

up to me. Maybe it was the way he held my hand when Papa said grace over the meal?" She looked at Tori. "I don't know really, but I know that I can't stop thinking about him."

"See I told you." Tori said. "And please don't ruin this by telling me that you're worried about Gin."

"Well," Ruby said.

"Rue, damn it," Tori said.

"It's not even like that Tori." Ruby said. "Relax, Jesus," she sighed. "Gin and Kamari just happened to walk in on us kissing."

Tori started screaming again uncontrollably. Ruby covered her ears at first and then she smacked Tori on the leg playfully as she attempted to make her stop. She started the truck and backed out of Tori's driveway and headed up the block.

"Tori if you don't stop." Ruby said, stopping at the light.

"Okay, okay, breathe Tori," she said. "My prayers have been answered."

"Oh Jesus," Ruby said, waiting for the light. "Don't start doing what the old folks do." She went through the light.

"Well, it worked didn't it?" She laughed.

Ruby glanced over at her and shook her head. "I'm not even gonna answer that."

"Don't," Tori giggled.

"You know," Ruby said, turning into her Papa's driveway. "The look in Gin's eyes was vengeful. It was so unlike her."

"Rue," she said. "We've been over this. Kameron wants you. It's that simple, and there's nothing you could have done to make him like Gin."

"That's what he said," she looked at Tori.

"See," Tori said. "Maybe Gin is getting it; you said she was with Kamari which is strange." She said.

"Strange exactly," Ruby removed the keys from the ignition. "She's up to something I know it." She sighed. "And whatever it is, she wants to hurt me, I can feel it."

"She can't hurt you Rue." Tori said. "And maybe by her spending time with Kamari, she'll see the light."

"Kamari really likes her. I just hope that she doesn't hurt him." Ruby said as her and Tori got out of the truck.

Ginger entered her front door only to hear her father yelling from the top of his lungs. She could only imagine who he was screaming at. She tried with no avail to contact her mother, but she didn't answer. She knew something was wrong. Whatever it was it had to do with her. What had happened to them? Since her father had returned from overseas, all they did was fight.

"Of course I blame you," he said. "You took my daughter's college fund and now I have to damn near liquidate everything to get it back." He slammed the phone down and looked directly into Ginger's face. "Baby listen," he said.

Ginger's bottom lip began to tremble; her eyes filled with tears. She rushed past her father and ran outside the door, jumped into his car and pulled off. She cried uncontrollably so much that underneath her chin became soaked with tears. She was furious at her mother and disturbed by her father for being so caught up into his career that he would allow such a thing like this to happen.

She wanted revenge. She wanted everyone that had hurt her in some way to pay; Ruby, Kameron, Tori, her mother and father. Somehow, she would see to it that they all did. She didn't know where to go. So, she parked behind Berry's and cried some more.

Her cell rang, but she didn't answer it.

It rang in desperation; first her father and then her father again; a repeated process that continued so much that she ended up shutting off her phone. A light tap penetrated the driver's side window. She jumped at first, wiped the tears from her face and eyes, and noticed that it was Solomon. She rolled down her window not in the mood which is how she approached him.

"I've got a lot on my plate right now Solomon. I can't be bothered right now." She said.

"Well," he said, "if it helps, I'm not in such a good mood myself. Kamari just informed me that Ruby and Kameron are an item now." His eyes carried a mixture; anger, shame, and embarrassment.

"Get in." She said, and unlocked the passenger's side door. "I guess it's no point in crashing her precious little surprise luncheon." She said.

"I think I'll go front her and old boy." He said.

"For what," she looked over at him.

"So, we just give up?" He looked at her strange.

"No," she looked at him. "We get even."

"That's what I'm talking about," he pumped his fist and twirled it in the air.

"Not like that," she turned to face him and suddenly the slit in her skirt revealed her honey colored legs.

Solomon felt a twinge in between his legs. He tried to fight it, but it got stronger and stronger. This couldn't be happening. He didn't even like Ginger. Somehow his eyes roamed up to her blouse which showed too much cleavage, and revealed a peek at her ripe breast, and that was it. He scooted closer to her and placed his hand far underneath her skirt.

She tossed his hand away at first, but it found its way back inside of her under ware and she couldn't help herself as she took pleasure to his touch. Solomon was a pro and he wasted no time in getting Ginger out of her panties and planted himself on top of her. The car rocked slowly at first, and Ginger's sandal gingerly started falling off of her feet. But, as Solomon gained his stride, the car went crazy in up and down motions as if it were going to tip over.

She yelled in pleasure from the top of her lungs and unconsciously wrapped her legs around him, sticking her acrylic nails into his flesh. She screamed the screams of Tiffney and Daphne, and all the others that had been privy to his irresistible tenderness with young ladies. Now, she could understand why they always came back, and under no circumstances did she want him to stop.

Nothing mattered now except how he was making her feel; Ruby had done herself a disservice when she had dumped him. Her father paced in panic. And mother like daughter lay in a foreign bed in a hotel room, calling out another man's name that wasn't her husbands. The consequences didn't matter at this point. What mattered was the insane pleasure that both the Garrett men gave to their women.

Chapter 19

Kamari looked at his hair in the mirror as he dressed and it was time for him to get a cut. He knew exactly who he would go to at Mr. Nelson's shop. He needed to talk to Solomon anyway about Ginger. She had a sudden change of heart which still baffled him. She never treated him disrespectful or anything, but their communication was kept to a minimum. He wondered what had happened that made her have wanted him. From what he had heard and from what he had seen, he knew that Ginger had it bad for Kameron. But Kameron had it bad for Ruby and hung around until she had caught his flu.

He had warned Solomon and he hated to have told him the dreadful news. The look on Solomon's face said it all. But after his anger had subsided, it was the most pitiful look that Kamari had ever seen. Solomon did care a lot for Ruby. It was a shame that he didn't know how to show her. However, now that he had Ginger, he would not make the same mistake.

"Son," Ben said to his Grandson Solomon. "You're awful quiet today. Is something wrong?" He asked.

"Nah," he lied. "I'm cool." He said, smacking his Grandfather's shoulder.

"Is something going on between you and Ruby?" He cleaned his clippers.

"We're not seeing each other anymore." He said.

"What?" His grandfather was shocked. "What happened?"

"Mosely's Grandson happened." He said. "I guess she felt she needed an upgrade since she's going to Stanford." He rolled his eyes. "But, it's cool." He lied again.

"Really," his grandfather looked at him. "You know I find that hard to believe." He sat his clippers down. "That girl was crazy about you, you sure you're telling the whole truth."

"Pop," he smiled through his pain. "I'll admit I was warned by Kamari first, then Tommy that he was after her, but I didn't take it serious, and the next thing I knew," he picked his clippers back up. "Kamari's telling me that he saw them at Fat Cats and they weren't just talking." He said.

"So, Mosely's Grandson stole your girl," he said.

"Yeah," he said. "I tried calling her several times and she wouldn't even answer."

"But, I'm still on what would make someone so into you just go after him," he said. "I don't get it."

"Me neither," he smiled a false smile. "If I knew that, she'd be mines and not his."

"So, you're just gonna let her go that easily?" He asked.

"Pops, I can't make her want me. You know." He finished cleaning his clippers.

"That's a good young woman there son, if it were me, I wouldn't give up on her so easily." He said. "But that's just me," he dried off his clippers and smiled as Kamari and the others came in.

Solomon's eyes nearly popped out of his sockets at the sight of Kamari. Seeing Kamari made him think of Ginger and the lustful interlude that they shared just last night. He tried to be calm. He tried to act like his normal self, but in looking at his boy, he saw Ginger.

He heard her screams. He heard her moans. He heard the

calling out of his name, and he remembered how had begged him not to stop. He quickly excused himself and went into the bathroom to get a hold of himself.

"Get it together Solomon. Get it together. You can do this." He said to himself and took a deep breath. He stayed in the rest room another few minutes. He flushed the toilet as if he had used it, and turned on the faucet as if he were washing his hand. He paused and then went out of the bathroom door.

"Yo, man," he said to Kamari. "What's up?"

"Nothing much man, just needed a cut," he smiled.

"I got you covered." He said and wrapped a smock around him. "So, what's going on?"

"Ginger man," he grinned. "I think she's really into me man." He said.

"Yeah, well," he cleared his throat. "That's cool man, that's cool."

Solomon turned on his clippers and began cutting Kamari's hair. He tried to change the subject bringing up about the

San Francisco Giants wanting Tommy to play for them. Kamari talked briefly on it, but went right back to Ginger. He tried with Boyd the next time, how he had hooked up with Mr. Fletcher's Great niece, and how he had committed to the Navy after high school. It was the same result. He spoke on it briefly and went right back to Ginger.

He was in love with this girl and everyone in the shop including him could see it. Ginger However was incapable of love. The only thing she appeared to have loved was Solomon making her howl in the back seat of her father's Benz. He could kick himself for what he had done. This, he didn't know how to fix either, and who could he confide to that would truly understand? He finished Kamari's cut and rushed him out of the chair and the shop.

The look on his Grandfather's face was odd. Kamari's facial expression was strange as he stood for a moment looking at Solomon. He had come there to talk about his girl and to talk about the night that they had spent together, but Solomon was acting weird. It was Ruby he knew it. He had hurt her and Kameron had consoled her and she was his now.

Kameron was a man and Solomon a wild child unable to fit in a grown man's shoes. He thought he could by how he dazzled young women in the bedroom, but it was more to a relationship than that. Real women liked to be courted by a man, in fact, they expected it. It was something about their décor that allowed a gentleman to see it and seize the opportunity; that was Kameron, a blood hound in waiting.

Kameron checked on his chicken and dumplings. He lifted the pot top and looked at how the dumplings and the chicken were summering in a rich chicken sauce. He lowered his fire and looked at his watch.

"Granny," he called out to his Grandmother.

"Yeah," she appeared in the kitchen. "Um," she said, "smells good."

"Thanks," he said. "It should, it's your recipe. Ah, listen," he said. "Could you keep an eye on this? I have to go get Ruby and I don't want to burn the chow." He said.

"Of Course," she smiled. "I'm impressed and she will be too." She said.

"I hope so." He grabbed the tulips from off of the table. "And, I hope she likes the dumplings?"

"It's my recipe isn't?" She smiled.

"Yes it is." He kissed her on the check and left out of the door.

Ruby had put on her little black dress that just happened to be a jay bird blue with a darling white sash that tied to the side of the dress. It was Ginger's design alright and it seemed to have fit the occasion. How she wished that Ginger and she were on better terms? How she wished that she'd really come to her senses? The last look in her eyes was cold and unfeeling, so unlike the Ginger she knew. This was not how their summer was supposed to turn out.

She sighed put on her lipstick; sprayed on her Red Door perfume, and put on her teardrop earrings that her Papa had bought her one year for a birthday present. Her cell rang and by the sound she knew that it was Tori and she laughed when she answered it.

"You were supposed to let me at least put on my shoes." She said.

"Put them on then," Tori teased. "What do you have on?"

"Can you believe it, the blue dress Ginger made for me?" Ruby grabbed her shoes from her closet.

"Lord bless the dress, and the lady wearing it," Tori said.

"Tori," Ruby laughed.

"What," she said. "You're off to a great start and you don't need her energy Rue."

"Will you stop?" Ruby sat on her bed.

"Okay, I'll stop." She said. "Anyway," she said. "I have some great news."

"What," Ruby paused from putting on her shoe.

"I got accepted into San Francisco State for the fall term." Tori said, and screamed.

"What," Ruby shouted as she jumped up and down in her room.

Precious heard Ruby's screams from her garden. She immediately stopped what she was doing and rushed into Ruby's room, only to find her being seventeen and too excited about something. She breathed a sigh of relief when she saw that she was alright.

"Girl, what is going on?" She said. "I could hear you all the way outside."

"Tori got accepted into San Francisco State, and she's going this fall." She said.

"Well tell her congratulations, and stop all that yelling and caring on." She shook her head. "You nearly scared me into a heart attack."

"Sorry," she said.

"You look beautiful by the way." She said, and fiddled with her hair.

"Thanks," she said. "Tori I have to go, but I am so happy for you. You know this means we're having a sleep over." She said.

"I'm down." She said. "Don't leave out any details." She said.

"I won't." Ruby said and hung up. "Yes!" Ruby clutched her first.

Precious stood in her daughter's room just looking at her. She was a flower in full bloom. It seemed like she had blinked and she was walking; another blink and she was a near grown woman about to take flight into the world. She lifted her chin and fiddled with her hair some more. The doorbell rang and Ruby and her mother left her room. Ruby answered the door with her shoes in her hand.

Kameron stood in front of Ruby with a bouquet of yellow tulips in his hand. Her eyes lit up as she took the flowers from him and he kissed her. Ruby invited him in and her mother took the flowers to the kitchen and placed them in a vase. She couldn't help but smile for she admired Kameron's persistence.

"You look beautiful." He starred at her. "Wow!" He said.

"Thank you." She said. "You're not so bad yourself." She gazed into his eyes.

"Thank you." He said, and kissed her again. "Not as beautiful as the lady standing before me." He found her lips again, and she liked it.

Precious cleared her throat. "Would you like to sit down?" She asked.

"Ah, I'd love to but I've got my Granny watching the dumplings." He said. "I hope you like chicken and dumplings." He looked unsure.

"She loves them." Her mother said.

"I do." She said.

"Good," he said looking at her.

"Well," Ruby said, but paused her speech as her father walked into the door.

Jacob smiled a father's smile when a daughter had her first real date. Kameron was a Mosely, but Ruby was his daughter and he checked him over in detail like a fine tooth comb. Kameron suddenly became a little nervous.

"Baby," he kissed his daughter.

"Daddy, this is Kameron, Kameron this is my dad." She said.

"Nice meeting you Mr. Wells." Kameron said, shaking his hand.

"You to son," he said, eyeing him the way a father would. "So, you're taking my daughter out?" He asked.

"Ah," Kameron said. "Actually, I'm making her dinner at my grandparents' house."

"Oh," he said. "Making dinner," he looked at his wife. "That's pretty serious," he looked at Kameron.

"Daddy," Ruby said. "Stop," she looked at her mother for help.

"Jake," Precious took him by the hand. "Do you want their dinner to get cold?"

"Yes," he said.

"Go," Precious laughed. "Go," she said, as she blow a kiss at her daughter.

Ruby took Kameron by the hand and rushed him out of the door. He opened the door to his Granny's CTS Cadillac for Ruby. As he got in on the driver's side, there was an odd look on his face. Ruby looked at him and smiled.

"It's okay if your folks want to come to dinner." He started the car.

"No," she said. "Pay no attention to my father."

Mrs. Cassidy sat the table for Kameron. The table setting carried a woman's touch. There were long stem blue and white candles lit. There were blue and white silverware to match the blue and white plates. She had set a bouquet of white daisy's and blue carnations in a dainty vase, adding a romantic touch to the patio.

She heard the door and she quickly stepped in the family room and sat as if nothing had happen. Mr. Mosely laughed and shook his head. He mouthed as Kameron unlocked the door. "I'm going to tell." Cassidy tossed a pillow at him as Kameron and Ruby walked into the door.

Ruby and Kameron laughed at their horseplay. Kameron paused in the family room entry with his hand locked into Ruby's. Mrs. Cassidy smiled at the sight of the two of them. In her mind, they looked so good together. She was proud that he had seen what she had always seen in Ruby and was not swayed by Ginger's flare.

She stood and hugged Ruby warmly and kissed her on her cheek. Mr. Mosely followed and complimented her on her attire. She thanked him and as she did, she saw the beautiful setting out back and her eyes danced happily in her head.

"Did you do that for me?" She turned to face him.

"Yeah," he said, looking at his Grandmother who winked. "I wanted it to be special." He said, hugging Ruby and mouthing to his

Granny a thank you. "Granny, Gramps," he said. "There's plenty."
He smiled.

"We appreciate that Grandson, but these old birds already
ordered us a catfish dinner from Fat Cats. You young people enjoy
yourself." He said as the doorbell rang.

"There's a surprise dessert in the refrigerator." Mrs. Cassidy
said.

"Thanks Granny." He said as he closed the sliding glass door
to the family room.

"Welcome." She said as she sat at the kitchen table with her
husband about to eat their meal.

Ruby stood for a minute or two admiring the stunning
scenery out back. It was perfect with a striking yellow moon that
hovered over their table, and a sky full of stars that blanketed their
table and shined like tiny crystals in the sky. It was lovely and she
was overwhelmed at how much he put into it, and how much he
obviously cared about her. Solomon had never done that for her, but
yet Kameron took the time. She was impressed.

Like a gentlemen, he scooted out her chair. She sat in it and he gently nudged her closer into the table. He sat alongside of her, blessed the food and then served her, then himself. The smell of the dumplings hit her nostrils and she tasted.

"This is so good." She said. "Did you really make this?"

"Yes, I did." He smiled. "But, I can see you don't believe me."

Ruby had to snicker. She really didn't believe him. The only men she knew who could tie an apron on and make your mouth water was her father and her Grandfather. Kameron looked to handsome to cook, but then again what did his gorgeous looks have to do with his skills in the kitchen? Kameron smiled at her and wiped his mouth. He excused himself from the table, opened the sliding glass door and called out to his Granny.

"Yeah," she paused from eating and came out to the patio where they dined.

"Please tell Ruby that I made these dumplings," he couldn't help but smile.

"He most certainly did." She said. "You know I wouldn't lie to you."

"Wow!" She said. "I'm impressed."

"Thanks Granny." He said.

"You welcome baby." She said. "There's a banana crème pie in the refrigerator." She said as she took her place back at the kitchen table.

Ruby smacked his hand playfully. He pretended that it hurt, but it didn't. She ate more of her meal and sipped on sweet tea. He ate and watched her. At times he couldn't believe that she was sitting on the patio with him, eating a meal he had cooked, and allowing him to be romantic with her. He had dreamed of it and wondered if it would ever happen. But, he was a Mosely and Mosely's never gave up on anything.

She was stuffed and so was he. Dessert would have to wait. She tried to help him remove the plates and silverware, but he wouldn't allow it. Before she could blink he had removed it all accept the lighted candles that crackled like a romantic fireplace. Ruby sat looking at the stars and rubbing her cool arms from the sweet breeze of summer.

Kameron draped his warm sweater around her shoulders and sat behind her laying his cheek next to hers. For a moment there was silence between the two of them. As his cheek rested on hers, she remembered what she had wanted in a man. Now that she respected stillness and had opened herself up to it; fate had memorized her request and handed Kameron to her.

She lay back in his firm chest, her eyes following the big dipper. For what she had wanted in a man, she couldn't believe that she had missed it in Kameron and had tried to force it in Solomon. She had waited in a long line for Solomon. But what she didn't know was that she was really waiting for Kameron. She didn't see it then, but destiny had made the foggy clear.

Kameron kissed her cheek and then her neck. "On nights like this, I could sit out and watch the stars all night." He said.

"Me too," she turned to face him and they kissed, the stars watching them.

"What do you work on in the loft?" She asked.

"Would you like to see?" He said.

"Yeah," she said.

She stood and he took hold of her hand and they walked a short distance to the shed. From a little girl she had always wanted to go inside, but every time she tried, her Papa would go get her, pick her up, place her in his arms, and suddenly she'd forget. Funny after all these years she was finally getting the chance to see it.

It was beautiful. It amazed her how thick wooden tree logs could be made into something as fine-looking as the shed. However, the way the place was decorated inside was an understatement to call it a shed. It was decorated with love, she could tell. There was a cozy brown sectional in the front room; a stone fireplace with cut wood in an iron tray waiting for the cold of old man winter. There were pictures of family hanging from the walls and on the table a big thick book that said dreams on it.

Upstairs she knew was the loft. She could see Kameron's work station from the bottom, and as she veered to the right to try to see more, he took her hand and guided her upstairs and she was amazed. There was a deck that seemed to open up to the universe and she could see why Kameron loved to work there.

"So," she said. "This is where you do all of your work."

"Yeah," he said. "Come here." He reached for her hand. "I want to show you something."

She came and stood next to him and he uncorked his drawings and spread them out on his oversized work desk. Her mouth opened and for a moment she was speechless. He had recaptured the entire strip mall and had turned it into a daunting Galleria. It encompassed every mom and pop shop in Oak Grove, but gave it a mall type feel. And he designed a restaurant row exclusively for restaurants, with a nice spot for his Gramps snow cone business in the off seasons; even the dollar theater and the Gingerbread had gotten an upgrade.

"It's wonderful Kameron." She said. "I can't believe it." Her eyes were stunned. "What made you do this?"

"My Gramps, Granny, you," he kissed her.

"Me," she smiled.

"Yes you." He kissed her again.

Before they knew it, they were engaged in lover's kissing. Kameron had slid his strong hands down to her lower hips and heated Ruby's body temperature. Ruby placed her forehead next to his and looked into his eyes.

"You weren't supposed to stop." He teased her lips.

"Um-hum," she giggled. "You could make me do something right now that I don't need to be doing." She kissed him softly.

"Really," he wrapped his arms around her waist.

"Yes," she said. "You still haven't told me why?" She looked into his eyes.

"Come with me." He said.

He grabbed a warm blanket and Ruby's hand and opened the glass door to the deck. He spread the blanket over them and she sat in between his legs; his arms draped around her waist. The stars seemed to have followed them as they looked into the beautiful night sky. Ruby snuggled up against Kameron's chest and wondered what she had ever saw in Solomon? Kameron of course was in heaven. He cleared his throat and began to answer her question.

"Oak Grove is that small town of yester year." He said.

"The small town that held throughout the course of time and that amazed me." He placed his cheek next to hers. There's a since of family here, community, and quietness that reveals things." He snuggled a little closer. "You just have to be open to it and listen for it and when you do," he said. "Truth unfolds." He said. "I had no idea what my project would be. But somewhere in the quietness of this little place, it found me; gave me that drawing in there and you."

Ruby sat massaging his warm hands and listening. She had lived in Oak Grove all of her life and none of that had ever dawn on her until now. How could she have missed it? She sighed and welcomed his lips to her cheek. By viewing the stars it felt as if she were seeing time.

Time it seemed raced by; while Ruby and Tori prepared for orientations for college, Ginger had found herself vomiting all over her fabric. She had thought it to be a nasty virus at first. But when it persisted, she found herself at the clinic, and she nearly fainted when Mrs. Cassidy had told her that she was pregnant.

Chapter 20

Ginger sat starry-eyed at the news of her pregnancy. She was numb for a minute and she couldn't speak or move. Mrs. Cassidy sat on a rolling stool and rolled herself over to Ginger and took hold of her hand. She tried her hardest not to appear shocked. But, her eyes told Ginger all that she tried to hide.

"Baby," she said. "You know that you have options."

Ginger sighed with tears in her eyes. "Are you sure?" She said. "Can you take the test again?"

"Baby," she held her hand. "I've done it three times. You're pregnant sweetie. I know you don't want to hear it, but you're pregnant."

"Oh my God!" She said. "I can't believe this."

"Baby," Mrs. Cassidy said. "I've got to ask." She said. "Do you know who the father is?"

"I'd rather not say." Her voice cracked and tears slowly dripped down her check. "Can you not tell my parents?" She said. "I know when they find out, they're going to flip."

"I won't say a thing." Mrs. Cassidy patted her hand. "Honey, if you need anything let me know. I've been in the baby business a long time, and I'm here to help." She said.

"Thanks," Ginger took a Kleenex from Mrs. Cassidy and left.

Her entire world seemed to have fallen apart. She sat in her father's car and cried. Her thoughts ran wild. How could she have been so stupid? Why couldn't she have swallowed her pride and talked to Ruby and Tori? What was she thinking? Without a shadow of a doubt she knew that it was Solomon's.

Ginger felt as if her head were about to explode. She had cried herself into a frenzy and it gave her a splitting headache. She blew her nose, dried her tears and drove a mile down the road to the lakeside. She parked and sat for a minute and then got out of the car and let the summer breeze hit her face. She debated whether she should tell Solomon or just make plans to get rid of it and tell no one. She sighed and out of frustration she called Solomon.

"Yo," he said in a glad tone.

"Solomon, its Ginger." She fought back the tears.

"I'm at the lakeside and you need to get here right away. It's important."

"Well, it will have to wait," he said. "I've got a couple of men who are waiting for me to cut their hair."

"Solomon, I mean it." Her tonality changed. "Get down here now."

"Look," he said. "You ain't my woman, and just cause we got busy in the back seat of your pops car, don't mean you can put no demands on me."

"I'm pregnant." She said.

He paused. His mouth nearly dropped to the floor, and for a minute his tongue couldn't move. He sunk into his own barber's chair and the men in the shop stopped talking looking at him. It was as if someone had said that his mother or his pop's had died. He rubbed his hand over his forehead in disbelief.

"Solomon, are you still there?" She said.

"Ah, ah, yeah, I'm on my way." He hung up. "Ah pop," he said. "I have to go and attend to something. I promise I'll be back." He rushed out of the door.

"That didn't look to good," Mr. Fletcher said.

"No sir," his Pop's said. "No, it certainly didn't." A worried looked stood in his eyes.

Cassidy finished up at the clinic. It was a busy day and she was somewhat exhausted. Ginger had rolled across her mind. She remembered delivering her at Mercy Hospital and now she was pregnant. Young people these days, she thought to herself. They could do adult things, but couldn't handle adult responsibilities. Her hope for her was that she would not do anything stupid.

Her cell phone rang and she answered as she got into her car. "Hello," she said.

"Hey girl," Pauline said. "I thought you had given up working at the clinic."

"Oh hush," she laughed. "They were down two doctors and I couldn't tell them no."

"Yeah right," Pauline laughed.

"Woman, if you ain't feeding me as tired as I am, then just hush your mouth." She laughed and started her car.

"I got teacakes and hot turkey sandwiches with my special

gravy and sweet tea." Pauline said.

"Say no more," Cassidy said. "I'm on my way over and I've got some juicy, juicy news and if it gets out, I know where it came from." She laughed.

"Oh lord," Pauline said. "Now, you got me curious." She said.

"I'm on my way." She pulled off.

Solomon rushed to the lakeside almost forgetting to put his Pop's truck in park. He found Ginger by a big oak tree and as he approached her, he had never seen her look so sad. He didn't know what to say to her.

He sighed, placed his hands in his pockets. "Are you sure you're pregnant?"

"Mrs. Cassidy did it three times." She said.

"Oh damn," he said. "Mrs. Cassidy was the one who told you." He took a deep breath. "You couldn't have gone to another doctor?"

"I didn't know that I was pregnant when I went there Solomon. I thought I had the flu." She said.

"You know she's gonna start talking and my Pop's is gonna know, then my mama, then, all of Oak Grove." He said. "Damn, this is messed up."

"Tell me about it." She said.

"You weren't on something?" He asked.

"We're you?" She yelled. "You are not going to put all this on me."

Solomon put his hands on the top of his head. He was dumbfounded. He couldn't believe that one casual night had made him a father. He was too young, just seventeen with hopes and dreams; now a bombshell had hit and he didn't know how to deal with it. What was his Pop's and mother going to think?

"So," he sighed. "What are you going to do?"

"I don't know?" She said. "I don't know?" She took a deep breath.

Cassidy sighed as she took a seat on Pauline's couch. She could smell the teacakes before she hit the door. She took comfort in sitting on the couch. She sighed and reached for a teacake on her plate.

"Lord this couch has never felt so good," Cassidy said.

"One of them days huh," Pauline said, as she took a seat across from her. "Girl, I know what that feels like." She said. "Helping that son of mines at the restaurant nearly wipes me out at times." She poured them both some sweet tea.

"I can imagine." She sipped on sweet tea. "When is it not busy in his place?"

"Ain't that the truth," she said. "So, what's the dirt?" Pauline bit into a teacake.

"Girl, you are not going to believe this." Cassidy said. "It stays here. I mean it." She said.

"Lips are zipped." She said.

"Ginger, you know that Maples girl," she said. "She came into the clinic today thinking that she had the flu. The child looked tired and said that she couldn't seem to keep anything on her stomach." She bit into a teacake. "I asked her, what was the last thing that she ate. She said it was a cheese burger with the works. Just to make sure that it wasn't food poison, I ran a couple of test and when the results came back child," she reared back in her seat.

"It tells me that she's pregnant."

"What!" Pauline said. "Little Ginger, pregnant, I'm speechless."

"Well so was I," she said. "And to make sure, I did it three times, each time the same result." She said.

"How did she react when you told her?" Pauline sipped tea.

"She broke down and cried. I felt sorry for the child." Cassidy said.

"Well did she say who the father was?" Pauline asked.

"She said that she'd rather not say, which leads me to believe that she knows who it is, but she's too ashamed to tell." Cassidy bit into another teacake.

"I wonder who that could be?" Pauline said.

"Who knows girl?" She said. "I just hope the girl don't do nothing stupid."

"I know it." Pauline said. "It doesn't take much for these young folk to go over the edge, and they always trying to be grown."

"Tell me about it." Cassidy said. "I know her parents will flip when they find out."

"If she tells them," Pauline said.

"That's the truth," Cassidy said. "See why I didn't want her with my Kameron," she sipped more of her sweet tea.

Um-hum," Pauline laughed. "Good lord," she said. "Ruby is gonna have a fit when she finds out; there practically like sisters, and I'm not gonna say anything." She said.

"Better not," she said. "Speaking of Ruby," she said. "Kameron cooked dinner for her and I made it all nice and romantic for them out on the patio." She smiled. "Ruby was flattered, and they had a wonderful time." She said. "Between you and me, I think that he's going to get that co-op, or whatever you call it. They've called him back twice. I've been praying girl for the lord to make a way for my grandchild to stay here." She said.

"God works in mysterious ways." Pauline finished her teacake. "Ruby was a miracle."

"I remember when she was born." Cassidy said. "She came in the world kicking and screaming. She had so much power in those tiny lungs. I knew she was gonna be special."

"You know I can't agree with you more." She said.

Jasmin had awaken and found herself nestled in Bobby's arms. She felt guilty for cheating on Marcus, but she was frustrated by their marital chaos and out of aggravation, she was driven to Bobby's bed. His bedroom skills were unbelievable, and she couldn't get enough of him. But, she was married with a near about adult daughter and she needed to go back and set her house in order; besides she had gotten almost two thirds of the money back. Marcus would have to be happy about that.

She showered off the scent of lust and put a fresh set of clothing on. Bobby had awakened with a huge grin on his face. He stared at her fixing her hair and putting her lipstick on.

"Please don't tell me that you're leaving." He lifted his body to the head board.

"I'm married Bobby with a daughter." She buttoned her blouse.

"And a husband who can't fulfill your needs," he said.

"Don't speak on stuff you don't know Bobby." She said.

"I know he doesn't make you feel the way I do." He pulled the covers back and placed his naked body behind her.

"Bobby don't," she said, weaken by his touch.

Ginger had awakened to more vomiting, and she felt like crap. The smell of food, and even to look at it made her stomach crazy. She did not want to spend the rest of the month or two puking. She had big dreams and she was not about to let some brat spoil it.

She was sure that Solomon would be overjoyed at her not wanting to keep it. But what about her parents, how would she tell them? More like it, how would she tell her father? Her mother was God knows where acting like some spoil brat who messed up, but still wanted her way; to hell with her.

She puked again, then she placed a drop in her mouth that Mrs. Cassidy had prescribed to curb the vomiting. She sighed hoping it gave her at least temporary relief. She felt the urge to puke curb a little and in sitting on her bed feeling drained and weak, she wondered what Tori and God forbid Ruby would think. She continued to sit on her bed thankful that the vomiting was subsiding somewhat. She arose, left her bedroom and went downstairs to the kitchen. She didn't expect to find her father there.

"Daddy," she said. "What are you doing down here?"

"I live here don't I?" He teased and kissed her on the cheek. "Listen baby I know you heard what happened, but I don't want you to worry. You're going to college and…"

"Daddy," she said. "I don't think that I want to be talking about this right now."

"Okay," he looked at her strange. "I just don't want you to worry." He said.

"I'm okay really daddy. When's mama coming home?" She asked.

"Soon," he paused unsure.

"Something wrong," he asked. "You need to talk to us about something?"

"No," she lied. "I…" she ran to the bathroom downstairs and threw up.

Ginger came out of the bathroom and slipped another drop in

into her mouth. Her father stopped buttering the bread and looked at Ginger with a concerned look in his eyes. His look made her nervous and she took a piece of the bread and buttered it, hoping to avoid his eyes.

"You need to let me take you to the clinic baby." He felt her head. "It looks like you're coming down with something."

"I'll be fine." She said.

"Well, you don't look it." He said.

"I'll be fine daddy."

"Why don't you let me call Mrs. Cassidy and maybe she can give you something." He said.

"Daddy, I'm fine. It'll pass." She said.

He looked at her again and he put down the butter knife and reached for the phone. Ginger's eyes became as big as light bulbs. She rushed over to the phone and snatched it out of her father's hand. His look was strange.

"I'm calling Mrs. Cassidy." He said. All that vomiting is not good. It makes you weak and dehydrated."

"Daddy put the phone down. I'm pregnant." She said.

Chapter 21

Marcus dropped the buttered bread on the floor. The butter knife fell into the sink and cracked a juice glass. He was speechless of course, and he had not found the words yet to say to his daughter. He breathed in a few deep breaths and balanced himself on the kitchen counter before he fell. He looked at her with an angry blank look and he sighed just staring at his daughter.

"You want to run that by me again, because I don't think I heard you correctly." He said.

"Daddy," she looked at him with sad tear filled eyes. "I didn't want to tell you but you were gonna call Mrs. Cassidy and I didn't want it to get ugly."

"Well it's about to get ugly," he said. "Have you lost your damn mind?" He said. "Something must have happened for you to come in this house," he yelled, "and tell me that you've gotten yourself knocked up."

"I didn't mean for it to happen." She began to cry.

"You never do," he paced in the kitchen. "Baby girl," he took a deep breath. "What the hell were you thinking? You're only seventeen years old." He shook his head. "What about college? What about your dreams? Damn it!" He said, rubbing his forehead.

"I'm sorry." She cried.

"Too late for that," he stepped into the buttered bread on the floor. "Who's the boy?" He asked.

"Solomon Garrett," she sniffled.

"Jesus Christ," her father glared at her. "Does he know?"

"Yeah," her voice was broken from crying.

"Ah, man," he sat down at the kitchen table with fresh tears in his eyes.

Ginger had never seen her father so hurt. It was as if someone had told him she had died. He sat in his own space weeping and it broke her heart in two. Seeing her father lose it like that was way too much for her and she rushed from the kitchen back to her bedroom and fell on her bed crying. What had she done?

Jasmine knew she was way in over her head. She had to end this affair between the two of them before something unscrupulous happened. She had to stop acting like a school girl and become better than the woman she was while Marcus spent his life living out of a suitcase. She looked over at Bobby and he was sleeping. She gently tossed back the covers and eased out of his bed. She picked up her clothes from the floor quietly, trying to leave before Bobby would wake up and then her cell rang loud and she jumped.

"Damn it!" She said, looking over at Bobby, but he didn't even flinch. She dug inside of her purse to answer it. "Marcus," she said, recognizing his cell and instantly she became nervous.

"You need to come home right now Jasmin wherever you are and stop playing these games." He said. "Our daughter is in trouble."

"What do you mean she's in trouble?" She looked over at Bobby. "Is she okay? Is she hurt? Marcus damn it, you're scaring me say something."

"She's pregnant." He said.

Jasmin dropped the phone. Marcus was still trying to talk to her, but she had checked out. She was the one who ignored her daughter's calls when she couldn't tell her the truth about her college fund. She was the one who ran off to Berkley like a child when Marcus and her weren't getting along. She had failed her daughter and now she was paying for it.

She by passed the shower and put on her clothes. She grabbed her belongings and tossed her purse over her shoulder and left. She reached her Mercedes and collapsed in tears while Ginger buckled in immaturity.

She had learned by trial and error that anger rested in the bosom of a fool. In a single month she had lost her two best friends, and learned that she was pregnant with Solomon's baby of all people. What would Ruby think of her? What would Tori and God forbid Kamari think of her? In a single summer she had ruined her life and gave her dream a plane ticket to nowhere.

Revenge had taught her a harsh lesson. It was no place for the inexperience, and to exchange hurting someone for the thrill of winning was emotional suicide. Kameron was never hers to begin with, and if she hadn't allowed pride and ego to cloud her vision, she would have seen it that day at Echo Park.

Once Ruby and Tori found out what she had done, it would

destroy what little that was left of their already tattered friendship. It would never be the same between them, like it was never the same with Precious and Yolanda who once shared Ruby's, Tori's and Ginger's sisterhood through friendship. But, Garrett men had a history of ruining the lives of women who fell for them. Her rash decision to get even had taken her from innocence to womanhood quicker than she could blink and she regretted it miserably. She was seventeen alone, and pregnant; all of her dreams and hopes hung from a cliff; Solomon's off of Mount Rushmore.

Solomon was in a funk. In a blink of an eye his life as he had known it changed remarkably. His way with girls had finally caught up with him. At the tender age of seventeen when life was supposed to be filled with crazy, fun filled memories that would last a lifetime, he had gotten a girl pregnant that he didn't even like, let alone love. His future was getting away from him and he didn't know how to catch up with it to try and fix it.

What would his mother think? What would his Grandpa think? It was killing him inside and he wanted to tell someone before he burst. His Grandfather was loading his truck to fish and he rushed out to help. He lifted the heavy things onto his truck and made sure that his gear was locked down in the back and wouldn't roll.

"Invitation is open if you want to hang with the old man." He said. "Fishing clears the mind son, sort of like a warm bath I guess." He hopped into his truck. "Why don't you come?" He said.

Solomon thought about it for a minute or two and hopped into his Grandfather's truck. As he did, he saw his blue wind breaker neatly hanging over his seat; a peculiar look rest in his eyes. How could he know? Was he that transparent, or had his Grandfather heard something in the wind? Had he prepared himself for a moment that he had lived through when his daughter Yolanda had gotten pregnant?

In the quietness of the lake, he had thought a lot about his life, and his playboy type behavior that had taken him from a boy to a daddy. In a weird way he felt a sense of peace, and he had never experienced that before except when he watched Ruby's Grandfather fixing things on his side porch which seemed to give him so much tranquility. He never knew why he'd stop and watch him, but now he knew. He wanted peace from a life that was way too chaotic. In watching Mr. Wells, he had found a part of it, but as he fished with his Pop's, it had opened him up to quiet. Somehow, he found the peace that he was searching for.

He looked at the reflection in the water and for the first time he didn't see his father. He saw himself. He saw his goodness and his flaws, and he knew that he didn't have to live in the shadows of Bobby anymore. The Bobby that lived inside of him for so long that day had died, and now the real Solomon could live.

Solomon felt a fish fight not to become dinner. It nearly got away at first, but his Pop had taught him well and he manipulated the fish and reeled in a huge cat. It brought a smile to his face despite what was happening in his young life. His Grandpa smiled to and smacked him proud on the shoulder.

"Pop," Solomon placed the fish on ice. "I've got something to tell you that you're not gonna like." He turned and looked at him.

"I figured as much which is why I wanted you to come with me and fish." He said. "Something about fishing," he looked at Solomon. "So, what is it son that's weighing on you so?"

Ginger's pregnant and it's mines. I'm sorry pop." He said. "I know you're disappointed in me." He said.

"Oh sweet Jesus," he said. "Solomon," he sighed and just looked at him. "I didn't want this for you. But ain't no use in crying over spilled milk. What's done is done." He looked at him. "How can I help you son?"

"What!" Solomon looked surprised. "I thought you'd be upset." He said.

"Disappointed son. Disappointed." He looked at Solomon. "What's that girl gonna do?"

"I don't know?" He said. "But I know that I had plans. I wanted to go to college and have a chance at playing pro ball." He shook his head.

"Well," he said. "Something else had plans below your belt." He sighed. "You gotta life here Solomon and a future, but you have to be open and brave enough to see it." He said. "You know son, I really want you to have the shop. You're good at it. The men respect you, and you could expand and do more with it than I could." He said.

"Pop," he said. "You built that shop from nothing. It's more than just a place to get your hair cut." He said. "It's a place where men converse and share life man." He tossed his pole back into the lake. "And, it's a shrine for Dodger history; I wouldn't know how to do that."

"You love football champ and you know a lot about it." He reeled in another nice size catfish. "Who says it just has to be history about baseball. I want you to bring in what you love, and hopefully past it down to your son, then he brings in something that he loves."

"I don't even know what she's gonna do." He said.

"Well, what do you want?" His grandfather asked.

"I want my life back." He said.

"Son," he opened the door of his truck. "You will never get that life back. The moment life came into that girls belly, the boy inside of you became a man."

Solomon looked at his Grandfather and took a deep breath. He sighed and looked toward the lake again and in that moment, he knew that his Grandfather was telling the truth.

No matter what Ginger decided; no matter what he decided, neither of their lives would ever be the same again. There was something about crossing that line of bringing a child into the world and adulthood that wouldn't allow foolish kids getting busy in the back seat of a car to ever be teenagers again.

Jasmine had arrived home finally, and she was speechless. When she looked at Ginger, she blamed herself, and at the same time she was cross with her daughter for falling prey to the Garrett's talent in bedroom endeavors as she had. She couldn't look at Ginger without crying as she slumped down on a chair in Ginger's room.

"I don't get it." Jasmin wiped her tears. "Are you trying to get back at me and your father?"

"No, mama," she said. "I made a mistake."

"Are you trying to purposely mess up your life?" Her mother wiped her tears.

"No," she yelled. "But sometimes I think that's what you were trying to do to mines."

"How can you say that?" Jasmin said. "I have always wanted the best for you."

"Oh really," Ginger said. "So, you run out on me and my dad, and you squander my college fund."

"So you told her?" She looked at Marcus.

"No, she overheard." He said.

"Baby, I'm so sorry, but I got it all back." She said. "I sold some of my art work." Tears rose in her eyes again. "And I promise, I won't ever leave you or your father again."

Ginger looked at her mother as if she didn't believe her. Why did it take her getting pregnant for them to act as a family? For an entire week she heard absolutely nothing from her mother, and now suddenly that she was in duress her mother shows up. Ginger was angry at her mother and when she needed her most, she vanished into thin air without a trace and she despised her for that.

Marcus took a deep breath and looked at Ginger. For now what Jasmin had said about getting Ginger's college fund back went over his head. His daughter was seventeen and pregnant and he was still trying to wrap himself around this mess. He took Ginger by the hand and sat her down next to him and he hugged her tight.

"You know that I love you so much." He said. "And, I fault

myself for this," he sighed. "Had I would have been more in your life…"

"Daddy don't." She said. "It's not your fault. It's not." She sighed. "My life was just falling apart at the seams. Kameron fell for Ruby instead of me, and I hated her for it. And you and mama fighting all the time," she said. "This is not what I expected when you came home to stay and work in San Francisco." She said. "Truth is, I got in over my head with Ruby and I wanted to hurt her. I wanted her to feel what I was feeling. It seemed like at the time everything that I wanted in life was being taken from me, and I guess I couldn't handle it."

"So Ruby and Kameron are an item now?" Jasmin looked surprised. "Some friend," her mother said. "What you do comes back." She said. "She will not touch a strain of hair in my head again." Jasmin acted immaturely.

A Surprise look found its way in Marcus' eyes as he looked at Jasmin. What would make her say such a thing? Whomever this Kameron was, he could not tell his heart who to love. His daughter should have understood that. He was upset that she didn't and now look what she had caused.

"I hope you're not telling me that you made out with Bobby's boy because you were trying to get back at your friend. Because…"

"Daddy please," she wiped her eyes. "I wanted revenge, but I didn't want to get pregnant." She sniffled.

"Ginger, baby," her mother said. "You're not keeping this child. I'm thinking that you have it and then we as a family put it up for adoption to some loving parents who tried and couldn't have children of their own."

"Wait, wait, wait," Marcus said. "Adoption, no," he said. "I could not live with myself knowing that my grandchild was somewhere in some foreign persons home growing up and that I could never see him or her." He shook his head. "Baby," he looked at her. "What do you want to do?" He said.

"I don't know daddy. All I know is that I want to go to college and I don't know how I can do it with a baby." She said. "I've really screwed up my life." Tears filled her eyes.

"Baby," her mother tried to comfort her. "It's going to be alright." She said.

"Mama don't," she shoved away her arm. "Don't," she said.

"Baby, come here." Marcus reached out to his daughter. "It's okay." He held her. "We'll figure this out together." He kissed her on the forehead. "But," he said, "I want to talk to Solomon, and his folks, and Bobby," he turned towards his wife. "Where's he at any way?" As if she knew.

Solomon sat quiet all the way home from the lake. It wasn't a sad silence, but a thinking one. So many things had crossed his mind, but the one that jumped out at him was the thought of keeping the baby. Yes he was seventeen, unlearned and untrained to be a father, but he wanted to give his unborn child a fresh chance that he never had. The problem would be convincing Ginger and his mother, but he would do it somehow.

In his silence, he discovered that the shop was where he belonged. It was the one place where he wasn't Bobby but Solomon. It was his quiet place. Pro ball was no longer his priority, but he was going to college somewhere and raise his child.

"Pop's," he said, as they pulled up. "I'm telling Ginger that I want her to keep the baby."

"What?" His pop looked stunned. "Are you sure that's what you want? Raising a child is not going to be easy son, but I'll be right here by your side to help." He said.

"Thanks," he smacked his Pop on the shoulder.

He was glad that his mother had pulled an overnighter at work. It gave him time to think just how he would tell her, and it offered him time to think about how he would approach Ginger about him raising the baby. He knew that with both of them he would have a fight on his hands, but he was determined, and somehow he felt through a careless mistake that the universe had given him a second chance.

Marcus tip-toed out of Ginger's room as she slept soundly. He walked softly down to his room and walked in on Jasmin throwing a towel around her naked body. He missed her in the bedroom as a husband. Seeing her nude had gotten him heated and wanted her. He walked over to her and wrapped his arms around her waist.

"Baby, what's happening to us?" He looked at her.

"We'll be fine, come on." She patted his cheek and quickly walked past him and pulled a lingerie out of her drawer.

"Will we?" He said, watching her put on her lingerie.

"Haven't we always been?" She turned to face him.

"I don't know." He drew her into him. "You never left me before." He kissed her.

"You threw me out." She said, and pulled away from him.

"I'm sorry." He said, taking off his shirt. "I over reacted. We saved hard for that money, and like you, I want the best for her." He climbed into bed with his wife.

"Then you know she needs to have it and put it up for adoption," she said.

"Baby, it's our grandchild." He kissed her neck. "You don't mean that." He kissed her neck again.

"Marcus, she's seventeen years old and we both want her to go to college and have a future. I worked my but off to sell my paintings and get the fund back that I borrowed," she said.

He scooted his body up to the headboard. "You must have sold them to very wealthy folks, or to some gallery." He said.

"It was a gallery in Berkley." She lied, "close to the University." She said.

"Really," he said. "What was the name of it? I'd love for us to go there so we could see your work. I'm glad you've started painting again." He kissed her again.

"Ah, yeah," she said. "You know off hand I don't remember the name of it." She lied again.

An eyebrow rose up over Marcus' left eye. Was she that stressed over Ginger's pregnancy that she couldn't remember the place that had given their daughter back her future? He yawned and scooted closer to his wife and kissed her neck again.

"Baby," she moved away from him. "It has been a long hard day. I'm still not processing this and I just want to go to sleep."

She had never refused his advances before. The old Jasmin would have ripped his tee shirt off and leaped on top of him and drove him crazy. Had they gotten there to where making love was a distant memory? Or, was it just a rough patch and stress due to Ginger's situation?

He sighed and kissed her forehead. "Okay, okay," he said, disappointed he wasn't going to wake up with a smile on his face. "I still say we talk to Yolanda and Bobby." He said. "As a matter of fact," he said. "I think I'll make a trip over to old man Nelson's shop and find out where Bobby's at." He lowered his body down to his bed.

Jasmin suddenly rose up with a fearful look in her eyes.

Chapter 22

There was a glow about Kameron as he made French toast and sausages. His Granny stood in the door facing of her kitchen watching him. She didn't know what it was but she knew something was up. Being old, and curious, she didn't hesitate to take a seat in her kitchen and find out what was behind that spark inside of him. She picked up a link and bit into it and looked at him and smiled.

"You're glowing." She put the other part of the link in her mouth and ate it.

"Ah," he was caught off guard. "I guess people shine Granny when they're around people they love." He kissed her cheek. "Where's Gramps?" He asked.

"I'm right here son." He said. "I could smell breakfast all the way down by that lake out there." He took his baseball cap off and sat, and ate a sausage link. "So, what's up?"

Kameron sat a tray of French toast, hash browns and sausages on the table. His Gramps took milk from the refrigerator, and Granny sat mugs around the plates and poured herself and her husband coffee. Kameron passed on coffee this time for milk with his breakfast. As always they bowed their heads at the table, but this time, Kameron said grace over the food. He had never done that before. Usually, he watched and listened to his Gramps, but this time for some reason, he felt it appropriate to take the lead.

"I'm just gonna come right out and say this." He fixed his plate. Both his Gramps and Granny paused from making their plates and looked directly at him. "I got the internship that I applied for." He said.

Cassidy dropped her fork on her plate and screamed. His Gramps smacked the table and echoed. "I'm proud of you son."

Her scream lead into her leaving her seat and wrapping her arms around his neck and giving him a big hug and kiss.

"There's more," he said. His Gramps stop eating and starred at him. "They were pretty impressed with my project and they've already offered me a job after I graduate, and…"

Before he could tell more, Cassidy reached around his six foot six frame and hugged him again as if she didn't want to let him go. His Gramps smiled his smile and from the look in his eyes it was obvious that he was tremendously happy for his Grandson. He stood, as he nearly had to pry Cassidy away from him to hug his Grandson.

"I am so happy for you." Cassidy said. "I only wished that you didn't have to leave." She said, resuming her seat.

"Yeah," his Gramps said. "We're gonna miss having you around, and it'll probably be a while before we see you again." He placed a slice of French toast in his mouth.

"That's just it," he said, swallowing hash browns. "I'm staying here."

Cassidy went nuts screaming and leaped out of her seat hugging her Grandson again. His Gramps mouth nearly dropped to the floor. And for a moment, he just looked at his Grandson. His eyes registered disbelief, but his heart expressed sheer excitement.

"I don't believe it." His Granny said. "I don't believe it."

"What about Cornell son?" His Gramps said.

"My advisor and the firm I'll be working with pulled some strings and I'll finish up at Stanford." He said.

"Does Ruby know?" His Granny asked.

"No, not yet, I'm going to surprise her." He said, eating more of his breakfast.

"I know she will love that." His Gramps said. "You really care about that girl don't you son?"

"Yeah I do." He said. "I love her." He ate more of his breakfast.

"Well," his Gramps said, finishing his plate. "Love's been kind to you. It's blessed you with one of the great ones."

"Amen to that," Cassidy smiled. "So, when did you know?" She asked, sipping her coffee.

"Last night," he said. "But, I didn't want to wake you." He finished his plate.

"I'll send for you things." Cassidy said.

"Granny you don't have to do that. It's not a big deal. I can do it." He said.

"You know she's not listening to you don't you?" His Gramps said.

"Yeah, I know." He laughed and finished his milk.

"So, how'd you stump them son?" His Gramps said.

"Wait here, I'll show you." He said.

Cassidy couldn't contain her joy. She hummed in the kitchen and as she soaked the dishes she sang and danced a little. Her husband laughed. Cassidy always carried a joyful spirit, but because of her Grandson's news, her joy was heightened.

"Can you contain yourself?" Her husband laughed.

"No," she turned from washing the dishes. "It's the answer to my prayers."

"Mines to," he said placing his and Kameron's dishes into the soapy water to soak. "Just never know what the good lord's gonna do when you ask him." He said.

"Ain't that the truth," she washed the plates. "Thank God he's got most of my instinct and some of yours." She laughed, looking at him.

"Oh," he laughed. "Since he made a decision that you like, he's got more of your blood," he said.

"Yeah," she teased and licked out her tongue. "Well," she said. "Thank God he didn't fool with that Maples girl."

"I feel sorry for the child." He said.

"Yeah I do to." She said. "Who would have thought that Ginger Maples would have gotten pregnant?"

"What," Kameron returned to the kitchen. "Did you just say Ginger Maples is pregnant?" He asked.

"Yes, I did." She wished she wouldn't have said it, but it was too late. "She came to the clinic yesterday thinking she had the stomach flu, and found out it was something else." She dried her hands on a dry cloth.

"Does Ruby know?" He said.

"No, I don't think so." She said.

"Wow," he said. "Who's the father?" He asked.

"Solomon Garrett." His Gramps said. "Ben told me himself in confidence."

"What!" Cassidy and Kameron said.

"Ruby will be devastated." Kameron said.

"Oh sweet Jesus," Mrs. Cassidy shook her head.

The news about Ginger and Solomon was slowly leaking out. Everybody in Oak Grove was talking about it. Mrs. Amy made a special hair appointment just to go into the shop and spread what she had heard, and to hear what she hadn't heard. Mrs. Fletcher was stunned and despite what was being said, she didn't want to believe it. And out of stubbornness she didn't want to believe it until she heard it from Jasmin.

"So, it's true," she said. "Oh good lord," she tossed her hand in the air and looked very displeased. "And where were you?" She said.

"I was selling my paintings in Berkley." She said.

"Oh, I don't believe that mess," she said. "You and that Godson of mines was fighting over your finances in which you didn't handle well while the boy was gone." She said. "Let's just be honest about it."

"I made mistakes yes," she said. "But, I will not shelter all the blame for my daughter getting pregnant."

"You are her mother and a mother needs to be there for her daughter girl." She became testy. "Out of all the young men in this town, I can't believe she would get pregnant by that Garrett boy." She said. "It's a shame. Now, all hope is lost for her and that

Mosely boy," she said.

"It may not have been any hope at all." She said. "From what I understand, the boy wanted Ruby and for what I don't know, but he does."

"You know she can't keep it." She said.

"Try telling that to her father." She said.

"Oh God forbid," she said. "You've got to talk some sense into him."

"I've tried." She said. "You know how stubborn Marcus can be."

"What would it prove in keeping the child?" She said.

"Mother Fletcher you are preaching to the choir." Jasmin said. "I don't know what to do." She said.

"Does Bobby know?" She said.

"I don't know." She said. "Why is everybody so concerned about Bobby?" She got touchy.

"Well excuse me for asking," She said. "I'm sure Yolanda is calling him right now, and I bet that will bring him out from Berkeley."

"Berkeley," Jasmin's eyes widen. "How'd you know he was in Berkeley?"

"How'd you know that Bobby was in Berkeley?" She asked with underlying intentions.

"I didn't." She said. "I heard you say it."

"Um-hum," she said. "Well," she said, "she won't be a Mosely now."

"Neither will Ruby," she said. "The boy's leaving in a month and their little fling will soon be over, and she'll have the egg on her face not my baby."

"Better an egg, then a baby," she said, standing walking with her cane to the door.

The doorbell rang and Solomon trotted from his room to answer it. His Pop yelled from the kitchen that he would get it, but before he got a step past the refrigerator, Solomon was opening the door.

"Come in." Solomon said.

Ginger wiped the souls of her feet on the welcome mat outside of Solomon's door. She entered his home like she didn't want to be there, and her eyes showed it. The rumor mill had started and soon Tori and Ruby would have heard the news and what friendship that they had would come to a sad end. She blinked away the tears thinking about it and faked a smile as she waved at Solomon's Grandfather.

"How you doing Ms. Ginger?" Ben Nelson tipped his cap to her. "Grandson, I'll be in my den if you need me." He said.

"So," she sighed, and rubbed her queasy stomach. "What was so important that you needed to talk to me about?"

"I want to keep the baby." He said.

"What?" Her mouth dropped. "Well I don't," she said. "I've got a future. I want to go to college, and I can't do it being mommy."

"Well then go to college," he said. "I want to raise my baby."

"You," she said, "raise a kid. This is the dumbest thing I've ever heard." She said. "I'm out of here."

"Ginger wait, please." He stood in front of her. "Just hear me out," his eyes were serious. "I don't care how stupid it sounds. I got a chance to do something right. My dad didn't give a damn about me so I guess in a sense I grew up not giving a damn." Tears formed in his eyes. "This is not about me." He said. "It's about him, and I am willing to give up everything even college for a while if I have to just to raise my son and give him what I didn't have."

Ginger was speechless. She couldn't believe what she was hearing. This was not the Solomon that had his way with girls, including her. What in the world had gotten into him?

"Please," he said, almost begging her. "I've got four thousand dollars to my name and you can have it and do anything you want with it." He said.

Ginger sat back down on the couch before she fell. "Are you on something?" She said, "because I don't believe what I'm hearing. Why would you do that?"

"Because I want my kid," he said.

Ginger thought about it for a minute. She could design her line, promote and market it all while carrying Solomon's kid. She could take courses online at the community college and build up transfer course as she was building her line.

And on top of all of that, she would be handed four grand. For whatever reason he was serious, she could tell by his eyes. She on the other hand was serious about her clothesline. Maybe this was her ticket to New York?

"So, let me get this straight," she said. "You're going to totally raise this kid, because I don't do breast feeding, or dirty diapers."

"It's on me, except for the breast feeding. He'll have to take a bottle." He almost laughed at her.

"And you'll really give me the four thousand dollars," she said.

"Yeah, it's yours. Two grand now and two grand after you have him." He said.

"Deal," she said. "And, it's a her," she said.

The front door opened and it was his mother. She smiled when she saw Ginger sitting on the couch opposite of Solomon. Ginger swallowed hard suddenly. She was nervous. She could tell by Yolanda's reaction that Solomon hadn't told her yet. She was surprised that her mother hadn't snapped and said something yet.

"So," she sat across from Solomon. "You're home early." She rubbed his head. "Nice seeing you again Ginger. You know you're always welcomed at my house."

"Mama," Solomon could see that Ginger was about to past out. "I got something to tell you, and I don't know how you're gonna take it." He looked at Ginger.

"Should I keep sitting or stand?" She scooted on the edge of the sofa.

"Mama," he sighed. "Ginger's pregnant, and we decided to keep it."

Chapter 23

Ginger could tell by the look in Yolanda's eyes that she was beyond furious. The cold stare that she gave Solomon and her ran chills up her spine. It made her nervous and she looked away from her. Yolanda turned her eyes from Solomon and stared at Ginger. Ginger could feel her knees buckling as she stood. She swallowed hard, and inched a step closer to the front door.

"Does your mama know about this girl?" She said.

"Yes ma'am." Ginger's voice was nervous and scared.

Yolanda sighed and put both of her hands in her face. It was Ginger's cue to leave, and she hurried to the door. Solomon tipped back his head, and mouthed. "Talk to you later."

When Ginger closed the door he sat briefly watching his mother. She was crying profusely and he could tell that she was hurt. He took a deep breath, and rubbed his forehead again.

"I know you're disappointed mama." He said.

She raised her head up and wiped the stream of tears that soaked her face. "Disappointed," she said. "What the hell were you thinking Solomon? Boy, you are seventeen years old. You are not ready to be nobody's father."

"I'm sorry mama. I can't go back and undo what's already been done." He said. "But, I'm going to raise my kid and give him what I didn't have."

His Pop left his den and entered the family room where they sat. She looked at her father with tear filled eyes. He took a seat next to his daughter and rubbed her back.

"Sorry is not cutting it Solomon. This is not some game. Being a parent is serious business." She frowned, and looked at her father. "I'm sure you know."

"Yeah," her father shook his head. "It's going to be okay baby."

"No, it's not, did you hear them, they want to keep this baby. Neither one of them know nothing about parenting."

"I know that mama." He said.

"Yeah," she blew her nose. "Then why the hell did you go and get this girl pregnant?"

"I made a mistake mama. I'm human okay." He turned to face her.

"Mistake, human, well, I heard those same words from your daddy when I was seventeen." She yelled at him. "I wanted better for you, so much better for you."

Solomon stood. His expression had changed from a boy to a man. He sighed almost like a snort, like a bull preparing to attack his prey. "I'm not you and I'm not him. And if you ever wanted better for me, I never knew it." He said.

"What?" She said.

"Oh come on mama," he said. "You were too busy reminding me of being just like him." He said. "And I believed you, and all the other folks around here who just couldn't separate Bobby from Solomon." Anger boiled in his eyes. "The only ones whoever accepted me was my pop sitting there; the old men at the shop, and Ruby." He said. "And I blew it, now I'll have to live with that pain for the rest of my life." His face was sad.

Yolanda stopped cold. For the first time in a long time, she realized that she was still angry at Bobby, and angry at herself for loving him. Through all of her pain, she never once considered that Solomon was innocent. He was a product of premature love which was like an anxious season that come too early, and threw the course of time off balance.

Beyond fury and unhandled affairs, she had wounded Solomon, and helped contributed to him acting out like Bobby, and for that she was sorry. Though she wished his circumstances were different, they weren't. The deed had been done and she needed to be there for her son now. Criticizing him wasn't going to undo what was already done. She had done enough of that, and look where it had gotten her. She stood and looked at him. She reached out her arms to him, and immediately he rushed to them.

She held him tight in her arms. He felt the peace upon him like he had at the lake. He embraced it; loving how it made him feel. Summer had challenged him and his mistake had grown him up. The peace that he had longed for and so much wanted had found him in the place where he least likely expected it to. The only thing she could do now was to be there for him.

"I'm gonna make you proud and Pop proud." He said. "I'm gonna make my kid proud and I'm gonna be everything to him that Bobby wasn't to me." He took hold of his mother's hand.

Ben hugged his daughter and then took hold of his grandson. Though it appeared to be a tragic situation, something greater than revenge had somehow created a silver lining. Yolanda kicked off her shoes and picked her purse up from off of the floor and tossed it over her shoulder. This is what he had always wanted from his daughter and finally she had showed up.

"Well," she sighed. "Let me go call your father and tell him."

"For what," he said. "I know he's gonna trip and I'm not trying to deal with him right now." He rubbed his hand across his face.

"Baby," she said. "He needs to hear from us rather than hear it from somebody else."

"Mama," he interrupted.

"Wait, let me finish." She said. "It wasn't just your father. I wasn't there for you the way I should have been. I know this is hard for you to hear, but if you don't want your child not to be haunted by the demons that troubled you, you're gonna have to forgive him and let the good lord do the rest." She stood. "You hear me."

"I don't know if I can do that." He said. "The way I feel right now, I don't even want him to see my kid or be a part of his life." He sighed.

"Time and space will heal a lot of wounds." His Grandfather said.

Solomon stood about to go into his room. So many things raced through his mind; in an instant life for him was different now. The world he thought so much was his had handed him a cruel lesson, but he would learn from it and make the best of it somehow. He knew that the rumor mills were spinning. He could imagine that every clothesline, backyard fence, and front porch was bombarded with gossip. He had made his decision and at this point, Solomon could care less what the people of Oak Grove thought all except for Ruby.

August had come in much cooler than expected. The lazy breezes of summer were cool signaling an early fall. Ruby had written in her planner the date and time she would arrive at Stanford

for orientation and the day her belongings would be moved into her

one bedroom apartment off campus. It excited her and at the same

time it scared her. But, her faith was stronger than her fear.

She took a deep breath and sat her orientation packet back

down at the kitchen table in the back part of the shop. She stood on

a small step ladder and replenished her supplies of shampoo and

conditioner and placed them in a small tub. The shop was flowing

with conversation as usual; Mrs. Amy leading the conversation.

"I just didn't want to believe it." She said. "Here I am

hearing that her and Kameron had a thing going, and come to find

out that she's pregnant with that Garrett boy's baby." She shook her

head.

"You're talking about that Maples girl." Odette said.

Ruby dropped the tub of supplies on the hardwood floor.

Their conversation stopped cold. They knew that she had heard.

They were sorry for it. You could tell. Ruby rushed down the

hallway; ran out of the back door and sunk into a comfortable lawn

chair out back.

What she had heard could not be true. Ginger pregnant and with Solomon's child, it was a nightmare that was seriously messing with her dreams. They hated each other. This had to be some sort of cruel joke. She didn't understand it. Tiffney and Daphne yes, but Ginger, it just didn't make any sense at all. Ruby was numb, and for a moment she couldn't think.

Now she knew that Ginger hated her, and it was obvious that it was cold, calculated revenge. She had loved Ginger as her sister since they were crawling around in diapers together. Ginger and she would switch colored barrettes in each other's hair. Ruby loved pink and red, Ginger blue and green, Tori purple and yellow. They would trade shoes and purses, and as they had all gotten older, they shared all their secrets under the sweet gum tree in Echo Park.

Ruby buried her face on the patio table and wept sore. Precious left the lobby and found her daughter sobbing and broken and sought to comfort her. She sat next to her daughter and rescued her in her arms. She was hurt she could tell and she was hurt for her. She had been in the same spot with Solomon's mother Yolanda and she knew how that felt.

"Hey," she held her. "Oh, baby," she kissed the side of her cheek. "I'm so sorry that you had to hear that, that way." She said, rubbing her back. "I'm so sorry." She rocked her in her arms.

Ruby cried profusely and clung to her mother more. The more she cried more she remembered Ginger's eyes and how vindictive they looked at Fat Cats after seeing her and Kameron together. What she had done was spiteful and in sync with betrayal and she had wounded her heart in a way that only someone who loved her could.

"Hey, her mother lifted up her face and kissed her daughter. "Baby, I know this isn't easy, and I know how you feel." She sighed. "I need to tell you something; something that I never even shared with your father." She looked deeply into her daughter's eyes.

"What's that?" Ruby sniffled.

"Moons ago," she smiled, "when I was about your age, I had a serious jones for Bobby Garrett." She said.

Ruby's eyes suddenly widen and her mouth opened. Her eyes were a mixture of shock and disbelief. "What?" She said.

"Yeah," she sort of snickered. She could snicker now

because time had healed her heart. Destiny had sent Ruby's father, and she was thankful that Bobby had found a way out of her life; unlike Yolanda she happily let him. "Like you," she said. "I was crazy about Bobby. I mean what girl wasn't at the time." She remembered. "Everybody warned me, everybody," she laughed remembering. "But," she shook her head. "I don't know? I guess there's something about the Garrett men." She looked at Ruby. "Anyway," she said. "At one time, Yolanda and I were just like you, Tori, and Ginger, best of friends."

"Really," Ruby sounded surprise. "What happened?"

"She got pregnant with Solomon and I was devastated." She said. "But, I got over it, and you will too."

"Oh mama," Ruby rose from her mother's shoulder with a fresh batch of tears in her eyes. "All I ever did was love Ginger, and I don't understand why she would hurt me like this." She said.

"Revenge and anger do strange things to a young girl's heart." Precious said.

Precious kissed her daughter and held her in her arms. Life had placed her there decades ago and decades later, she was comforting her daughter like her mother had done her. Of course in the act of being a mother, she wanted to give Ginger a piece of her mind, and in a mother's way, she wanted to ring Solomon's and Ginger's neck for hurting her daughter so. However their own pain would come with altering their dreams, and being sworn into parenthood too soon over silliness and vengeance.

Unfortunately, every girl at seventeen had experienced such a thing; even she had. It was the mark of womanhood and the first test of coming of age, and going from a girl to a woman. Sadly, there were wounds to follow; wounds that would heal, wounds that would linger, hurt, and cause a lifetime of regrets. Despite her pain, she knew her daughter and of course she would heal. But, it was the forgiving that she worried about. She would be there for her but she realized that the lesson she would learn from this was something that only time and God could teach her.

Kameron stood at the back door. He could tell by the way Ruby was cuddled in her mother's chest that she had heard the news. Unfortunately he had arrived too late to break it to her. His face was as sad as hers was. Even he knew how much she cared about

Ginger; so much so, that she tried vehemently to get the two of them together despite his feelings for her.

Whatever respect he had for Ginger, he had lost it. For he could not wrap himself around the idea of a best friend seeking such calculated revenge. He knocked softly on the back screen, both Precious and Ruby turned to see who was there.

"Hey," her mother got up from her seat and hugged him. The look in his eyes said that he knew and that he was there to support Ruby. She patted his shoulder softly, kissed her daughter and left, returning inside the shop.

"Hey," he wiped away her tears. "I'm so sorry." He kissed her. "I really don't know what to say to you to right now, except that I'm here for you." He wiped away more of her tears. "I love you." He hugged her. "Come here." He said, taking hold of Ruby and sitting her on his lap.

Ruby lay on Kameron's shoulder sobbing. It wasn't that she was crying because she still had feelings for Solomon. She didn't. Ginger had hurt her to the core of her soul and she had done it with a malicious intent because Kameron had chosen her over Ginger as if that were her fault. Why couldn't she have been like Tori when Kamari had chosen Ginger over her? They had talked about life under a sweet gum tree in Echo Park, but she couldn't talk about being rebuffed by Kameron; her pride again.

Kameron held on to Ruby like he held on to life. He placed his cheek next to hers not caring that it was wet. He had to get her out of that funk because seeing her cry tore away at his heart. Solomon and Ginger had altered his plan. He was going to surprise her at the luncheon that he had invented, not knowing that fate had its own plan.

"I think I have some great news that will cheer you up a lot." He said.

"What is it?" She said, lifting her head from his chest. "Sorry I soaked your shirt." She looked at her tears forming puddles on his shirt.

"It will just put hairs on my chest." He winked, then smiled.

And, that was all it took for her to smile. His dry humor had even cranked out a tiny laugh. Sadness was finding its way to foreign soil and its exit was nearing. Out of concern, Mrs. Amy and

Mrs. Odette had peeped out of the kitchen to check on Ruby. After all, it was their slip of the tongue that had caused Ruby to fall into a gloomy mood. Unfortunately, things like that happened at beauty shops, but it was not their intention to hurt Ruby.

In spite of her youth she was one of them, and they loved her. She didn't know it but they had all groomed her for this. Like dust she would rise, and find her rightful place, and soar.

They stood looking at Kameron comforting Ruby and Ruby taking solace on his lap. Something bigger than foolish reprisal sat amongst them and something greater than even the two of them could imagine had taken the time to bind them long before they were born. Odette and Mrs. Amy could see it, and even old Mrs. Fletcher could see it and though she hated it, it was nothing that she or anyone could do.

"So, what is it that you have to tell me?" Her mood was rapidly changing.

"I got the internship, and I'm not going back to New York." He gazed into her eyes.

Ruby's eyes enlarged and her mouth nearly dropped to the

floor. She leaped from his lap and started to scream, and she threw her arms around his neck hugging him. Precious and all the other ladies in the shop came racing to the back to see what all the commotion was. However, Mrs. Amy, and Odette were blocking their view. However, Precious and Pauline managed to squeeze in between them to observe what was happening.

"See," he wrapped his strong arms around her waist. "I knew I could make you smile." He kissed her.

"But, what about Cornell," she said.

"What about it?" He teased.

"Kameron," she playfully smacked him on his muscular shoulder. "I'm serious." She said.

"I think Stanford has enough room for me." He said.

Ruby wrapped her arms around him; leaped in his arms and began kissing him. Suddenly she had left behind all the pain. What had broken her had freed her. She had been warned at Fat Cats that day that a fierce storm was coming. But a secret life wrath awaited.

There was a crowd of little women who stood at the back door watching love bloom. It had reminded them of their days of attraction; a blissful youth that only came once in a lifetime and chose its people carefully. There was no denying that Ruby and Kameron were two of those people; epiphany's of love, chosen by the universe long before both of them were ever born.

It was a sight to see and not to miss it, Precious tip-toed over the other women to witness what she had already seen in their eyes. It was love coming to bud. It snatched her daughter up like it had Precious when she was her tender age. There was nothing she could do about it. Like, there was nothing Jasmin or Marcus could do about Ginger having the baby and turning all parental rights over to Solomon.

None of the real adults involved in either Solomon's or Ginger's life liked the decision that either of them had made. Jasmin had harsh criticism of her daughter and made her feelings known. Marcus was angry with Ginger's decision. He too gave Ginger a piece of his mind. But Ginger didn't care, she made it clear to her parents that she wanted nothing to do with the child after it was born. After what her parents had put her through, she didn't care how they felt.

In spite of how she felt about Solomon, he had given her more than what her mother had offered her. He had given her hope by giving her four grand, more than enough to start the line of clothes she had always dreamed of developing.

Solomon's Grandfather Ben didn't like that arrangement either. It said a lot about Ginger in his opinion, but it even said more about his grandson. He had saved long and hard for that money and in an instant he was willing to give it all just to have his unborn child. However, his mother, and father were furious. Bobby entered their home; a place he hadn't been in years. It was awkward to say the least. But, he needed to be there, and he wanted to support his son if he would let him.

Yolanda looked at Bobby as he approached her. He was still handsome; still maintained his football physic and in a way that she would never admit, she still wanted him. He bent his tall frame to kiss her cheek, but in all the pain that he had caused her, she turned from him. He could feel her coldness towards him and though he didn't like it, he knew that he earned it. He was nervous about how Solomon would greet him, and as Solomon came into the family room to see him, there was blind hatred in his eyes and Bobby felt it.

Solomon set next to his mother and just stared at his father. He had his face; thick eyebrows, wide nose that was tailored for his face. He had gotten his looks from his dad. The only thing that was Yolanda's was his eyes. They were hazel; round, and in search of, now he had found it. It was sad he thought that the man who sat in front of him was a stranger with a tag on called dad. He didn't know him and now he didn't want to.

"So," Solomon's tone was rough with his father. "What do you want man?"

"I came for you son. Your mother…"

"Don't call me that," Solomon's tone was angry. "You lost the right to be my dad years ago man. So, you can just go back to the rock from wherever you crawled because I don't need you now, and I don't want to see you again."

"Solomon," his mother said. "He's still your father."

"No he's not," he said. "My pop in there," he pointed to the kitchen, "is my dad."

"I screwed up son I know." He said. "But…"

"But nothing," Solomon said. "There is no excuse you could ever give me that would get you off the hook from being my dad." He stood. "You screwed me up man. But, you know what, I'm not going to screw my kid up like you did me. From changing his first diaper, to tossing his first baseball, I'll be there. And, I'll give all what I have just so he can be happy, and not have to go through the bull shit I did." He began to cry.

Bobby's face was soaked with tears. He soon learned that the little boy he had left was now a man and he didn't know how to get back into his life though he really wanted to. Ben placed an arm around his grandson and massaged his shoulder and pulled him into his chest. He didn't blame Solomon for lighting into his father. He had abandon the boy for football, women and booze.

Now the harsh reality had hit him, and he was an eyewitness to losing his son. He took Solomon into his den and closed the door Bobby wept sore, even Yolanda felt sorry for him

"The boy hates me." He wiped his tears."

"What did you expect?" Yolanda said.

"I screwed up okay." He looked at her. "If I could do it all over again," he said.

"But you can't," she said. "I made a lot of mistakes with him to." She sighed; "always comparing him to you, when I shouldn't have. I feel that I'm partially to blame for him getting this Maples girl pregnant."

"Well, I'm all to blame," he shook his head. "Did you say Maples?" He asked.

"Yeah, why," she said.

"Ah, nothing," he said.

"It's never nothing with you Bobby." She said. "Well," she sighed. "It's not my business anyhow. I'm just so pissed at Solomon for paying this girl to keep this baby." She took a deep breath.

"Wait, wait, wait," he said. "Paying who to have a baby," he looked stunned.

"Long story short Ginger didn't want the baby, Solomon did and the only way she agreed to carry it to term was for him to fork over all of his savings, four thousand dollars' worth."

"He's a minor." His father said. "He'd have to get our consent."

"He'll be eighteen before the baby is born."

"So," he said.

"So he will be a consenting adult." She said.

"Like mother like daughter," his demeanor changed.

"What's that supposed to mean?" She said.

"Nothing," he rolled his eyes.

"He's adamant about doing it. He really wants his kid. In all honesty, her parents don't like it either." She said. "Poor Marcus is furious."

"Damn," he said. "You know that's extortion."

"Solomon suggested it from what I understand." She said.

"What?" He said.

"So, daddy and I are just going to replace it in a different account without him knowing it." She said.

"No, no, I'll do it." He said.

"You don't have to do it Bobby." She said.

"Yeah, I do." He rubbed his forehead. "I haven't done right

by my son and I don't care if he hates my guts for the rest of my

life. I'm going to do the right thing by him and my grandkid." He

said.

Yolanda was stunned. For a brief moment she couldn't

speak. Bobby cared about Bobby at least that's what he had always

shown her. Solomon's grilling had stung him in places that he

probably never knew that he had. It hurt she knew because the

Bobby she saw didn't know how to show emotion. And if he would

have for some reason, his tears would have been stone. She had

learned Solomon was different only today had she discovered that.

Ginger looked at herself in the mirror and even though she

was far from showing, it was hard to believe that a real baby was

in there. However, every time she barfed in a brown paper bag, she

was reminded of the life growing inside of her. The sad thing was

that it was part of Solomon's life that grew inside of her belly.

It was all so crazy. Who would have ever predicted a summer like

this?

The rumors were circulating like lightning speed. She was

positive that Ruby and Tori knew about the baby that had been conceived on a useless moment of stupidity. She could only imagine how much they couldn't stand her, especially Ruby. It was bigger than Solomon. It was betrayal in the worst since.

They had been friends since they were in diapers, and had shared so much. Now, they were as distant as the five fingers and nothing about them or between them would ever be the same. She had blown it and it hurt. And after the baby was born, she would leave Oak Grove for New York and hitch her wagon to the stars; at least that was her hope.

She hadn't even tried to call Ruby or Tori since she had gotten pregnant. She knew that if she attempted to do that they would see her number and not answer it. She couldn't blame them. She had offended Ruby in a way she never dreamed of, and she was too ashamed to tell her that she was sorry and pregnant with Solomon's baby.

She had to tell Ruby that she was sorry but it would have to come through somebody else, Tori. She wanted a clear conscious going to New York so she would take her scathing from Tori. Tori's cell rung and she answered, not paying attention to the caller.

"Hello," Tori said.

There was a pause on the other side of the line. Tori said hello again, and again, and as she was about to hang up; Ginger finally broke her silence.

"It's me Tori, and please don't hang up." She said.

"Ginger," Tori said. "You've got a lot of nerve calling me after what you did to Ruby."

"So, you know?" She said.

"Everybody knows." Tori said.

"Even Ruby," she asked.

"I'm certain that she does. But, what do you care? And to think I used to love you as if you were my own sister."

"Tori I'm sorry for what I did. It was wrong." She said.

"No, Ginger, it was stupid, and you knew that it would hurt Ruby. Was Kameron that important that you would deceive your best friend? And the sad part about it was that you didn't care."

"I do care. You're wrong." She said.

"Really," Tori said. "If you cared Ginger, you wouldn't have done it in the first place." She yelled. "I have to go."

"Wait," Ginger pleaded.

"What," Tori said.

"Could you tell Ruby that I am so sorry?" She cried.

"Why don't you tell her that yourself?" Tori said and hung up.

Chapter 24

Solomon had found himself in the same bind that Ginger had. He was sure that Kamari had heard about his girl getting pregnant and beyond being devastated he was searching his soul to try and figure out who the father was. So many things roamed through his mind; did he know? Would he lay his hands on him? But, what scared him most is that no matter what Kamari did or didn't do their relationship was over. And, he had only himself to blame.

At the same time, he had Tommy and Boyd to think about to. Like Kamari, they had probably heard something to, and how would he approach them? The men had started coming into the shop. The look of embarrassment decorated his face and he couldn't bear to look them in the face at first. He was sure that he had disappointed them as much as he had disappointed himself, his mother, and his pop.

He wanted to go and hide. As a matter of fact, he wanted to leave the shop and not come back. However, he knew that hiding wouldn't solve anything. He looked away from all of them including Mr. Fletcher, but he looked right at him and threw his arms around him and hugged him like a seasoned old man with life written on the pocket of his shirt. From Fletcher's hug came the embrace of tested old men that had battled many hardships in different facets of their lives and had overcome. Each hug lifted his spirit up somehow and now he could face whatever came from Kamari knowing that he would break his heart, but that time and support would eventually heal it.

"No matter what people may say," Mr. Fletcher said. "You keep your eyes on God, and keep your head up." He patted Solomon on his shoulder. "Missteps in this lifetime only beat you down if you let it." He said, and handed him a bag of barbecue potato chips.

"Amen," echoes came in the shop from the other men.

"Just a step in your journey," Tommy's grandfather, old man parker said.

"That's the truth," Mr. Fletcher said. "We don't love you no less son." He said.

"See," Ben said. "That's what I've been trying to tell this boy." He cleaned his clippers. "What's done is done, and ain't nothing you can do but move on and do the best you can do."

Solomon opened his bag of chips that Mr. Fletcher had given him. He hadn't done that before. He knew that it meant something; almost like rites of passage, but how did he deserve that when he had fathered a child out of wedlock? Nonetheless, he began to eat them and so did the rest of the men in the shop, including his Pop. Now, he knew what it had meant.

Just when his spirit had calmed, Kamari pulled up in his father's Tahoe. Kamari had a certain pulling up that distinguished himself from either Tommy or Boyd. The tires somehow sounded as if they were bumping to his loud music and the brakes like they were snapping their fingers. But this time it was silent and when he looked up and saw Tommy and Boyd beckoning him to come outside the shop door, he felt something was wrong. He patted Mr. Fletcher on the shoulder and told him that he'd be right back.

"No rush man," he said. "This old cat will just be chewing the fat with the fella's." He ate more barbecue potato chips.

"Cool," he smiled. But Mr. Fletcher was good at making him grin.

Solomon paused at the closing of the screen door out front. Their eyes looked weary and in all honesty it looked as if both of them had gotten run over by a diesel truck. He was almost afraid to ask them what was wrong. So, he paused briefly and placed his hands in his pocket; a nervous jester. He noticed that Tommy had a manila envelope in his hand and he was just holding it as his arms were folded across his chest. He couldn't help but wonder if it were for him.

"I assume that you know that Ginger is pregnant." Tommy said.

"Everybody's talking about it man." Boyd said. "And of course lots of rumors are flying," Boyd's look was almost depressing.

"Ah, yeah, I heard." He said knowing that by their tonality that they knew he was the father, but somehow wanted him to come clean. "There's something that I need to tell you guys." He said, clearing his throat.

They looked at him with a distasteful gaze. He had over

 stepped his bounds and severed a friendship that was meant to last.

How could they forgive him when he had butchered their hearts to?

In a moment of lust and irresponsibility, he had changed what they

all knew: laughs, girls, hanging out and friendship. He had brought

bitterness where love and aspiration reigned.

What Solomon had done had affected all of them and in an

odd way, it had ushered all three of them into manhood slightly

before they wanted to be. Their days of being boys had ended and

their lives of being men had just begun. Tommy was more prepared

for it than Boyd.

He had to welcome maturity early on after his folks had

passed on and left him with his elderly Grandparents' who had taken

the role as his guardians and raised him. Without recognizing it,

Grandpa Parker had introduced him to baseball the sport that he had

come to love while getting haircuts at Ben Nelson's shop. From the

early age of five to the tender age of seventeen he played baseball,

and without a doubt he knew what he wanted to do.

His Grandmother had grown tired of the college scouts blowing up her phone. She had gotten tired of digging out college packets in her mailbox about their college and baseball program. Beyond baseball, his Grandparents' had given him a roof over his head, love, and taught him a trade; running the storefront on their small farm. For Boyd it was different. He never knew his mother and his father was too preoccupied with being angry at her for leaving him. Unfortunately, he never really focused on Boyd.

Laughter was his medicine. He had learned early on that he needed plenty of it and the only way he could get it was to make others laugh so he did. Laughter somehow kept his spirit calm. In a strange way it administered unto his spirit, and it gave him hope somehow. Now, he had to find hope in what looked like a hopeless situation.

When Solomon cleared his throat again, they knew what he would say. "The baby that Ginger is carrying is mines." He hurried and said it as if that would make it easier.

"That's low man," Boyd said. "How could you do that?" Tommy shook his head. "You knew how he felt about her man.

"That was messed up."

"See," Boyd said. "That's why I never liked that girl. I tried to tell Kamari she was evil."

"I thought you had more class than that man." Tommy said.

"Okay," Solomon said. "I messed up. I screwed up. I…"

Boyd interrupted him. "Keep going." There it was; that moment of raw humor that through Boyd leaked out in the most turbulent situations.

"How do you think it's going to make me feel to tell my boy that I got his girl pregnant?" He said with a deep melancholy in his eyes.

"Well," Boyd said. "You won't be telling him in person. He left today." Boyd's eyes became sad again.

Solomon was dumbfounded, and amazed. He sunk to the steps and held his head in disbelief. He needed to cry but the tears wouldn't come out. What had he done?

"Where…"

"Atlanta Georgia," Tommy interrupted him. "He wanted us to give you this." Tommy handed it to him. That's when Solomon broke down and cried.

Unlike Solomon, Ruby was tired of crying; tired of beating herself up, and tired of sheltering trouble that wasn't hers. Of course she was disappointed by Ginger's act, but she wouldn't allow herself to be bitter and permit some sick sort of vengeance to take hold of her spirit.

She waited for Tori underneath their favor tree in Echo Park and she felt at peace. The summer breeze swept across her face and as she paused in her thoughts it seemed how funny this whole summer had turned out. Tori honked her horn. Ruby stood and walked to greet her. They embraced each other and took solace under their favor tree. Tori had brought food, drink and goodies. Tori sighed as she took a seat on the beautiful quilt Ruby's Grandmother had made.

"So you've heard right," she said, handing her a turkey and ham sandwich.

"It depends." Ruby said, biting into her sandwich. "So much is going on."

"Ginger's pregnant." She said. "But you knew that right?

Please tell me you knew that."

"Yeah," she said. "I overheard the ladies at the shop talking. I don't think they wanted me to hear it for some reason." She wiped her mouth, "probably because the baby is Solomon's." She shook her head. "I still can't believe it."

"Tell me about it." Tori stop eating her sandwich. "And to think she was supposed to be our best friend. I don't get it. What made her go that far?"

"Revenge is a cruel beast." Ruby said. "She wanted to hurt me. She wanted to rip my soul from my flesh. I could see it in her eyes that day when she saw Kameron and me together at Fat Cats. I knew it was coming. I just didn't know how or when."

"Wow!" Tori said. "You know she's keeping it."

"Yeah, I know." Ruby said. "I hear Solomon if you can believe it wants to raise it."

"Shut up." Tori said.

"Nope," she said. "I got it first hand from the ladies at the shop."

"So, Gin is just going to give him her baby with no strings attached?" Tori inquired.

"I'm sure she's getting something out of it, but who cares." Ruby said. "It's her bed to lie in."

"None of this bothers you," Tori asked.

"When I first heard the news, I was numb." She said. "It felt like someone had stabbed me in the heart with a hunting knife." Ruby sighed remembering. "I thought I knew her, but I guess I never really did. I thought that we'd all spend the rest of our lives together, and become delightful old ladies with so many good memories. But," Ruby paused, "sad that it's not meant to be."

"Maybe not for the three of us, but you and me will have so many good times, and recollections, and we'll start with college this fall." Tori blinked away the tears. "I am so sorry Rue, so sorry." She cried. "I want you to know that I will never ever hurt you like that." She wept. "You're my friend and my sister and I love you." Tori broke down.

Ruby hugged Tori and wiped away her tears. "I feel sorrier for her than I ever could for me." She said. "I'm fine Tori, and I know that you would never in a million years do anything to hurt me." Ruby looked at her. "I've done a lot of thinking and I realized that I got what I wanted this summer. I found love and so much more." She sighed. "I've cried so much that I don't have any tears left inside of me, and I'll be damn if I start crying again."

She hugged Tori tight and cleared the leftover tears from her face. Somehow fate had given them a new beginning and the pain that had temporarily blocked their way had someway fallen off a cliff. It was strange, but in a moment of craziness the friend that she loved as her own sister had betrayed her and that she would never understand.

She turned her back on Ruby; forgot that they had a seventeen year history. Sorrow had forced her to be quiet and in her stillness she leant on reflections. The blinders had come off and she was able to see Solomon for what he truly was, not for the man she had longed for him to be.

She had gotten a good look at what hate could do and she wanted no part of it. As her eyes had finally opened, it was apparent that the qualities that Solomon lacked, Kameron had been blessed with; to think that she had almost missed it gave her goose bumps, and it made the tiny hairs on her arms stand at attention. However, she had learned from tragedy and from misfortune, and she discovered what the old folks had already known.

Ginger's vengeance had become her curse and now Solomon's child would be hers forever. All of her dreams of going to college in New York would be put on hold. Against her own will, she would be stuck in Oak Grove for a while, but the life she so much wanted would have long moved on.

The thought of her wanting to be with Solomon so much made her want to vomit now. What if fate would not have saved her, then she would be stuck with a thick belly carrying Solomon's brat and Stanford would never have known her. Thank God an angel was on her shoulder.

"Have you seen Solomon since all this took place?" Tori finished her sandwich.

"Please," Ruby said. "I am too through with him." She took the last bite of her sandwich. "You know the more and more I think about it. Ginger and Solomon suit each other, and they've got more in common than we ever did." She finished her sandwich.

"I never in my wildest dreams would have imagined that this would of ever happened to Ginger." She said.

"Tell me about it." Tori opened up a sweet tea. "You know folks are going to be talking."

"Um-hum," Ruby said. "As My Big Mama always said, when you lay down with dogs you get up with fleas."

"Ain't that the truth," Tori said as they high fived. "Any way," she said. "Guess what?"

"What," Ruby opened up a can of sweet tea.

"Tommy's going to Berkley this fall." Tori got excited.

"What? What happened to UCLA?" Ruby asked.

"He said he could play baseball anywhere, but…"

"I'm getting it." Ruby smiled. "He wanted to be close to his Boo."

"Yes," Tori leaped up and did the happy dance.

"Speaking of news," Ruby put her sweet tea down. "Kameron got the internship, and he's transferring to Stanford for fall." Ruby pumped her fist in the air and made a cheerful noise.

Tori leaped up in celebration. Favor had found them and had blessed them. The first new memory had begun. Tori and Ruby both celebrating joyously and forgetting about the reprisal that tried to stop them. The tree that had hosted three had sadly drifted to two but they didn't seem to mind it. Life had moved on and had taken them with it

For whom they were, and who they would become, it was a story she would regret telling. The man of her dreams bedding down with one of her best friends, and forgetting his oath he had pledge to her; an oath meant a lot at seventeen. It was funny, when he made that promise Ginger never once crossed her mind. It was Tiffany and Daphne who she had worried about. Never did she think in her wildest imagination that Ginger would have been the one who hurt her heart, and deceived her over a man who was never meant to be hers.

Solomon was in no way predestined to be hers. Sadly, she discovered that in her deepest pain. She wanted him to be different. All because she had constructed this man and had placed Solomon's face on him. When Kameron had come along and fitted the bill, she missed him, but destiny had not.

She didn't have an explanation for it really except to say that something grander had opened her eyes and guided her on the right path. In her days of agony, she had learned a lot about her little town and it was horribly sad that she had to understand it through such distress. But she was thankful that she had settled down enough to get it. Prior to her heart being injured she found no need to be still; that was for the old folks in the town.

The old Ruby only wanted quiet when she was writing, reading or sleeping; now she welcomed stillness as her friend. This summer had challenged her in ways no other season in her life had. Betrayal in its worst fashion had threatened the core of her goodness and altered her life forever. But something beyond her understanding had prepared her for this moment. Long before her heart was crushed, she had been around older women who had suffered affliction and had shared how they had gotten over with her. Without even knowing it, she had embraced their lessons. When calamity had struck, she came prepared.

Kameron sat out his drawings on his desk. It was time for his Gramps to see them and he wanted to know what he thought of his idea. Mosely walked heavy footed up the stairs. He had gotten much older and the stairs winded him a bit. He took a seat in a spare chair in the loft and took a couple of deep breaths.

"Got to forgive the old man Grandson, not as young as I use to be and them dog gone stairs wind me so." He chuckled.

"Sorry about that Gramps," he said. "I could have just brought them down."

"No, no," he waved his hand. "This is where you work, where something greater than yourself speaks to you, and as long as I can walk, I'm coming up in here." He said.

Kameron moved his desk over towards his Gramps. He scooted his chair next to his and began to show him what he had been working on when he wasn't helping him on the truck. In his drawings, he had redefined Oak Grove and give it a face lift. The eyes of his Gramps said wow and his little old lips were speechless. He couldn't believe what he was seeing. It was Oak Grove on steroids.

The Gingerbread Mall would become the Galleria and increase five times its normal size. All the small time vendors who had storefronts or tiny pubs would be gifted with large retailer space and loads of foot traffic. Oak Grove would not be just a small coastal town that folks past through, but it would be a coastal oasis in which everybody would stop, enjoy and spend money. How did Kameron know? What had prompted him to draw up his Gramps vision and go as far as to pitch it to a firm and make it become a reality?

It brought old man Moseley to tears. After so many prayers and waiting so many years, his prayers had been answered. Mosely smacked his Grandson on his shoulder. He was proud and honored that Kameron had thought so much of his dream that he would take steps to build it. He couldn't believe it.

"So what do you think Gramps?" Kameron asked.

"It's my dream Grandson." He said. "You made the old man proud."

"Thanks." He said. "I see how hard you work and all the folks here who run their own businesses. I can't help but think where they would be with an Oak Grove revitalized. We're going to make it happen Gramps." He said.

"Yes we will." He said. "I can't wait until your Granny sees it."

"Yeah, me to, by the way where is she anyway?" Kameron moved his desk back.

"Out shopping with Ruby's Grandmother," he said.

Kameron's eyes lit up. But they always lit up every time Ruby's name or someone associated with her was mentioned. He couldn't help it. She had hold of his heart like no one ever had. Moseley saw in his Grandsons eyes what he had eventually saw in his own when he had fallen for his Granny decades back. He knew what he needed to do and he grabbed the keys from the rack. He tilted his head towards the front door and somehow Kameron knew to follow.

They hopped in the truck and drove a few miles down pass the lake. His Gramps stopped and park the truck. It was a part of Oak Grove that he hadn't seen; raw, undeveloped land and it seemed perfect for him and his Gramps vision.

"Back then I suppose that I was the only one here dumb enough to buy this piece of land." He smiled. "Oh," he laughed. "I got talked about real bad. But I think I knew something that nobody else knew."

"What's that?" Kameron said.

"That you'd come along and build my dream right here on this piece of land that nobody at the time would give a nickel for." Moseley looked at his Grandson.

"I don't understand." Kameron said, with a confused look standing in his eyes.

"This is all yours now. I'm giving it to you all two hundred and fifty acres." He said.

"What?" Kameron was stunned.

Chapter 25

To Jasmin's surprise, Bobby had shown up at her home and sat comfortably in her living room chatting with Marcus. When she and Ginger stepped into the front door and she saw Bobby talking with her husband Marcus, she dropped a bag of groceries and a jar of pickles broke and splattered all over the floor.

"Damn it." She said, her nerves all over the place.

"Mama," Ginger said. "What is wrong with you?" Ginger stooped to help her mother with the cleanup.

"Ginger," she slightly raised her voice. "Get up. Get up." She said. "You are not supposed to be bending or stooping in your condition." She frowned. "Have you lost your mind?"

"I was just trying to help." She said.

She looked and saw Solomon's father and immediately she could see Solomon. Her father and Bobby both rushed into the kitchen when they heard the loud blast from the breaking of the glass jar. Marcus saw the juice from the pickles in the middle part of the floor. He excused himself and got Ginger out of the kitchen.

"Baby girl," he said. "Get out from around this glass now."
He said.

"Just putting the milk in the refrigerator," she said.

"Go keep Bobby company." He said.

Marcus set the broom aside and took Ginger's hand like he
use to when she was a little girl and guided her over the broken glass
and the mess. Bobby watched and he was envious to say the least.
His son hated him. Ginger adored her father he could tell. He
looked over his shoulder and saw Jasmin watching him.

He knew that stare. She didn't want him there. They had
history together; good history and she didn't want it out. As he
looked at Ginger, he saw Jasmin's, spicy attitude, and willing to do
anything to get what she wanted at the likes of emptying his son's
bank account.

She wasn't Solomon's type he could tell. But, it was what
was beneath her skirt. Unfortunately he had handed down his lust
from women to his son, and now it had come back to haunt him.

Ginger was uncomfortable sitting in the family room with
Solomon's father. Her memory of him was vague. He never hung

around Solomon or Yolanda much after they divorced and to think

the child she was carrying would have part of his blood made her

sick. It made Jasmin sick to see him sitting on her couch across

from her daughter. Suppose he had said something. She watched

them nervously.

"What is he doing here?" She asked Marcus.

"Baby," he swept up the last dust pan of glass. "He's the

baby's grandfather come on, and he came to offer whatever help that

he could, and he apologized, not that it was all Solomon's fault." He

said. "Breaks my heart to say it."

"He needs to leave." She said. "I don't know why he felt the

need to just rush in from Berkeley when he's never bothered to be a

part of his son's life at all." She fumed.

Marcus paused from getting the mop and bucket from the

utility closet by the pantry. For years no one knew where Bobby had

hung his hat. Every time he had heard anything about him it was

always that he was here the last time I heard, never he's up in so and

so now. So how did his wife know?

"How'd you know he was in Berkeley?" He asked.

"Ah," she had to think quickly, "Mother Fletcher." She said. "She mentioned it to me the other day."

"Funny she didn't mention it to me," he said. "And I was just at her house the yesterday." He said. "Her whole talk was about Ginger having a baby and how sorry she felt, and what could she do to help us." He raised any eyebrow. "Bobby has never been one of her favorite people." He lowered his voice. "So I'm not feeling that she would be all that interested in his whereabouts."

"Mother Fletcher keeps up with everything that goes on in this town. We know this." She said. "The point is I don't want him around my daughter."

"It doesn't matter what you or I want." He mopped up the pickle juice. "He's the baby's Grandfather, and our daughter wants his son to raise our grandchild." He ran the mop over the floor again. "He wants the same thing that I want. He wants us to help them raise this baby."

"Solomon I'm sure does not want his wayward daddy in his life now. And though I don't care for the boy, I can't blame him." She said, seeing Bobby eye her.

He put the mop and bucket back where he had gotten it. He stood in front of his wife looking deep into her eyes. Something was wrong he knew it. She had refused him on more than one occasion, and when they did have their moment in the bedroom she made love to him like she was performing her bedroom activity with someone else.

She prayed silently as they entered the family room. She detested what she had done and it seemed as though Marcus may be on to her and have figured it out that she slept with another man, that man being Bobby. She had fought it hard not to call out Bobby's name. So, she dug her nails into Marcus' flesh and groaned in Bobby's honor. She was determined to keep her secret at all cost.

Marcus sat in between Ginger and Jasmin. He rested a strong arm around his wife's shoulder. He kissed Ginger's hand and she loved it.

"I was just telling your daughter that I'd be more than willing to finance her business venture regarding her clothesline." Bobby said. "As much as Solomon wants to help…"

"Listen," she snapped at him. "We don't like this agreement any more than you, but if this is his way of supporting his unborn child and my daughter's dreams than he should help if it does drain his account dry."

Marcus and Ginger both looked at her. Ginger had never seen her mother act like that before. She was always diligent and appeared to know how to speak to people. What had happen? And what was it about Bobby that her mother detested, or was she taking it out on Bobby that Solomon had gotten her pregnant?

"I should go." Bobby said. "I see that I've upset your wife and I really didn't mean to." He said with a smirk look on his face.

"Baby," he looked at her. "I think you owe the man an apology." He said.

"Sorry," she said and got up and walked out of the front door.

Marcus and Ginger looked clueless. Bobby stood with a smile on his face knowing that he had gotten to Jasmin, and knowing that he had the ammo to get her to undo what Ginger had done. Below his belt had spoken to her and his presence made her anxious and she caved just the way he had wanted her to.

"I am so sorry about that man." He stood along with him. "Say Bobby," he said. "Where you laying your hat at these days?"

"Berkeley," he said. "You didn't know?" He pretended to look confused.

"Man," he said. "I just got back from China myself." He said, "takes a while to catch up."

"I hear you man." He said and stretched out his hand for Marcus to shake. "I helped your wife sell those beautiful paintings she had." He shook his hand and left out of the front door.

Marcus' demeanor changed and so did Ginger's. The truth had hit him head on like a train wreck; for Ginger it had made her more spiteful and now her own mother would be added to her black book list.

Precious closed her shop early. She swept and placed all of the soiled towels into the bin. She placed her purse over her shoulder. She took her keys off of her station and took a deep breath.

She had never paid attention to the calendar that sat on her station. For seventeen years, she didn't need to. Now she did, Ruby was leaving soon. Ruby had grown up it seemed within a blink of an eye. She was off to Stanford to construct the life she had dreamed of and fought for. She didn't have the heart to hold her back.

Make no mistake, she was proud. But, in being pleased she was a mother and she was already missing her daughter though she hadn't left yet. She too had learned a lot about her daughter this summer and so she could send her off into the world with confidence that she would take flight and soar. She kissed the date that she would leave and blinked away the tears. As she left out of the front door of the shop, her cell rang. She dug inside of her purse and answered it.

"Yeah, Jake," she wiped away a lingering tear. "What's up?"

"Are you sure that you're okay with this?" He asked.

"Yeah, yeah," she wiped away more tears. "She deserves it."

"Is she at the house?" He said.

"Yeah, the girls our at the house making brownies for their

men." Precious laughed.

"For who?" He said.

"Jake," she laughed. "Stop it. You know he's a nice boy and one with a future."

"And one that's suddenly going to Stanford," he said. "I think we should move up there." He said. "I'm serious."

"Will you go do what you need to do before the girl heads over to the lake?" She said.

"Alright," he said. "I love you."

"Love you more," she said and hung up.

Tori stood over Ruby's mother's oven and melted chocolate for the brownies. Ruby sat cracking nuts and placing them in a bowl. Tori looked over her shoulder. "Did you hear about Kamari?"

"Yeah," she said, "heard the ladies at the shop talking about it. You know nothing gets by them."

"Tell me about it." She laughed as she continued to stir the chocolate. "Think we'll be like that when we get old." She snickered.

"Probably," she laughed. "You more than me," she teased.

"Yeah right," Tori laughed. "You work at the shop and they have definitely weaned off on you." She turned the fire from under the chocolate and started mixing the brownies.

"You would say that." Ruby laughed.

"Is it not true?" Tori reached for the nuts.

"Hush," Ruby laughed.

"It's going to be weird not having Kamari here. I can't believe he left for Atlanta on Thursday, and that he's going be attending Morehouse this fall instead of USC."

"I still can't believe it." Ruby said. "It had everything to do with Ginger." Ruby placed the brownies in the oven. "Kamari was his best friend."

"Ginger was ours." Tori ate a nut.

"True." Ruby said. "What Ginger did to me, I would not wish that on anyone." Ruby dipped her finger in the chocolate. "They're gonna be good Tori. The guys will love them."

"Of course they will," Tori ate a brazil nut. "And to think that when summer begin, I was dreading it."

"Why?" Ruby said.

"Because I didn't know what my life would look like after high school," she said.

"And now, you're going to San Francisco State," Ruby smiled.

"Yeah," Tori said, "funny isn't it."

"Yeah," Ruby checked the brownies and pulled them out of the oven. "I would have never guessed that I would have found the one thing in life that I was so afraid that I wouldn't find."

"What was that?" Tori said.

"Love," Ruby spread a dry cloth underneath the brownies.

"I don't know how you could have thought that." Tori hunched her shoulders. "You have a heart the size of the Mississippi Rue. Look," she said. "You were willing to give up Kameron to our best friend just so she could be happy."

"Because I loved Gin, and now I just feel sorry for her." Ruby pulled a jar from the bag on the counter.

"That's what I'm saying Rue, and because you wanted the best for her, look what happened to you." Tori started cutting the brownies in squares.

"Kameron is so in love with you." Tori said. "And the fact you're going to have him all to yourself at Stanford." Tori continued filling their jars. "Tell me that wasn't fate." She snuck Ruby a brownie.

"Yeah," Ruby sat starry-eyed. "I'm glad that something was working because I could of easily been Ginger."

"Please," Tori finished putting brownies in both jars.

"I thank God every day for saving me, and for giving me Kameron." She placed the jars in a nice size picnic basket without the flap.

"Rue, he is so fine." Tori said.

"Tell me about it." Ruby said. "Tommy too," they both smiled.

Tori sat the basket on the table. Ruby soaked the dishes and loaded them into the dishwasher. Out of the blue, there were three loud honks in Ruby's driveway and a loud thump at her front door. A strange look stood in both Ruby's and Tori's eyes and they carried those looks to the front door.

"Kameron and Tommy I bet." Ruby unlocked the front door.

"Probably," Tori said.

"Daddy," she looked clueless. "What are doing here?"

"I live here." He joked. "Come test drive your new truck." He smiled.

Her mouth dropped and she leaped into her father's arms and squeezed him tight, screaming wildly.

"Girl," he said. "Are you gonna choke me to death, or go drive that thing?"

"Oh my God," she said. "Oh my God," she leaped out of his arms and dashed to the truck with Tori behind her.

In all the excitement, she hopped in her truck forgetting her purse. "My Purse Tori, my purse." She looked around for it but it wasn't there. She rushed out of the truck, and her father was waiting with her purse in his hand. "You might wanna take this?" He teased.

"I love you." She was on the verge of tears.

"I love you more." He hugged and kissed his daughter.

Christmas had come early for Ruby. The truck she had dreamed about owning was officially hers. She couldn't believe it.

It stood before her as happy as she was waiting for her to climb in and introduce herself. It was perfect; the right color, a candy apple red with gold spoke wheels, and loaded with extras.

All this time she had thought that her dad wasn't listening. But, he was. She just didn't know it. Usually she would have picked up on it, but she was surrounded by noise; unwarranted commotion that blocked her from the peace that would have allowed her to be in tuned with her senses. But that had been her life, until Kameron had come along.

It was funny how he had come from a big city stained with noise, but yet he brought quietness to Oak Grove that she hadn't known. Oak Grove was a quiet place where the universe spoke in ways that the young folks couldn't hear at first. When it spoke to them, it was like a foreign language that they couldn't understand. But, when it did speak to them, it spoke to them in the only way that they could comprehend; noise.

However, when they were hurt enough, wounded enough and beat up enough, they were forced to be still. The language that was once foreign became clear. Now, they could understand. Suddenly they knew what the old folks knew. In all of her excitement, she finally recognized that she and Tori had forgotten the jars of brownies that they made for Kameron and Tommy.

However, she had been shocked out of her mind by her new truck and her mind had drawn a blank. Ruby pulled up in front of the Moseley's place. She saw her Papa, Mr. Moseley and Kameron loading chairs, and tables in the back of their trucks. Ruby parked behind them and hurried out of her truck.

"Papa, papa," she said. "Look, look at my truck."

"Looks almost as good as you," he said. "I told your big head daddy to hold out for the red one." He laughed.

"So, you knew he was going to get it," she said.

"Does anything about my Grandbaby get past me?" He pinched her cheek and then kissed it.

Moseley whistled. "Stop traffic with that one," he walked around it. "I suppose now I'll never see that Grandson of mines." He winked at Kameron.

Kameron had also took noticed of the truck. But, he had more so took notice of the lady driving it then the fire red Silverado.

Kameron stunned Ruby by jumping in the back of the cab. He could be so silly at times but she loved it and she smiled. The gaze that she had once given Solomon was now his magnified. Tori leaned on the passenger side door watching.

"It's you for sure." He jumped down and stood in front of Ruby. "I love it." He said. "But, not as much as I love you." He kissed her. "I have to go help with the tables and chairs. See you later." He snuck in another kiss.

"Okay," Ruby grinned.

"I have a surprise for you." He said, sneaking in another kiss.

"What," she said. "Tell me what."

"It's a surprise." He said. "Later," he kissed her again.

"Ah boy," his Gramps said. "You can lip smack that little girl all you want later. We've got work to do." He laughed.

"Gotta go," He kissed her again, and hopped into his Gramps truck with the biggest smile on his face.

"Bye," she waved.

"I counted four kisses." Tori Said," or was it five, heck, I lost count." She teased. "Oh do I wish I could be a fly on the wall in your apartment at Stanford." She said.

"Hush," Ruby got back into her truck.

"Somebodies in love," she closed the door and the seatbelt snapped her in.

Mrs. Fletcher had declined the invitation to go to the luncheon turned dinner that Cassidy had been planning for a while now. It had grown from just celebrating Ruby's success to Tori's, Kameron's, Tommy's and Boyd's. She had hoped that when such an event took place that Ginger would be the bell of the ball. Marcus was her Godson and Ginger getting a Moseley and going off to college in style made her look grand and accomplished.

But, Ginger had fallen prey to lust and the Garrett's men spell and it had gotten the best of her. She had shamed her parents and her. Oak Grove would talk on it forever and she wanted no part of it. And to think of all the hard work that was left dormant and in vain, Ginger practically placed Kameron in Ruby's arms. Ruby was privy to old women and their stories. Ginger was not and needed an adult to help her play a woman's game.

She was sure that lady folk would talk about her to. In fact, she could just imagine the hurtful things they would say and the lies they would tell. She was done. Age and experience had taught her when to quit. She would sit on her refurbished recliners Big Jake had done for her; share a bowl of popcorn with her husband and watch "The Haves and The Have Nots."

At one time, she would have been out there with Cassidy, Pauline, Mrs. Amy, and the other's decorating, cooking and of course gossiping as she knew they would. But fate had tossed disappointment in her hand, and she quietly accepted defeat. After all, it was Ginger's cross to bear not hers.

However, Jasmin felt as if it were hers to bear rather than Ginger's. May be this was God's way of paying her for her sin. She had given herself away the moment she laid eyes on Marcus and he knew that she would. "Bastard," she paced out back; now what was she going to do. Here she was with a pregnant seventeen year old daughter whose dreams were placed on a serious hold.

What had happened? Where did she go wrong? She felt like

a complete failure. Things would never be the same for Ginger, or any of them really and she was to blame.

Marcus stepped out back on the patio and she could tell by the look in his eyes that he knew about her and Bobby. He placed his hands in his pockets and blinked away the tears, but they rolled down his cheeks anyway.

"After our Daughter has this baby," he said. "I want you out of my house." He yelled at her. "In all the traveling that I did, I never once cheated on you." He couldn't hold back his tears. "I don't want to see your face, and I do not want you in my bedroom." He said. "You can take up residence in the guesthouse." He turned his back and walked away.

Jasmin trembled all over. Twenty-three years of marriage gone within a snap of finger. All over one careless night. Marcus could not have meant what he said. He was angry and hurt. But he loved her. Bobby would pay. She would see to that.

It was a perfect night for a dinner by the lake. The sky a perfect blue and clear. There was a sweet summer breeze in the air and the blue lake rippled softly. The night seemed to have borne celebration in it.

The tables were set; red and white candles and napkins that said congratulations on them to match. There were red plates, white handled silverware that coordinated the table setting. Big balloons white and red hung from the branches of the tall trees. Kameron had done that at his Granny's request.

Precious had styled Ruby's and Tori's hair. Tori wanted a French roll, Ruby a flip. Ruby had picked out a red velvet strapless dress with a dainty cover up, and Tori a blue dress with spaghetti straps; a slit in the back and a shawl that matched. They both had accomplished what they wanted in the course of one summer: Tori found her dream; Ruby had found love, and Ginger heartache. It was strange how everything had worked out.

Boyd who was late to everything had showed up early and with flowers for the ladies and gifts. Boyd seemed more grown up since Kamari had left. He joked still, but there was something about him that was serious now. Against his father's wishes, he had committed to a four year bout with the Navy after high school; his reasoning, he could see the world, and go from there.

Boyd greeted Ruby and Tori with a kiss on their cheeks and a mixed bouquet of flowers. He bought a writing set for Ruby, and a cookware set for Tori. And for Tommy, he couldn't resist the joke of giving him a baseball glove with his autograph in it. It said. "Watch me; I'm going to be famous." Tommy couldn't help but laugh. It was the Boyd that he was used to, and though he laughed at what he wrote, he believed him somehow. He joked with Kameron to and had given him a float that said, "Get out of town."

Kameron howled in laughter. It was the funniest thing. He got the joke instantly and his laughing made everyone at his table laugh. From a short distance the older people watched them; it was them at their age in a sense. Cassidy stood and asked for everyone's attention.

"You know," she said. "This was supposed to be a luncheon done weeks ago for Ms. Ruby on behave of my Grandson trying to win her over." She laughed. "I see that he did."

Kameron smiled and gazed into Ruby's eyes and kissed her. Underneath the table he folded his hand into hers. He turned back and looked at his Granny.

"But, it grew into something greater." She said. "Tonight we are honoring all of your accomplishments: Ruby, Tori, Tommy, Kameron, and Boyd." Boyd seemed shocked that she mentioned his name. "This dinner is to say we love you and we are so proud." She began to cry. "We know that you all will do great things." She sat and wiped her tears.

"Remember where you come from and don't get stupid." Mrs. Amy said. "I'm proud of all of you."

"Just remember when it gets tough out there that you have several shoulders to lean on," Odette said. "We'll always be here for you."

Precious mouthed to Ruby." I love you." Ruby mouthed I love you back, and Tori's mother blew a kiss at her daughter and waved.

"Eat up," Moseley and Big Jake said in unison.

Kameron honored Ruby as he made her plate: Barbecue chicken, greens, dirty rice, and a healthy slice of cornbread. He made himself the same. Tori fixed Boyd's plate while Ruby fixed his dessert; peach cobbler. While Tori made Boyd's plate, Tommy had made hers and his. To look at the both of them, it was obvious that each of them had found the right girl for a lifetime.

As Ruby and Tori talked to each other, Kameron and Tommy found themselves looking starry-eyed by the women that destiny had given to them. Before Tori could wipe away the melted cheese on her lip, Tommy swiped it with his finger and placed it in his mouth; an excuse for Tori to kiss him. Kameron on the other hand licked barbecue sauce from Ruby's fingers, and then serenaded her lips with a kiss. Tommy had loved Tori since the second grade. Kameron loved Ruby when he had first seen her at Echo Park when her interest was elsewhere.

On the other hand, Ginger sat on her front porch with sadness in her eyes. Mr. Opportunity had showed himself to all of them and somehow Tori, Kameron, Ruby, Tommy, and even Boyd had managed to grab his hair from the front. Unfortunately she and Solomon had grabbed him from the back and he laughed at them. They had moved on all of them even Kamari and he didn't even bother to say goodbye although she needed him to. They sat where she was supposed to be sitting. And, Ruby had the man that she so much wanted to be hers and they had forgotten her.

She placed her hand on her tummy and felt the life that grew inside. They may celebrate now, but she would make each of them pay later. Her dream may have been delayed, but it would not be denied. She watched in anger and in envy and when the tears rolled down her cheeks she didn't bother to wipe them away. She just let them fall hopelessly to the ground.

"Mrs. Cassidy," Ruby said. "This is wonderful. Thank you." She wrapped her arms around her and kissed her.

"You welcome baby." She said.

"So when are you leaving," Odette asked. "I know our Tommy is leaving the week after next." She said.

"Me too, and Tori," she said. "Thank you too Big Mama." She kissed her and hugged her. "Thank you Papa. I love you." She kissed him.

"You look beautiful tonight baby." Her Grandmother smiled.

"Yes she does," Kameron said, wrapping his arms around her waist.

"I don't believe I gave you permission to embrace my baby like that." He joked as he ate.

"Big Jake," Mrs. Cassidy said. "I don't want to have to hurt your boy." She playfully smacked his shoulder.

"Papa," Ruby laughed.

"Oh, so now you gonna tell my daddy on me," he said. "I'll take back that truck." He laughed.

"No you won't," she said.

"I have something that I have to show you." He whispered in her ear. "Remember the surprise I was telling you about?"

"Yeah," Ruby smiled.

Solomon frowned as he sat and watched Kameron love Ruby the way he couldn't. He didn't know if he detested himself more, or Kameron for moving in on what should have been his. He didn't have the guts to face Ruby or talk to her after what he had done. Maybe this was fate mocking him and giving him a swift kick in the butt. He sat stewing at his own self mostly.

Kamari had left because of him. Now, Kameron was sitting where he should have been, and Tommy and Boyd seemed down with him. It seemed so unfair, but he had caused it.

They were destined to fall in love and now they both knew it. She had learned the hard way that when one interferes with fate, there is huge price to be paid. He had discovered that something bigger than his reputation with the ladies was working in Kameron's favor and it hurt like hell. Unfortunately, there was nothing he could do about it.

"Are you ready for me to show you the surprise?" He asked.

"Yeah," she said again, turning to face him.

"I need to borrow your daughter for a few minutes?" He said.

"No," Ruby's father said. "Absolutely…"

"Stop it." Precious laughed, smacking her husband on the hand. "Go."

Kameron stopped in his tracks, looking back at Ruby's father. Ruby took his hand and waved goodbye to her friends and everyone else. Tori winked at Ruby, Ruby winked back.

"I don't think you dad likes me." Kameron said.

"He likes you." She started her truck. "He's just trying to mess with you.

Ruby backed back and made a funky kind of U-turn. She headed towards the Moseley's house but continued further. She drove past the Gingerbread Theater and Echo Park. After a mile or two past the park, Kameron asked her to stop. She put her truck in park and felt Kameron's hand taking her out of her truck.

"Okay," she said. "What are we doing out here?"

"This is the surprise." He wrapped his arms around her waist again.

"I'm not getting it." She looked back at him.

"Gramps gave all this to me." He placed his check next to hers.

She turned completely around to face him. "What?"

"And I want to share all of it with you." He drew her into him and kissed her.

"You do." She was surprised.

"Yes," he gazed into her eyes.

"But, what would you do with it? And, why did he give all

of this to you?" Her eyes were innocent.

"Well," he looked at her. "I'm going to build his dream here and re-develop the entire Gingerbread Mall scene here."

"Your project," she said.

"Um-hum," he kissed her.

"But, what will you do with the rest of it?" She asked.

"I was thinking on the east end that borders the other half of the lake that we'd build our home there. Anything you want." He said as they engaged in a kiss.

"What?" She said, appearing surprised at what he said.

"I have loved you since the first time I laid eyes on you in Echo Park that day." He said.

"Really," she looked at him, and she could see that it was true.

"I know that this may be premature and I know that we haven't known each other very long. But I love you, and I want to spend the rest of my life with you." He looked directly into her eyes. "I'll wait until you finish Stanford if I have to; as long as it takes." He gazed into her eyes. He dropped to one knee. "Ruby Wells, will you marry me?"

Ruby was stunned and at first all she could do was shake her head in a yes motion.

"Is that…"

"Yes, yes," she lowered her body to his and kissed him. "Yes!"

He lifted her in his arms and carried her back to her truck. "We have to tell my parents." She said.

"I know." He kissed her.

"And you have to ask my dad," she said.

"Um-hum," he kissed her again. "Right now, he said."

"He'll say yes." She said. "Mama will make him."

"He's in here with the champ and I'll wear him down until he does." He grinned.

The full yellow moon shined its light upon them as if they were the only two that existed in the world and finally in Oak Grove it was quiet.

The End

www.ingramcontent.com/pod-product-compliance
Lightning Source LLC
Chambersburg PA
CBHW051428260626
47162CB00001B/3